THE RAKE'S REBELLIOUS LADY

Anne Herries

MILLS & BOON®
Pure reading pleasure™

All the characters in this book have no existence outside the imagination of the author, and have no relation whatsoever to anyone bearing the same name or names. They are not even distantly inspired by any individual known or unknown to the author, and all the incidents are pure invention.

First published in Great Britain 2008
Harlequin Mills & Boon Limited,
Eton House, 18-24 Paradise Road, Richmond, Surrey TW9 1SR

ISBN: 978 0 263 86293 5

Set in Times Roman 10½ on 13 pt.
04-1208-90609

Printed and bound in Spain
by Litografia Rosés S.A., Barcelona

THE RAKE'S REBELLIOUS LADY

Chapter One

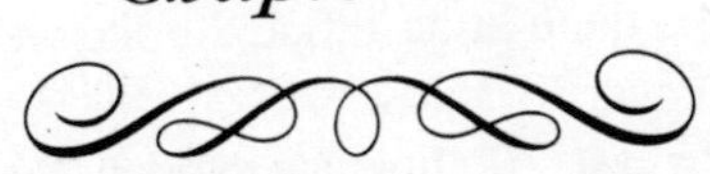

'My word, Freddie, that pair of yours are out-and-outers,' George Bellingham said, admiring the thoroughbred chestnuts that Sir Frederick Rathbone was driving in Hyde Park that May morning. 'You are an excellent judge of horseflesh. I shall come to you next time I decide to improve my stable.'

George was walking, Sir Frederick having pulled over to oblige him. He now offered the reins, inviting him to climb into the high-wheeled phaeton.

'Care to try them yourself?' he asked. 'They have as sweet mouths as any you'll find in London. I was lucky to get them. Came from Farringdon's stable. He sold them to me after a run of ill luck at the tables.'

'Had some of that myself recently,' Bellingham said, pulling a wry face. 'We can't all be as fortunate as you!' He looked thoughtful for a moment, then, 'It surprises me that Farringdon sold them; I thought they were his pride and joy.'

'Needs must when the devil drives, I dare say.' Freddie laughed, a gleam of mockery in his dark eyes. He was a handsome devil, arrogant, wilful and the bane of match-making society mamas, for at eight and twenty, he had managed to avoid all the traps set for him with consummate ease.

'Lucky at the tables, unlucky in love, is that not what they say?' Freddie's look challenged and provoked his friend. He did not add that the chestnut horses had been in settlement of an overdue gambling debt and that he had offered to take them at an inflated price well above their true worth.

'Not in your case!' Bellingham retorted. 'Your latest high-flyer is a beauty, Freddie. There isn't a fellow in London who doesn't envy you the magnificent Yolanda.'

'An expensive hobby,' Freddie remarked grimly; his mistress might be a spectacular beauty, but she had a decided partiality for expensive baubles. 'As greedy in bed as out. To be honest, I weary of her. She is too predictable.'

'Good grief, man! What do you expect? She is a courtesan of the first line. They say she has consorted with crowned heads in Europe—perhaps even Bonaparte himself!'

'You don't say?' Freddie said, pulling a face. He had heard the rumour and knew it to be untrue, but could not resist teasing his friend. 'Why did I not know this before? Boney, indeed! I do not know whether to be flattered or horrified.' He shook his head as he returned to the subject of his mistress. 'I dare say she is well enough in her way, George, but she is not… Perhaps I am too particular.'

'You would not want a simpering society miss? Perhaps the lovely Miss Avondale—if you are on the catch for a wife?'

'God forbid! That insipid fairness—and that lisp! I would be bored within days—hours!' Freddie laughed mockingly. 'No, I have no thought of marriage, George. Yet I sometimes yearn for a woman I can talk to as I do to you. A partner in more than a physical sense.'

'If such a woman exists, she's mine,' Bellingham said, taking up the challenge instantly. 'A woman like that *would* be something out of the ordinary. I might consider marrying her myself.'

'Come, come, old fellow,' Freddie chided, for his friend was four and thirty, and a confirmed bachelor in his own words. 'She would have to be special indeed to tempt you.'

George nodded, but looked thoughtful. 'As you say, though I have wondered of late…' He shook his head as the horses moved restlessly, impatient at being kept waiting. 'Since neither of us is likely to meet such a lady, it is mere speculation.' He gave the reins a little flick, allowing the high-spirited horses to move on at a trot. 'Do you attend Almack's this evening?'

'Good grief, no!' Freddie said, revolted at the idea of such a wasted evening. 'When you see me there you will know that I have discovered the paragon we spoke of.' He laughed softly deep in his throat. 'I believe that you may safely assume that hell will freeze over first.'

'Oh, you will fall in the end,' George murmured, more for the sake of provoking his companion than anything. He grinned at Freddie. 'You don't care to sell these beauties, I suppose?'

'No—but I will wager them against your greys.'

'On what?' George was surprised. His greys were very good horses, but not the equal of the chestnuts.

'That a woman who could tempt me to marriage does not exist.'

George grinned, for they were in the habit of making such bets, and often on a simple thing like the turn of a card,

Freddie the winner at least three out of four times. However, he bore his friend no ill will; he could afford to gamble, and, often, the stakes were trivial. 'I'll willingly put my greys up against your pair—but we must have a time limit.'

'Christmas,' Freddie said, a wicked glint in his eyes. He had made the bet for sheer devilment, as a cure for the slow, creeping boredom that had come over him of late.

'Done!' George cried instantly. 'But you must attend all the main affairs of the Season, no running off to hide in the country or disappearing to your club until you've met all the new hopefuls.'

'Fair enough,' Freddie agreed. 'But I draw the line at Almack's. When you see me there you will know that you have won your bet.'

'Indeed I shall,' Bellingham said for he knew his friend too well. 'I would not be attending myself, except that my sister is bringing her daughter to town and I have agreed that I will escort them. I assure you that Miss Julia Fairchild is not the lady you are seeking. She is seventeen and a shy child, so I must do my best for her—but we have the whole Season to look forward to, Freddie. Who knows what may happen?'

'Precious little, if past experience serves me true,' Freddie said and wondered why he had made such a bet, when it meant that he would have to attend many tiresome affairs that he usually avoided like the plague.

He yawned behind his hand, wondering what he could find to do with his evening. There was no denying that he was bored with Yolanda and a visit with her did not engender any feeling in him. It would be best to make an end. His tastes had altered of late, and he thought that it might be time to start making changes to his lifestyle.

He would buy the lovely Yolanda a handsome present, perhaps the diamond necklace she had been angling for these many weeks. Yes, he would give her the necklace and make an end to it.

'Mama, do we truly have to stay with Aunt Louisa?' Caroline Holbrook asked of her mother that morning. It was more than two years since Caroline's father, the Honourable Mr Anthony Holbrook, had passed away, and his grieving widow was only now coming to terms with her situation. 'Could we not take a house for ourselves for the Season?'

'You must know that that is impossible.' Marianne Holbrook sighed deeply. She was a thin, pale lady with a fragile air. Having given her husband two sons and a daughter, she had suffered a series of unfortunate miscarriages, which had left her a semi-invalid for some years. Her bereavement had taken its toll of her too and, never a strong-minded woman, she had fallen under her elder sister's influence. 'Your father died owing considerable amounts of money, and your brother has had difficulty in holding the estate together. I do not feel able to ask him for such a large amount of money.'

'Poor Tom probably hasn't any to spare,' Caroline said regretfully. She was fond of her eldest brother and had no wish to make life more difficult for him. She sighed because it seemed that there was no escape for her. Her aunt, Lady Taunton, had married to advantage and though she had been widowed a few years previously, she was in possession of a generous independence, which enabled her to live as she chose. It was kind of her aunt to offer to pay their expenses, but she had such an overpowering manner that Caroline was dreading the experience. 'Couldn't we afford a short stay—if I did not spend too much on my clothes?'

'Please do not be difficult, Caroline,' her mother requested. 'I have a headache coming on. You know my health is not what it ought to be. I should not be able to escort you to all the balls and affairs you would wish to attend.'

'Forgive me, Mama,' Caroline said, suddenly feeling wretched for upsetting her mother. 'I suppose we must accept, but I hope that Aunt Louisa will not try to dictate to me, especially on the subject of whom I should marry.'

'Of course, my dear, but you must choose someone suitable—if you receive offers, of course.'

Marianne Holbrook gazed at her daughter doubtfully. She was certainly very striking, though not in the particular fashion of the day, which seemed to be for slight, fair girls with gentle manners. Caroline was a flame-haired temptress with a seductive mouth and challenging green eyes. She was tall and filled with a restless energy that made her mother feel distinctly weary around her. Sometimes, she wondered how she had managed to give birth to such a spirited creature. She must be a throwback to the old marquis, Caroline's grandfather, now a recluse, who had been a rake, a gambler and highly disreputable from all accounts. Certainly she in no way resembled any of Marianne's family.

'You married for love, did you not, Mama?'

'Yes, and have regretted it since,' Marianne said ruefully. 'Louisa married for position and wealth. I chose a younger son with only a small estate and have suffered the consequences. I should not wish to see you in a similar situation.'

'Poor Mama,' Caroline said. 'But I think you were happy enough while Papa lived, were you not?'

'Yes, perhaps…' Another sigh escaped her mother. 'Yet I do not care to see my son worn down by worry. And Nicolas has gone to be a soldier. I cannot sleep at night for thinking of him in danger.'

'The war with Bonaparte is surely over, Mama, for he has been confined on Elba,' Caroline said. 'Besides, Nicolas is not the kind of man who would be happy staying at home. You know that he was always into some adventure when a child.'

She and Nicolas had been born a matter of eleven months apart. Although not particularly alike in looks, for he favoured their mother, they had been kindred spirits. It was Nicolas who had taught his sister to climb trees, to swim in the river in her shift and to ride her horse astride. All of these unladylike pursuits had of course landed her in hot water first with her nurse, and later her governess. She had learned to be more sensible as she grew older, but secretly envied her brother his freedom.

'You always encouraged him in his wayward behaviour,' her mother said a little unfairly. 'But I suppose you are right. A mother may not keep her son in leading strings for ever. However, it is my duty to see you settled with a husband and a home of your own, and therefore we shall accept Louisa's invitation to stay with her in town. It is my intention to go up next week.'

Caroline gave up the attempt to dissuade her mother. It was not often that Mrs Holbrook set her mind to something, but on this occasion it seemed that she was determined. However, Caroline was equally determined that she would not allow her aunt to dictate to her in the matter of the gentleman she accepted as her husband—if anyone actually offered for her, of course.

* * *

'Very suitable,' Lady Taunton said, approving her niece's attire for that evening. 'Yes, I was right to insist on mainly white for your gowns, Caroline. The emerald you favoured would have been too bold with hair like yours. It is a pity that you are not more like your mama, but it cannot be helped.'

Caroline gritted her teeth, but kept her thoughts to herself. She had been in town for three days now and already she was finding her aunt's overbearing manner hard to accept, especially in matters of dress, which should surely have been her choice. She believed the white gown was less becoming than the emerald she had wanted, but her aunt was paying for most of her clothes and there was little she could do but accept her choices. Mrs Holbrook wanted only to keep the peace, and Caroline was forced to mind her tongue.

'Well, come along then, Caroline,' Lady Taunton said and swept ahead out to the waiting carriage, leaving her niece to follow in her wake. 'It is a pity your mother did not feel up to attending the ball this evening, but she will be better resting at home with her maid to cosset her.'

Caroline did not answer, for she knew it was not required. Her mother had accompanied them to a musical evening and two small dinners, and then declared herself exhausted. It was clear that she had abandoned the task of finding her daughter a husband to her sister, and that she would not bestir herself unless it was truly necessary.

During the carriage drive to the house of Lady Melbourne, who was holding one of the most prestigious balls of the season, Caroline was forced to endure another lecture from her aunt.

'I dare say I have no need to remind you not to be too free

in your manners, Caroline,' Louisa Taunton droned on. 'It was a fault I observed in you when you were younger, but I expect that you have learned how to behave since you left the schoolroom.'

Caroline made no reply; she felt that if she did she might say something rude, and therefore it was best to say nothing at all.

'Did you hear me, Caroline?'

'Yes, Aunt, of course.' Caroline folded her hands primly in her lap.

'Indeed,' Louisa Taunton said, eyes narrowing suspiciously. 'I do hope you are not sulking. I cannot abide gels that sulk.'

'No, Aunt, I am not sulking.' Caroline held on to her temper by a thread. If she was forced to endure much more of this, she would rather go home and never marry! She was fuming inside, and found it difficult to produce more than a polite smile when she was introduced to her hostess. However, as she followed her aunt's progress through the reception rooms, her mood began to lift.

Music was playing in the furthest room, which was the ballroom, and there was an atmosphere of excitement that communicated itself to Caroline. She looked about her, admiring the lovely gowns some of the ladies were wearing, and the flash of costly jewels. Overhead, a shower of sparkling light fell on the company from the massive chandeliers.

'Caroline, pay attention,' Lady Taunton said, recalling her thoughts sharply. 'This gentleman is Sir Henry Forsythe and he has just asked you for the honour of the next dance.'

'Oh…thank you,' Caroline said, relieved that the gentleman was in his middle years and quite attractive. She dropped a curtsy. 'How very kind of you.'

'No, indeed, Miss Holbrook,' Sir Henry said with a smile of approval. 'It is my pleasure and my privilege.'

Caroline gave him her hand, feeling a little spurt of excitement as he led her through to the ballroom. The black cloud that had hung over her dispersed as she was swept into the throng of dancers, and suddenly she was feeling wonderful.

The feeling continued after the dance ended, because she was besieged by gentlemen begging for the favour of a dance and her card was filled in no time at all. She laughed as she gazed up at her partners, for most of them were young and some were rather handsome.

The hours seemed to fly by with never a dull moment. She was the centre of a small group of ladies and gentlemen for the whole evening. It was not until the dance before supper that she was claimed by a gentleman she had rather liked when he asked for the privilege earlier.

'George Bellingham,' he told her, making his bow. 'You were kind enough to grant me the pleasure of this dance, I believe?'

'Yes, I remember,' Caroline said, giving him a dazzling smile. 'I have been looking forward to it, sir.'

'Have you?' Bellingham raised an eyebrow, a quizzing look in his eyes. 'But you have danced with all the young bucks, Miss Holbrook. I fear I cannot compete with the likes of Brackley or Asbury.'

'Indeed, I disagree, sir,' Caroline said at once, forgetting her aunt's strictures not to be too free in her speech. 'I do not think you need fear either of them—they are young rattleheads, are they not? Charming, of course, but interested only in horses and sport.'

'But one the heir to an earldom, the other to his uncle the

Marquis of Northbrooke.' Bellingham's mouth twitched, for she had described the pair of young bucks to perfection.

'Oh, that!' Caroline made a face at him. 'As if I cared for such things. I think a gentleman of your mode might possibly take an interest in poetry and reading, as well as sport, of course. Do not think I have anything against such pursuits, for my brother Nicolas is a rare goer at many things and I have enjoyed fishing for trout with him.' Her face sparkled up at him as she recalled her childhood adventures with pleasure.

'Have you indeed?' George was intrigued—she was not quite in the ordinary way. He recalled his wager with Freddie Rathbone and smiled inwardly. 'You must tell me more…' He was disappointed as the music ended. 'Oh…it has seemed but a minute…'

'Do you not think time always flies when one is enjoying oneself and drags when one is forced to do something utterly tedious?'

George disguised his laughter as a cough. It was on the tip of his tongue to ask her to have supper with him, but as soon as they left the floor, she was surrounded by four splendid young bucks dressed in the height of fashion, and all with the same question in mind.

'Miss Holbrook, may I take you in?'

'Ignore Brent, Miss Holbrook. I am sure you promised the privilege to me.'

'Oh, Asbury, she damned well said nothing of the kind—she is promised to me,' another gentleman claimed entirely falsely.

'No, no, gentlemen,' Caroline said and laughed, her eyes dancing with mischief. 'I have promised no one, but I shall yield to the gentleman who can quote Richard Lovelace to me—accurately, mind.' She looked at them expectantly.

There was stunned silence for a moment, their faces falling as they struggled to bring a word to mind; though most had subscribed to books of more modern authors, they were unable to remember the lines of the seventeenth-century poet.

'Stone walls do not a prison make,
Nor iron bars a cage;
Minds innocent and quiet take
That for an hermitage;
I'll have freedom in my love,
And so in my soul am free;
Angels alone, that soar above,
Enjoy such liberty.'

'Oh, well done, sir!' Caroline clapped and turned as the deep voice finished his quotation. 'That was excellent…' Finding herself having to look up at the newcomer, she discovered that he was the most devastatingly handsome man she had yet met. His hair was the colour of a raven's wing, almost blue-black where the light from the chandeliers touched it, his eyes very dark, just now mocking her, his mouth strangely enticing as it curved in a smile that made her heart jerk and then race on at frightening speed.

'Good evening, Miss Holbrook,' Freddie Rathbone said and offered her his arm, a glint in his eyes as a murmur of protest came from the other gentlemen when she took it. 'The honour is mine, I think. Better luck next time—George, gentlemen.' He inclined his head to them, his manner a nice blend of mockery and arrogance, as if he had claimed the prize by right.

Caroline laid her hand on his arm. She was laughing inside, though she did her best not to show it. 'I do not believe we have been introduced, sir?'

'Sir Frederick Rathbone at your service,' he said and smiled at her. 'I came late and was reliably informed that your card was full—young Asbury supplied the details. You must be aware that you have made a hit with that gentleman, and a few others, I dare say.'

'They have been amazingly kind,' Caroline said, a faint blush in her cheeks. She did not often blush, but there was something about this man's gaze that made her a little uncomfortable. He seemed to demand her thoughts, and she was not sure that she wished to share them with him. There was something about him that seemed to challenge her. To accept that challenge might prove dangerous.

'Come, now, no false modesty,' Freddie said, his eyes seeming to dare her to respond in a way that was not at all fitting. 'You must know that you are a sensation. I might almost say you are the belle of the evening, perhaps of the Season, though it is early days yet, I think.'

'This is my first ball,' Caroline said, her enthusiasm bubbling over. 'I have been lucky enough not to sit down for one dance as yet, but I do not think I am the only lady to have been popular this evening.'

'True enough, but people are talking about you. Everyone wishes to know where you came from—perhaps you were wafted here from some distant paradise? You are a siren come up from the depths of the sea to weave your spell over us poor mortals…'

'You mock me, sir,' Caroline reproved. She was a little uneasy—there was something about him, a glint in his eyes that told her he might be dangerous if she were to like him too much. And yet despite that she was drawn to him, much like a moth to an open flame. She tilted her head, deliberately challenging him. 'If we are to speak of looks, I dare say yours have won you more than your fair share of attention from the ladies? And if you should be wealthy, of which I have no idea, I am sure you are much sought after—unless you are already married, of course?'

'Oh, rich as Croesus,' Freddie said and grinned at her. Her bold manner was immediately attractive to a man of his humour, intriguing him. He wondered how she would respond to his teasing. 'And not married—a fact that some find irresponsible, for it must be the first object of a gentleman to marry, must it not?'

'Must it?' Caroline said, wrinkling her brow. He *was* clearly mocking her. She threw him a daring look, a flicker of defiance in her eyes. 'I do not see it. Much better to remain unwed unless it is for the further happiness of both partners—do you not think so? It would be tedious to marry just for the sake of it, I imagine.'

'Absolutely,' Freddie said, much amused. He had not met such frankness in a young lady of her class before and found it refreshing. 'Unfortunately, the match-making mamas of too many young ladies do not see it from your point of view. Now, what shall we have of this fine supper provided for us, Miss Holbrook? Please do not say you are not hungry. Surely you must fancy some of that delicious ham—or the chicken? Perhaps with a few green peas?'

'I would prefer one of those savoury pastries, and a syllabub,' Caroline said. 'But you must certainly have some of that beef, sir. It is rare and I know gentlemen like their beef that way—at least Nicolas does and so did my papa, although my other brother, Tom, likes the first slice from the cut.'

'Your father is dead, Miss Holbrook?'

'These two years past,' Caroline said and sighed. 'I miss him sorely, sir, but, truthfully, I miss my brother more. Tom has taken on the estate, of course, but Nicolas has gone to become a soldier. I just wish that I might have gone with him. I think it must be a fine thing to wear a handsome uniform and march to the sound of the drums.'

'Do you, indeed?' Freddie hid his smile at her naivety. 'I have had my share of it, Miss Holbrook. I can assure you that it is not all drums and flying colours.'

'Were you with Wellington when Napoleon was defeated?'

'No, I had resigned my commission, but I was with him at Salamanca.'

'Truly? Did you resign because you were wounded?'

'I was wounded several times, but I resigned because my father died and I had commitments at home.'

'Ah, yes, you are the elder son, I assume. I think poor Tom wishes that he were Nicolas at times. He has all the burden of the estate, while Nicolas may do much as he pleases.'

'Within reason, I dare say, but he will have to make his fortune—or marry into one. I dare say he has not much fortune of his own?'

'Oh, no,' Caroline said candidly, unaware that she was being quizzed for information. 'None of us has. Poor Papa was not a good manager, you see.'

'Ah…' Having gained all the information that Asbury had not been able to give him earlier, Freddie was satisfied. The girl clearly needed to marry well, which in her case should not be difficult, even without a fortune. She was undoubtedly beautiful and her easy manner had made her a favourite with the gentlemen. He found her amusing company himself, but could not help wondering if there were some artifice behind her easy manner. It would be interesting to discover more about her. 'Now, we must eat, Miss Holbrook. Please seat yourself, and I shall arrange for our supper.'

Caroline saw that a table by the window was still free, and she went to sit there. Before Sir Frederick could bring her her supper, Mr Bellingham came and sat down, supplying a third chair for himself.

'Freddie looking after you?' he asked. 'Decent chap, but rather stole my thunder. I was recalling what I know of Lovelace when he jumped in. I dare say he won't mind my joining you. We are close friends, you see.'

'I set the question, thinking that you might answer it,' Caroline said truthfully. 'I particularly like his letter to Lucasta—do you know it?'

'"Tell me not, Sweet, I am unkind..."' George quoted, raising an eyebrow. 'Is that the one?'

'Oh, yes, written to Lucasta when he was about to go to war. I find that period so romantic, do you not agree? I have a book at home, which tells the story of a lady defending her home in her husband's absence. It was a brave age, less polite than today, I imagine.'

'Yes, indeed,' George Bellingham agreed and smiled.

'George,' a voice said from behind him. 'What is this, my dear fellow—stealing a march on me?' Freddie waved the servant forwards who had brought various plates of the delicious food on offer. The servant deposited them and bowed, leaving the company to serve themselves. 'Please do join us...feel free to eat whatever you wish, but not the syllabub.'

'Very well, I shall,' George said, impervious to the sarcasm in his friend's voice. 'Miss Holbrook and I were discussing Lovelace—and the Civil War, a brave age.'

'Really?' Freddie said drily. 'With the whole country in arms and most of the aristocracy ruined for years?'

'Oh, you have no soul,' Caroline said, throwing him a challenging look. Her eyes were bright with mischief, making both men aware of her wayward spirit. 'The men were so gallant, and the ladies very different from the ladies of today, would you not say?'

'In what way?' Freddie asked, a gleam in his eye as he realised that his friend had been quoting her views, not his own. It seemed that this young lady was not afraid to voice her opinions.

'Oh, we are hedged about with convention,' Caroline said. 'I think it was easier to speak one's mind then than now.'

'Indeed?' Freddie was hard put to it not to answer in kind, for she was speaking quite freely. 'What would you like to say that you dare not, Miss Holbrook? Please do not hold back, for you are amongst friends. Neither George nor I will censure you.'

'Oh...' She looked into his eyes and saw the mockery. 'Have I been speaking too freely? My aunt forbade it, but I have been used to speaking as I find with my brothers. Forgive me.' A faint blush touched her cheeks.

'No, indeed, you have not. I find your frankness refreshing,' George assured her hastily. 'Do not let anyone tell you that you should be otherwise, Miss Holbrook.'

'Yes, well, perhaps I should not be quite so open,' she said, belatedly realising that her aunt might be right in some instances. 'Do you go to Almack's this week, sir? I believe I am to be given vouchers.'

'Then I shall certainly be there,' George said and shot a look of triumph at his friend. 'But I believe Freddie has other engagements?'

'Yes, I fear I have,' Freddie said and gave his friend a look that spoke volumes. The challenge was fairly joined and both men were enjoying themselves. 'But I shall be at Lady Broughton's rout—do you attend?'

'Yes, I believe so,' Caroline said. 'Indeed, we have so many cards that I am not sure how we shall manage to attend a half of the affairs we have been invited to.'

'You will no doubt simply make an appearance at some and then go on as many of us do,' Freddie said. 'But I shall engage to dance with you at least twice at the rout, Miss Holbrook. Please mark your card for me as you will.'

'Thank you, sir…' She looked at Mr Bellingham, for she sensed a friendly rivalry between the two and was amused by it. 'And for you, sir?'

'I believe two would be suitable,' he said, 'and I should like to take you driving in the park—perhaps tomorrow afternoon, if you have no prior engagements?'

'I know we are engaged for the evening, but I think there is nothing as yet for the afternoon. I shall be delighted to drive out with you, sir.'

'I shall look forward to it,' George assured her and glanced at Freddie. Their habitual rivalry was good-natured, but often quite fierce, and their friendship was all the stronger for the occasional clash of temperament.

Freddie was eating his supper. He made no comment, apparently leaving the field for the moment, though George did not doubt that he would re-enter when he chose.

Caroline looked up and saw her aunt bearing down on them. 'Gentlemen, I think my aunt may need me.'

The gentlemen got to their feet as Lady Taunton descended on them, but she smiled and indicated that they should sit. 'Please continue with your supper, gentlemen. I came only to see if my niece wanted to accompany me to the rest room?'

'Thank you, Aunt.' Caroline rose obediently, for she knew when she was being told to do something, however charmingly it was put. 'Excuse me, Mr Bellingham—Sir Frederick. I shall hope to see you at the rout we spoke of.'

She followed Lady Taunton from the room and up the stairs to the bedrooms that had been set aside for the comfort of the ladies, waiting for the tirade to begin. However, when they were alone, her aunt smiled at her.

'You have done well, Caroline. Mr Bellingham is a wealthy gentleman, though some think him a confirmed bachelor—but of course Sir Frederick is one of the catches of the Season. He has been for years, of course, but so far has shown no inclination for matrimony. If you were to receive an offer from either of those gentlemen it would be highly satisfactory, though Sir Frederick is the better catch of the two. He is his uncle's heir, you know—and will be the Marquis of Southmoor one day.'

'I am sure that they were just being gallant,' Caroline replied. 'They wanted to pass the time pleasantly.'

'I am not quite so certain,' her aunt replied, looking thoughtful. 'Rathbone's godmother is a friend of mine. I do not think you have met her—Lady Stroud?' Caroline shook her head. 'No, I thought not. She told me that he has been attending more of these affairs recently, something he hardly ever does. I imagine that must mean he has set his mind to taking a bride. You have clearly caught his eye. It might be to your advantage to make a push, Caroline.'

'We share an interest in certain poets,' Caroline told her,

'but I dare say that is all we have in common. Besides, there were many others who asked me to dance, and to take supper, Aunt.' Her aunt's untimely interference was irritating, for she had only just met the gentlemen in question.

'Yes, of course. You must not show neglect in your manner to any gentlemen who take an interest in you, my dear—but bear it in mind that Rathbone is a good catch.'

Caroline did not answer. Her aunt's words had the opposite effect of the one she had surely hoped for. If anything were calculated to set Caroline against someone, it was being pushed in his direction.

Freddie looked across the card table and sighed inwardly. He had been holding the winning hand for the past few minutes, but was reluctant to declare it. He would have preferred not to play Farringdon, but had been unable to refuse the challenge, having won from him only a few nights previously. He was aware that the fool was playing out of his depth, and could probably not afford to pay a half of the notes he had so carelessly thrown on the table. He toyed with the idea of throwing his hand, but that was against all the rules of play. Farringdon must learn not to gamble beyond his means.

He took a card from the pack; it was the one card that could improve his hand, which was now virtually unbeatable. He discarded and then laid his cards on the table. A groan broke from two of the other players; they complained of his incredible luck, but did so with a smile and a careless shrug, for both were well able to pay what was owed. Freddie looked at Farringdon's white face as he sat staring at the cards in disbelief.

The other gentlemen got up and left the table almost immediately, in search of wine or food, but Farringdon sat on, almost as though he were frozen to the spot.

'It will take me some time to raise the cash,' he said in a flat voice, the seriousness of his situation showing only by a slight nerve flicking at his right temple.

'Yes, of course,' Freddie said, gathering up the various gold coins and notes that had been tossed on to the table. 'Unless you would wish to toss for double or quits?'

'No, no, I think not,' Farringdon said with an attempt to seem casual. 'It is a temporary thing, Rathbone. I should be able to settle in a few weeks.'

'Yes, of course. There is no hurry, none whatsoever. You may take as much time as you please, sir. Will you drink a nightcap with me? It is my intention to walk home.'

'Thank you, no,' Farringdon said and got up. He left the table and walked from the gaming club without looking from left to right, his face set in a frozen expression that gave no indication of his state of mind.

'Have you won again?' George Bellingham wandered over to Freddie as he sat on for a moment in contemplation. 'Farringdon looked desperate. I heard a rumour that unless he finds some way to come about he may be forced to sell his estate.'

'The damned fool should have cut his losses earlier,' Freddie said with a frown of displeasure. 'I have no desire to ruin any man, George, and if he comes to me with the truth, I shall return his notes to him. However, he must retire from the tables. He should take a bolt to the country and stay there until he has the funds in his pocket. The rule is that if you can't pay do not play.'

'A gaming debt is a debt of honour,' George agreed immediately. 'Why do you not put the poor fellow out of his misery, Freddie? Send the notes back to him if you mean to do it.'

'He needs a lesson,' Freddie said. 'Had he lost to Markham or Lazenby, they would have demanded payment within the month. If I give him his notes, he may be tempted to play again with someone less lenient than I.'

'Well, yes, there is that to it,' George said. 'But he will hate you if you show him leniency—it will damage his pride.'

'Then he must hate me,' Freddie said. 'The man is not ruined yet—not while I do not press my claim. No, no, Farringdon must come to me, and then we may settle this thing like gentlemen.'

'Well, I dare say you are right, though you may make an enemy,' George said, and then grinned at his friend. 'Tell me, what did you think of *her*?'

'I am not certain what you mean?' Freddie said with a lift of his mobile brows, though he was perfectly aware of George's meaning. Caroline Holbrook had made her mark with him, even if he was not prepared to admit it. There was something very appealing about her, which had drawn him to her despite her youth.

'Miss Holbrook, of course,' George said. 'Do you not think she is everything we spoke of the other day, Freddie? She has beauty, a liveliness of spirit that one cannot but admire, and when she smiles the room seems to light up. Enchanting would not be too strong a word.'

'Ah, I see you have been smitten. When am I to wish you happy, my dear fellow?' Freddie raised his brows

'Oh, as to that…I am set in my ways, you know. I am not certain that I should be comfortable married to any lady…but I must admit that, if I were tempted to change my ways, I might ask Miss Holbrook if she would do me the honour. Not that I expect she would accept me. I am too old for her—and she may take her pick of a dozen or more gentlemen, I dare say.'

'All this on the strength of one ball?' Freddie looked incredulous. 'She is not quite in the usual style for one so young, I give you that, George—but you have met lively young ladies before.' He refused to allow that Miss Holbrook was anything out of the ordinary, even though she had unaccountably lingered in his thoughts these past few days. He had not yet decided if that ingenuous manner was genuine or whether it hid something rather less pleasant. The girl had been frank about her lack of fortune—but was she a fortune hunter herself? For the moment he was inclined to stand back and watch as others fluttered about the flame.

'Yes, of course,' George said. 'I am not sure what it is, Freddie—but does she not strike you as being remarkable?'

'She has an amusing turn of phrase,' Freddie conceded. 'But is that artlessness real or assumed? I am reserving judgement for the moment. You will not see me at Almack's just yet, George.'

'I shall certainly attend,' George said. 'Sally Jersey has been giving me hints for ages. She thinks I should bestir myself to find a wife before I sink into the murky waters of old age.'

'Good grief,' Freddie said, revolted. 'You are in your prime, George. But if you fancy the little Holbrook filly, I shall not stand in your way—though I warn you she has scant fortune.' Now why had he added that piece of information? It could make no difference to George, who had fortune enough not to need a rich wife.

'Where did you hear that?'

'She told me herself.'

'Well, you may be right, though…' George shook his head. 'It matters not a jot either way. I am not on the catch for a fortune. I may not have your luck at the tables, but I am not done up yet.'

'I never imagined you were, my dear fellow,' Freddie said, amused as much by his own feeling of pique as George's enthusiasm. 'Do you care to walk with me?'

'I have my carriage,' George said. 'Let me take you up, Freddie. It has started to rain.'

'Has it? I had not noticed,' Freddie said. 'Very well, then. I had thought to stretch my legs, blow the cobwebs away, but I do not care for a soaking.'

The two men smiled at each other, in perfect accord as always as they went out of the club and into the waiting carriage. Neither of them noticed the shadowy figure watching as they were driven away.

Chapter Two

'Damn it, Jenkins—' the Marquis of Bollingbrook glared at his valet '—I am not yet in my dotage. When I ask for brandy, I do not wish it to be mixed with water!'

His valet's face wore a martyred air, for, having served his master, man and boy, he was not like to resent his outbursts of temper. Especially since he, above anyone at Bollingbrook Place, understood the pain behind the anger.

'Begging your pardon, milord,' Jenkins said, 'but it was Dr Heron as told me your lordship ought not to drink so much.'

'Damn his impertinence and yours,' the Marquis said with a grunt of displeasure. 'Pour a smaller measure if you will, but do not ruin the damned stuff!'

'No, your lordship.' Jenkins retained his impassive stare. The Marquis was prone to severe bouts of painful gout, which another, more critical man might have considered a judgement for his sinful past—sins that had haunted the older man for too long. Jenkins, however, was devoted to his master, besides being privy to secrets that others did not share. 'It shall not happen again.'

'See that it doesn't.'

'I am sorry, milord.'

'No need to be sorry.' A weary smile settled over the old man's features. He knew that of late he had become almost impossible to live with. There had been a time when he was a very different man, but he had lived too long trapped in the pain of his memories. 'Damned if I know how you put up with me, Jenkins. It's a wonder you haven't walked out before this. I've driven my family away. None of them visit me these days.'

The Marquis had fathered three sons, all of them by different wives. He had been unfortunate in losing the last of them, a beautiful young lady many years his junior. She too had died shortly after childbirth from a putrid chill. The Marquis had not been the same since her death. However, the loss of his youngest son had almost finished him.

'Wouldn't know what to do with myself if I retired, sir,' Jenkins answered in the same flat tone as before. 'Can't blame your family for not visiting. You lost your temper and banned them from the estate the last time.'

'Do you think I don't know that?' Bollingbrook growled. His foot was causing him excruciating pain and there was nothing to be done about it. 'But I didn't mean her, damn it!' A look of regret came into his eyes. 'Caroline is the best of them all. She is very like *her*, do you not think?'

Jenkins understood perfectly. 'Yes, very like, my lord. You could write and invite her to stay…'

'Her mother and aunt have taken her to London,' the Marquis muttered. 'Had a letter from that wilting lily last week. Damned if I know what Holbrook ever saw in her. I blame her for his death, you know. Another woman might have steered him to a safer path instead of weeping buckets in her bedchamber! Still, water under the bridge now.' He glared at his valet. 'I won't have Caroline forced into a marriage she doesn't care for. I suppose her mother is feeling the pinch. That is my fault, of course. Should have done something for her. I ought to have done something for Tom before this.'

'Why not invite him here?' Jenkins suggested, braving his master's fierce stare. He knew him too well to quail in his boots, though others had been known to flee before such a look. 'If I may take the liberty, milord? Send him to town to look after his sister. He can keep you informed on her situation.'

'Excellent notion,' the Marquis agreed. 'He's not as weak as his mother, though I prefer Nicolas. Full of spunk, that lad! However, Tom is Holbrook's heir, so I must do something for him. Bring me pen and ink, if you will. I shall write the letter now.'

Jenkins obeyed, setting the well-used, mahogany writing slope on the Marquis' lap, as he sat in his high-backed chair before the fire.

'Is there anything else, milord?'

'Not for the moment. I shall ring for you later.'

Left to himself, Bollingbrook opened the secret drawer of his writing slope and took out the miniature of his third wife. Angelica was the only one he had loved, though there had been many women before her, some of them acknowledged beauties, but none at all had followed her. He had loved her dearly, and believed that she would survive him for she had been so much younger. She had been the delight of his life, and when he'd lost her he had wanted to die and to be buried in her grave with her. Only her dying wish had prevented him from taking his own life.

'Look after our son; look after Anthony,' she had whispered as she lay slowly wasting of the putrid fever. 'Love him for my sake, I beg you.'

He had loved Holbrook for her sake and his own—and he loved Caroline too because she was so like his lost wife; she had the same vitality, the same brave heart. For the rest of his family he had scarcely any affection. He disliked his eldest son, Sebastian. He thought it a damned silly name, and would have disinherited him if he could, but would find it difficult to break the entail. He liked Claude slightly better, but not enough to want him to visit.

The Bollingbrook estate must go to his eldest son by law, and Claude must have the London property. He had lived there for years and it would not do to put him out. Yet he had some money and property that had not come to him through the estate and was his to dispose of as he pleased. He would divide it equally between Caroline and her brothers. He should have done it before, but it was still not too late. Despite the constant pain, he was sound of mind and there were a few years left to him yet.

Caroline dressed in a green-striped carriage gown. At least she had been allowed to choose this for herself, she thought with some satisfaction. She knew the colour suited her and she was pleased with her appearance as she went downstairs.

Louisa Taunton was still in her room, but she knew of and approved Caroline's engagement to go driving with Mr Bellingham that morning. She had given her permission without hesitation.

'He will no doubt bring his groom with him. However, it is quite respectable to drive out unaccompanied with a gentleman of Mr Bellingham's reputation. I have known him for some years, and a more likeable gentleman could not be found, I am sure.'

'Yes, Aunt. I thought you could have no objection to the outing. He is a gentleman of good taste, would you not say?'

'Indeed,' her aunt replied and looked thoughtful. 'But he has no immediate prospects of a title. It is unlikely it will happen—there are several cousins before him—whereas Sir Frederick will undoubtedly inherit his uncle's title, as the present marquis has no living sons or grandchildren and he is not likely to marry again at his time of life.'

'I think I prefer Mr Bellingham,' Caroline replied, 'should he take an interest—but I do not think we should count on it just yet, do you?'

She spoke innocently, yet with a look in her eyes that her aunt suspected. Lady Taunton was no slowtop and she was well aware that her niece resented her interference.

'I am only reminding you of possible options,' Louisa said tartly. 'I believe that Sir Frederick might be on the catch for a wife, whereas Mr Bellingham is unlikely to marry. Everyone knows that he is too set in his ways.'

'Is that so?' Caroline asked sweetly. 'Well, I dare say there may be others, Aunt. We must be patient, must we not?'

'You are impertinent, miss,' Lady Taunton said with a sour twist of her mouth. She thought that if Caroline were her daughter, she would have beaten some of that sauciness out of her long ago. 'Do not ruin your chances to spite me, Caroline. You may get less than you imagine, despite your success so far.'

'Oh, I do not let such foolishness weigh with me,' Caroline replied. 'I dare say I shall be fortunate to receive any offers at all.'

'Well, you will make a push for Sir Frederick if you have any sense,' her aunt said and dismissed her with a wave of her hand.

Caroline was not sure why it should make her so out-of-reason cross that her aunt was trying to influence her decision. As yet, of course, there was no decision to be made, for she was barely acquainted with any of the gentlemen she had met. Perhaps it was her aunt's eagerness to rush her into marriage for the sake of a fortune that she found so distasteful. It had soured what might be simply a pleasant acquaintance. She shook her head, thrusting the irritating thoughts to the back of her mind as she heard someone arrive at the door.

The footman opened the door to admit Mr Bellingham into the elegant hallway. He was looking extremely fine in his blue coat and pale grey breeches, a beaver hat now removed from his fair curling locks. His face lit up as he saw her descending the stairs, clearly ready to accompany him.

'Good morning, Miss Holbrook. May I say how charming you look?'

'Thank you, sir. We have a beautiful day for our drive, do we not?'

'Very pleasant. There is a slight breeze but it is quite warm.'

They went outside to where his curricle stood waiting, his groom at the horses' heads. Drawn by a pair of fine greys, it was a smart affair with yellow-painted spokes to its wheels, and Caroline felt privileged to be taken up by him. He handed her up himself and then took the reins, the groom jumping up behind.

During the drive to Hyde Park, they made polite social conversation, but once they were within the park, they turned to poetry and books they had both read. From there it was an easy matter to progress to other pursuits they enjoyed.

'Do you ride much at home, Miss Holbrook?'

'As often as I can, before breakfast if the weather is good. My father put me up on my first pony almost as soon as I could walk—and of course I rode with Nicolas most days. I miss him greatly now that he has joined the army, but I know that it was what he wanted.'

'Nicolas is the younger of your brothers, I believe?'

'We are but eleven months apart in age. My elder brother Tom manages the estate, of course. I am fond of Tom, but it was Nicolas with whom I shared so much.' She laughed as she recalled some of the naughty escapades that had landed her in hot water when she was younger.

'Yes, I see,' George said. 'It is natural that you should feel closer to Nicolas with him being so near in age.'

'It is more than that.' A husky chuckle escaped her. 'Nicolas was sometimes a little high-spirited, and he encouraged me to do things of which my governess did not always approve. We escaped our tutors together, and he always shouldered the blame as much as he could, though I confess that the ideas for our adventures were not always of his making.'

George smiled inwardly. Her laughter was infectious and he thought her enchanting. She seemed to have no fear of speaking out, though some of her revelations might displease the old tabbies who considered themselves the arbiters of good taste and decorum.

'You were fortunate in having such a companion, Miss Holbrook. I, on the other hand, was an only—' He broke off as he saw who was approaching them on foot. 'There is Freddie. I think we must pull over for a moment…'

Caroline made no comment. She knew that he could not neglect to acknowledge his friend, but would have preferred to drive past with a polite nod. Something about Sir Frederick Rathbone unsettled her, whereas she was perfectly comfortable with Mr Bellingham.

'Good morning, George—Miss Holbrook.' Freddie's dark eyes dwelled on her face. With that flame of hair peeping from beneath her chip-straw bonnet, which was tied with green ribbons to match her gown, she was certainly a beauty. She would not lack for suitors, he thought, and wondered why the idea of her being pursued by all the young bucks should be slightly irritating. 'Are you enjoying yourself, Miss Holbrook?'

'Very much, sir, thank you. I have seldom seen a finer pair than Mr Bellingham's greys.'

'You haven't seen Freddie's fine chestnuts,' George said, generous to a fault. 'Miss Holbrook is a great rider, Freddie, and a judge of horseflesh. You must take her up in your phaeton one of these days. I am sure she would enjoy it.'

'Oh, yes, I should,' Caroline said without pausing for thought. 'Nicolas let me drive his phaeton sometimes, and we once raced a friend of his around the estate…though perhaps I ought not to have said so? I believe it might be frowned upon by some?'

'You have just damned yourself in the eyes of the old tabbies,' Freddie said, amused. Her way of confiding in one was attractive, for she did it with such innocence that one could not help being charmed. 'But fear not, Miss Holbrook. Neither George nor I shall betray you.'

'Thank you,' Caroline replied, a faint blush making her look touchingly vulnerable for a moment. That was the second time he had said something of the sort. Had he taken her in dislike? She lifted her head defiantly, meeting his gaze.

'I think my tongue will land me in trouble one of these days. I should learn to curb it, but it runs away with me.'

'No, no,' Bellingham assured her, but Sir Freddie remained silent. His silence made her feel that he disapproved of her and that made her want to challenge him. For why should he censure her? She had done nothing outrageous, and his manner had pricked her pride. 'Though you might offend the tabbies without meaning to.'

'Who are these tabbies?' Caroline asked innocently, though she was well aware of their meaning. Her eyes were bright with mischief, bringing a laugh from George and a thoughtful look from Freddie. 'Please do tell, for I am all at sea.'

'You are a minx,' Freddie told her and now there was a hint of amusement on his lips, which caused her heart to flutter oddly. 'I think you mean to tease us, Miss Holbrook. George, I shall not keep you. I am certain you are wishing me to the devil.'

'Not a bit of it.' George smiled. 'All is fair in love and war, they say. I shall see you later at White's…' The words died on his lips, for at that moment Caroline gave a little cry and jumped down from the carriage, lifting her skirts clear to avoid stumbling as she ran across the grass. 'What the devil is she doing?'

Sir Freddie did not answer—he had seen what had caused Caroline to risk life and limb and dash off so suddenly. A youth was tormenting a puppy, kicking at it cruelly, and the creature was yelping with pain. Without reference to George, he set off after her, arriving just as Caroline rounded on the youth in a fury.

'How dare you?' she cried as the animal cowered away from yet another blow. 'Stop that at once or I shall teach you better manners, sir!'

'What yer gonna do, then?' the youth asked, leering at her. He was a dirty, ragged boy and his face was smeared with dirt. 'Can't stop me. Master told me to get rid of it—and he'll kill me if I go back with the flea-ridden brute.'

'Then go back without it,' Caroline said. 'Touch it again and I shall have you beaten!'

'Yeah? How yer gonna do that, then?' the youth asked, squaring up to her. He lifted his fist as if he would strike her, only to have his arm caught in an iron grip. Looking up, his face turned white beneath the dirt and his eyes darted to Caroline in fear. 'Call him off, miss. I weren't gonna hurt yer.'

'No, you certainly were not,' Caroline said, head up, eyes glittering. 'For I should have hit you with my parasol. Let him go, sir.' She addressed Freddie in a tone of command. 'He may run back to his master and say what he will. This poor thing shall not be tortured again.' Turning her back on them as though neither were of the least importance, she did not notice Sir Freddie give the youth a sharp clip of the ear before sending him off. Caroline was on her knees beside the puppy, stroking its head softly as it whimpered and shrank away from her hand. 'Oh, you poor little thing. He has hurt you so, but he shan't do it again—no one shall, I promise you.'

'The creature may well have fleas as well as broken bones.'

Caroline turned to look up at Freddie. 'The fleas are a matter of indifference to me, and may soon be cured with a warm bath—the broken bones are a different thing. He must be looked at by someone who understands these things and then…' She faltered, for she had suddenly remembered that she was a guest in her aunt's house. Lady Taunton would not welcome a bedraggled puppy in her home. 'He is not the prettiest dog, perhaps, but he deserves to be cared for, do you not think so?'

Freddie bent down and picked the puppy up carefully. He ran gentle hands over its quivering body, but, though it whimpered at first, it seemed to quieten at his touch.

'I believe he likes you,' Caroline said. 'Do you think—?'

'Oh, no,' Freddie said instantly. 'I do not wish to be saddled with a mongrel—and he most certainly has fleas.'

'I was going to ask only if you could direct me to a place where I can arrange for him to be cared for until I can claim him. I can pay for his keep and when…when I go home he shall come with me.' Her eyes were bright and filled with unconscious appeal that placed him on his mettle. Freddie struggled and lost. She saw it in his eyes and gave him a dazzling smile. 'I promise I shall claim him as soon as I can.'

'Very well,' he said reluctantly. 'I shall take charge of the wretched thing—but only until you can find a home for it. I have several dogs at home and they would make mincemeat of the creature. It can go to my stables. The grooms will know what to do for it.'

'You are generous, sir. I am grateful.'

'The dog remains your responsibility,' Freddie said gruffly, for something in her look had touched him. 'You should be aware that your dress has become stained, Miss Holbrook—and I would advise you not to throw yourself down from a carriage so precipitously in future. George was about to move on and you might have been injured.'

'What can that signify?' Caroline asked with a toss of her head. She bent her head to kiss the puppy's neck. 'Please take care of him, won't you?'

'I have never neglected any animal,' Freddie said a trifle haughtily. 'I do not think you need fear for this one.'

'No, of course not. And thank you for your assistance, though there was no need. I should have hit him if he had tried to attack me.' Her eyes flashed defiantly.

'Next time I shall remember,' Freddie said, a flicker of amusement in his face. 'I think you should go now, Miss Holbrook. George's horses begin to fret.'

'Oh, yes, I had forgot,' Caroline said and flushed. 'I did not mean to sound ungracious—thank you.'

She ran towards the waiting curricle and was handed up by George while his groom held the now impatient horses.

'You know you owe your good fortune to her, don't you?' Freddie murmured, scratching the puppy behind its ear. It had now settled in his arms and he was inclined to optimism about its condition. Painfully thin, it had obviously been starved, but with some good food and care… 'Ridiculous!' he said aloud, causing a passing lady to stare at him. 'I do not know who is the greater fool.'

Freddie stood watching as his friend drove on by with a wave of his hand. The girl was an original, there was no doubt of it. She would either become the latest rage or fall foul of some sharp tongues. It would be interesting to watch her progress.

He was not likely to be caught in her toils though, he told himself. She was lovely, intelligent and lively, and it seemed that she was both brave and compassionate, but he was not in the market for a wife. Though Miss Holbrook had certainly enlivened what had looked like being a damned dull Season before her arrival. He tipped his hat to a passing acquaintance, deciding to visit the club of a certain pugilist he favoured after he had handed the puppy to his groom. He was feeling oddly restless and in need of some exercise before he kept his appointment with George later that afternoon.

Tom Holbrook frowned over the letter from his grandfather. He had not been expecting it, but he was not averse to visiting the old gentleman. He had never been afraid of Bollingbrook, as some of his cousins were, though he had thought it wise to hold his tongue. The Marquis had a volatile temper, and had never hidden his dislike of Tom's mother.

Left to his own pursuits with nothing but a pile of debts to keep him company, Tom had been thinking that he might take a trip to town and visit his mother and sister. It would not bother him to make a small detour to visit his grandfather. The Marquis had said there was a matter of business to discuss, which did not sound promising. It was quite likely he was to be taken to task for putting up a part of the Holbrook estate for sale, but there was little else he could do in the circumstances. Tom had been forced to sell or risk losing everything, for his father had made some foolish investments.

He instructed his valet to put up a travelling bag for him and send his trunk on, and then had his groom bring round his curricle.

Within three hours of receiving the letter from his grandfather he was walking into Bollingbrook Place. It was an old house, but both the building and grounds were immaculately kept, which Tom knew must be expensive. The estate was clearly flourishing. Tom had not given much consideration to it in the past, but now he wondered where his grandfather's money came from.

'Master Tom, it's good to see you, sir,' Jenkins said. He

had just come into the hall as the footman opened the door and smiled his approval at the young man. 'Milord wasn't sure you would answer his call, but I thought you might—and here you are.'

'Of course I came,' Tom said. 'He threw Mama out with instructions never to darken his door again, but I was pretty sure that he didn't mean it. How is he, Jenkins? The gout playing him up as usual?'

'His lordship is in some pain,' the valet told him, 'but not as bad this morning as it has been for the past few days. I try to keep him from his port, but you know how it is, sir.' Jenkins sighed heavily, his long face wearing an expression of extreme martyrdom.

'I do indeed,' Tom answered and grinned; he knew the man had much to bear, but he also knew that nothing would prise him from the Marquis' side. 'May I go up and see him, do you think? His letter sounded important.'

'I believe it would do him good to have company, sir. He dwells too much on the past when he is alone.'

'I'll go up, then,' Tom said and nodded to Jenkins as he ran up the stairs. Outside his grandfather's door, he paused and knocked, waiting until a gruff voice invited him in. 'Good morning, sir. How are you?'

'No better for your asking,' the Marquis grumbled, but then thought better of it. He had, after all, invited the young man to call. 'Not so bad, thank you, Tom. It was good of you to come to see me.'

'I had nothing better to do,' Tom said frankly. He saw shock and then amusement in his grandfather's face, for it was unlike him to answer so. 'I was considering taking a trip to London, thought I might escort Caroline to some of the affairs, save Mama the trouble—that's if she has troubled herself, which I dare say she may not very often.'

'I take leave to doubt she will do so at all,' Bollingbrook growled. 'Featherhead! Still, she produced the best of my grandchildren—the rest of them are a pack of ninnies! I won't have them here; they argue and whinge and I can't stand that at my time of life. However, I want to see that gel of mine—Caroline. It's an age since she was here. I know she's gadding about town at the moment, and I don't want to spoil her fun, but I should appreciate a visit when she can spare the time. I want you to tell her that, Tom.'

'Yes, sir, of course. I shall go up in a few days—that's if you will put up with me in the meantime?'

'I hope you won't run off too soon,' the Marquis said gruffly. 'I didn't get you here just to talk about Caroline. I have some things to discuss with you. It concerns the future—you, Nicolas and my gel. I have been remiss, but I intend to put things right. In fact, I have already had my lawyer here and the thing is done, a day or two back as it happens. It can't be explained all in a moment. Concerns secrets that most of 'em don't know—and are not to be told, do you hear me?'

'Yes, sir.' Tom was surprised and yet flattered that he was to be let into that part of his grandfather's life that was never spoken of, though he knew the old reprobate had been a high-flyer in his heyday. 'You may rely on me to do as you wish on the matter.'

'Good, thought I might,' the Marquis said. 'Do you see that chest in the corner? The one with the iron bands? It is locked and this is the key.' He took it from his waistcoat pocket and held it out to Tom. 'Open it and bring me the packet you see lying on top. You may study it at your leisure, and then we shall talk…'

* * *

Caroline saw that Sir Frederick had entered the ballroom, which was overflowing with people and far too hot. He had such presence and such an air that she could not help thinking him the most distinguished man of her acquaintance, and her heart suddenly beat a little faster.

His gaze seemed to travel round the room, and then settle for a moment on her. She dropped her own gaze immediately, for she would not like him to think she was staring, even though she had been. However, in another moment her next partner claimed her and she was whisked into the middle of the dancers. For the following few minutes, she forgot about Sir Frederick; when she was returned to her aunt's side, he had moved from the place he had been standing earlier. Perhaps he had preferred the card room, she thought, deciding to put him from her mind.

'I should like to tidy myself,' Caroline told her aunt. 'Would you tell Mr Asbury that I shall be only a few moments, please?'

'Yes, though you must be quick,' Lady Taunton said with a look of disapproval. 'It is rude to keep partners waiting.'

Caroline left the room immediately, going upstairs to the room that had been set aside for the ladies. She made herself comfortable as quickly as she could and left the room, beginning to descend the stairs once more, but as she reached the bottom she met Sir Frederick. He had been about to go up, but stood to one side to allow her to pass. Caroline did not know what prompted her, for she ought simply to have nodded and passed him by, but some little imp was on her shoulder.

'You do not dance this evening, sir?'

'I seldom dance unless I particularly wish to,' he replied. 'And George told me that I had no hope of securing a dance with you, since your card was full soon after you arrived.'

'I am afraid that is so,' she said, 'but there are others who may have a space left, sir.'

'Of little use when I came only for one purpose.'

Caroline caught her breath. Was he saying that he had come merely to dance with her? Surely not! She smiled at him and went to pass him, but now he would not permit it and caught her arm, his fingers seeming to close on her like bands of steel so that she could not move without pulling away from him. His touch seemed to burn her and she trembled inside, wondering why he should have such an effect on her senses.

'You wanted something, sir?' She looked back at him, eyes wide and clear, a hint of challenge in their depths. 'But perhaps you came to give me news of the puppy we rescued?'

'Well, it would seem my groom has taken rather a fancy to the creature, which fawns on him in a ridiculous manner, and would like to take it home for his children—if you have no objection?' Freddie raised his brows. 'I was not sure what you would wish—unless you expected me to care for it personally? I am assured it will be well treated.'

'That is excellent news.' Caroline smiled. 'How very kind of your groom to take the poor little scrap in. Tell him that I am grateful for his kindness.'

'So would you like to name the pup or shall we leave it to Jacob and his children?'

'I should think his name ought to be Lucky,' she said, 'for he undoubtedly is to find such a good home, but it must be for your groom to decide, sir. I am in your debt for relieving me of what might have proved a problem in my present circumstances.'

'Yes, indeed you are,' Freddie said, his expression seeming to mock her. 'But I fear that if I asked you to walk with me in the gardens for a few minutes you would refuse.'

'We hardly know each other well enough for that, sir.'

'We do not know each other at all, Miss Holbrook.' He let one finger trail down her arm, sending a *frisson* of sensation shooting through her. For a moment as she stared into his dark eyes, she felt as if she were drowning, being sucked down and down into a swirling pool and out of her depth. 'I am not sure that it would be to the benefit of either of us to be become more intimately acquainted…despite our mutual interest in a lucky dog.'

'Then please allow me to pass,' Caroline said and gave him a frosty stare. Until that moment she had been revising her opinion of him, and liking what she had discovered, but now she was once again aware of the danger of allowing herself to like such a man. If she were foolish enough to develop a *tendre* for him, he would be sure to break her heart. 'My partner is waiting and I am already late for our dance. As you said, all my dances are taken.'

'Just so,' Freddie said, releasing her. He felt the reserve in her and mentally drew back. If he were not careful he would find himself drawn into a situation that could lead to only one end. He liked her enough to enjoy a light flirtation—but marriage? No, he had no thought of it! He reverted to the mocking stance that was his habitual manner. 'You intrigue me, for I do not believe that you can be all that you seem, Miss Holbrook. You have made an impression. I dare say you could marry one of several gentlemen, all of them titled and wealthy.'

'Do you think so, sir?' Caroline lifted her head. 'Perhaps you imagine that I wish to marry for fortune and position? If that is so, I think you may regard yourself as safe. I believe a marquis is as high as you can aspire in the future? I have only to encourage it and I may become a duchess one day…' She walked off, her back straight, leaving Freddie to watch her in wry amusement.

The devil of it was that she was probably right! He was annoyed that she intrigued him, holding his thoughts more often than he liked. What was it about her that had caught his attention? She was a beauty, but there were other ladies as lovely who aroused no more than a flicker of interest in his mind. It seemed that the only way he might free himself was to develop the acquaintance, for he was sure to find her out in the end. She could surely not be as innocent and pure of mind as she seemed.

Caroline returned to the ballroom. Had she been a cat, her tail would have been twitching, for he had managed to get beneath her skin. Sir Frederick Rathbone was a sight too sure of himself for her liking. He had deserved a set down, and that was the only reason she had spoken in a way that might be seen as bragging. It was true that a young gentleman, who was the second in line for a dukedom, had paid her considerable attention, but she would not normally have dreamed of drawing anyone's notice to it—and she had no intention of encouraging Sir Frederick to make an offer. Indeed, she had done her best to discourage it.

She wished that she had thought of some other way to put Sir Frederick down, for she did not wish him or anyone else to suppose that she was hanging out for a title. It was the furthest thing from her mind. At the moment she did not precisely know what she wanted from a husband. He must be an educated gentleman, able to discuss poetry and literature and to appreciate music and art. She thought that he must also have a sense of humour, for she did not think she could bear to be married to someone who was serious all the time.

For a moment her thoughts turned to Sir Frederick. She smiled at the thought of him giving into the seduction of a helpless puppy, allowing it to inveigle its way in to his good graces. Perhaps he was not as reserved or haughty as he sometimes seemed…and perhaps she did quite like him after all. At the back of her mind the thought hovered that, perhaps if her aunt had not been so very keen to see her marry Sir Frederick, she might have liked him quite a lot…

The next morning, Caroline had almost forgotten the little incident of the previous evening. She had decided to go to the lending library to take out a book one of her new friends had told her about. She went early, escaping without her maid, though she knew that her aunt would not approve of such behaviour. However, since the library was only a few streets away, she thought that it was quite safe for she would be at home again before her aunt was aware that she had been out.

It was as she emerged from the library, her parcel of books held by the string the assistant had obligingly tied for her, that she almost bumped into the man she had been thinking about despite her struggle to put him from her mind. He lifted his hat to her, and she could not but admire the way he looked in his dark green riding coat and pale breeches. It would seem that he had been riding earlier, for he still carried his whip. It was impossible to avoid him, so she smiled and wished him good morning.

'You are about early, Miss Holbrook.' He glanced at her books, a flicker of amusement on his lips as he saw that she had chosen not only a book of poetry, but also a rather lurid gothic novel that was just then causing quite a stir amongst the younger ladies. 'Ah, I see you have fallen victim to a great piece of nonsense, mistakenly described as excellent stuff.'

'You do not like Ann Radcliffe's work, sir?'

'I do not find it particularly entertaining,' Freddie said, 'though I can see it might appeal to the female mind.'

Caroline's eyes glinted with anger. 'I think you are patronising, sir. The female mind is equally capable of understanding more worthy works of literature, but a novel of this kind is meant for entertainment.'

'Yes, I dare say,' Freddie said, amused by how easily she had risen to his bait. 'Personally, I prefer the Marquis de Sade—but that would not be fit reading for a young lady, of course. If you wish to read gothic novels, may I recommend Gregory Lewis's novel *The Monk* to you?'

'Had I not already read it, I would have been pleased for you to do so,' Caroline said, lifting her chin. She suspected that he was teasing her and it brought a hint of defiance to her lovely face. 'I thought it a little shocking, but it was very well written, did you not think so?'

'Indeed, yes,' Freddie said and laughed softly, for he had read the hint of challenge in her eyes. She looked just like an angry kitten! 'Have you not guessed yet that I am teasing you, Miss Holbrook? It is a fault in me. My godmother often takes me to task for levity. She says that, if I were ever to conquer the need for such foolishness, I might become a better man.'

'Yes, of course,' Caroline said, sheathing her claws. 'Then may I take it that you have read Mrs Radcliffe's book *The Mysteries of Udolpho*?'

'Indeed, I have, some years ago,' he agreed. 'I found it

the best of her work—though I dare say others are tolerably readable.'

'I have not yet found it on the shelves,' Caroline said. 'It seems to be popular still, even though it was published some years ago.'

'Ah, then perhaps I may be of service to you,' Freddie said. 'I believe I still own a copy. Allow me to lend it to you, Miss Holbrook…'

Freddie became aware that she was not attending. Her eyes seemed to be fixed on something behind him, and he turned, taking in the incident instantly, for he saw the young boy being attacked by a group of older boys. Seeing that Caroline was about to plunge recklessly into the path of an oncoming dray wagon, he took hold of her arm, restraining her so violently that she yelped with pain.

'Forgive me,' he said, 'but I beg you, leave this to me. Stay here!'

The instruction was given in such a severe tone that Caroline remained where she was while he crossed the road, dodging between the traffic. She watched as he spoke to the lads, sending them off about their business, and noted that he slipped a coin into the hand of the one that had been attacked.

'What happened?' she asked as he returned to her. 'Was he much hurt?'

'It was merely a spat amongst brothers,' Freddie told her. 'The boy had lost some money one of the others had given him to buy their supper—nothing for you to be distressed about, Miss Holbrook.'

'You gave him money,' she said. 'That was kind of you, sir.'

'It was an easy task.' He gave her a severe look. 'May I

recommend you to be less impulsive, Miss Holbrook. You could easily have been injured just now.'

'You are good to be concerned for me,' she replied with a toss of her head. 'I assure you that I was aware of the wagon and felt that I was quite able to avoid it. I am not one of those fragile young ladies who faint at the slightest thing, sir.'

'Indeed you are not, but your behaviour is sometimes reckless in the extreme,' he said severely. 'If I may say so, Miss Holbrook, you are far too pretty to end your life crushed beneath the wheels of a heavy-goods wagon. But before you grow cross with me again, I believe I had just asked if I might lend you a book you wished to read?'

Caroline hesitated, for he had seemed critical, but her desire to read the novel overcame her pique. 'Thank you, I should like to read it for it has been recommended to me by a friend.'

'I shall send it round to your aunt's house,' Freddie said. 'In the meantime, may I walk you home?'

'You are kind, sir,' Caroline replied, 'but I am but two streets from my home and I dare say you have other things to occupy you.'

'Then perhaps we shall meet again soon.'

Freddie tipped his hat to her and set off down the street.

Caroline successfully managed to slip back into the house without being discovered by her aunt, though Mrs Holbrook had been to her room to inquire for her and was a little upset that she had been out alone that morning, even though it was merely to the lending library.

'It will not do for you to visit these places alone in town, my dear,' she scolded her daughter, though without malice.

'I am not sure it is safe, for who can tell what might happen to you, dearest? You might be snatched from the street and then I should never see you again.'

'Oh, Mama!' Caroline laughed. 'I do assure you that I was quite safe, and the only person I met was Sir Frederick, who had been out riding.'

'Oh, well, I suppose it was perfectly respectable,' her mother said. 'But I know that your aunt would not approve, my dear.'

'Aunt Louisa does not approve of anything I do.'

'Caroline!' Marianne reproved her daughter with a shake of her head, and then sighed. 'But do you know, I do not believe Louisa approves of much I do either.'

'Oh, Mama!' Caroline said and went into a fit of giggles for she had never expected to hear her mother say such a thing. 'Do be careful or she will give us both the most frightful scold.'

'I dare say she may,' Marianne said. 'Do you know, I think I shall accompany you this afternoon. You are going to visit some friends, I believe?'

'Yes, Mama. Mr Bellingham has asked me to take tea with his sister, Mrs Fairchild, and her daughter, Julia, and I have agreed. If you come with me, Aunt Louisa need not, and I know she had another appointment for she spoke of my going with just my maid.'

'If I come with you, there will be no need for a maid to accompany us,' Marianne said. 'Now, my dearest. The reason I came to look for you was that I have received some silk I ordered from the merchant a few days ago, and the seamstress is coming later this morning to discuss styles and fashions. Do come and look at the fashion plates she left for me to peruse. I need your advice.'

Caroline followed her mother obediently to her bedchamber, where various bales of silk were spread out on the bed. She was delighted to find that her mother had purchased some colours as well as grey, and there was not even a black ribbon to be seen.

During the next hour before the seamstress arrived, they had a pleasurable time discussing the styles that would most suit Marianne, and the colours she ought to choose for each ensemble.

Caroline left her mother when the seamstress arrived, retiring to one of the small parlours overlooking the garden at the back of the house to read her book. She returned to her bedchamber before the bell sounded for nuncheon and she was joined by her aunt and her mother, to partake of a cold meal.

After they had eaten, Caroline went up to change into an afternoon gown of pale green. She put on a bonnet tied with matching ribbons and a pelisse of creamy white, adding a pair of white gloves and a green reticule. She had hardly reached the bottom of the stairs when Mrs Holbrook joined her and they went out to the carriage.

'Well, this is nice, my dear, just the two of us,' Marianne said. 'Perhaps we should do this more often.'

Caroline forbore to answer that they might do it as often as she chose. It was nice to see her mother looking better and to know that she seemed to have begun to throw off her grief at last.

Mrs Fairchild welcomed them to her At Home, and invited Mrs Holbrook to sit opposite her, while Caroline shared a small sofa with Julia. There were only three other guests: Mr Bellingham, Mr Milbank, a gentleman of mature years, and also a gentleman Caroline had not particularly noticed before this day. She was introduced to him as Mr Farringdon, a man of some thirty-odd years, attractive but not as gentlemanly in his manners as Mr Bellingham in Caroline's opinion. He seemed to her to be ill at ease, and she disliked the way he spoke to her, as though trying to claim an intimacy that did not exist.

When Julia got up to help her mother by serving tea and cakes, Mr Farringdon came to sit beside Caroline. He began by being very complimentary to her, remarking on her dress and asking if she was enjoying her stay in town. Caroline replied politely, but did not smile or allow her tongue to run away with her as she so often did. She was glad when Julia looked at him expectantly, and he was obliged to relinquish his place to her. He took his leave soon after, and Caroline was pleased that he had gone. The tea party now became more intimate, and she was entertained by Mr Bellingham, who was relating a saucy tale that was going the rounds of London's drawing rooms.

'Well, you can imagine what Prinny made of that,' George said. 'He asked the lady to remove herself if she could not control her excess wind and she went off with her cheeks the colour of puce.'

'Oh, how embarrassing for her,' Caroline said. 'We should not laugh, for it must have been awful for her.'

'Think of poor Prinny. He was seated next to her, you know. I think it must have been just a little unpleasant for him.'

'Oh, my dear,' Mrs Fairchild said. 'I am not sure you should repeat that tale in mixed company. You may have offended Mrs Holbrook.'

'Not offended,' Marianne said. 'Surprised might be a better word—for I had not thought the Regent would mind his words to that extent...'

Silence greeted her sally, and then they all laughed. It was unlike Marianne to make a jest, but she had certainly attempted it and was given generous approval for her efforts.

'There, you see, it was quite acceptable,' George said and turned his attention to his niece. 'I am glad that you did not encourage Farringdon, Julia. I have every reason to believe that he is hanging out for a rich wife. From what I hear, he is all but done up.'

'Oh, I need no warning against that gentleman,' Julia declared. 'He asked me if I would take the air with him at Mrs Peterson's musical evening, but naturally I refused.' She laughed, a look of unusual naughtiness in her eyes. 'In any case, I believe he has turned his attention to Caroline—so I shall not receive a proposal after all.'

'Oh, dear, I do hope not,' Caroline said and gurgled with laughter. 'If he has hopes of me, I fear he will be sadly disappointed on two counts. I do not care for his manner so very much—and I am not the heiress he needs.'

'Caroline, my love,' her mother reproved. 'You are from a good family, and you have a small trust fund from your father. And your grandfather may give you something when you marry.'

'He might if he chose,' Caroline said. 'But I do not expect it.'

'I dare say your face is your fortune,' Julia said and looked at her admiringly. 'I wish I were as beautiful as you, Caroline.'

'Oh, I am not beautiful,' Caroline said, 'and you are very pretty, Julia. You must know that you are?'

'Pretty is not beautiful—is it, Uncle George? Caroline is beautiful, do you not think so?'

'Oh, most certainly,' he replied obligingly. 'But Caroline is right, Julia. You are very pretty, and you have your share of beaux so you do not need to pull caps with each other.'

'Oh, we shan't do that,' Julia said. 'I like Caroline best of all my new friends, and I intend to see a lot of her while she is in town.'

'Do you intend to stay in London long, ma'am?' Mr Milbank asked of Marianne. 'I myself have come only for a short visit. I find Bath suits me better and I have only come up to visit my tailor—there is no one to rival a London tailor, you know.'

The conversation immediately turned to the merits of various tailors of note, and the time passed quickly. Indeed, they stayed for much longer than the polite twenty minutes, and Julia was reluctant to let Caroline leave.

'You are coming to my dance tomorrow evening, are you not?' she asked. 'Please, you must say yes, for if you do not I shall be so disappointed.'

'Yes, of course we are coming,' Marianne said before her daughter could answer. 'We are looking forward to it very much—but now we must go. Lady Taunton has arranged a dinner party this evening, and we must not be late.'

She stood up and Caroline followed her, Mr Bellingham coming out into the hall to say goodbye to them.

'It was a pleasure to have your company,' George told her. 'It is seldom that one gets the chance to talk as we have this afternoon. I do not dine with Lady Taunton this evening, but I shall look forward to seeing you tomorrow evening. May I beg that you will reserve two dances for me, Miss Holbrook?'

'Yes, of course,' she said. 'I shall be honoured, sir.'

She followed her mother into the carriage, accepting Mr Bellingham's hand as he came to assist her. She sat forwards and waved, and then relaxed against the squabs as they were driven away.

'Well, that was very pleasant, was it not?' Marianne said. 'I thought I should be quite tired, but do you know, I feel very well. I think the air in London must agree with me. It is not as damp as the air at home, I believe.'

Caroline thought that it was perhaps being out in company that had helped her mother recover her spirits, but she said nothing. It was too soon to be sure of anything, and she would not embarrass her mother for the world.

When they arrived home, Caroline found a package waiting for her on the hall table. She knew immediately that it was the book Sir Frederick had promised her, and picked it up with a pleased smile. He had brought it as promised, which was kind of him, and improved her opinion of his character even more.

She was a little sorry that she had not been at home to thank him personally, but decided that she would send a polite note of thanks to the address on his card, which was tucked inside the package. As she went upstairs to rest before changing for dinner, she wondered if she would see Sir Freddie at Julia's dance…

Lady Taunton was somewhat indisposed the following morning, and announced that she would not be able to attend the dance that evening.

'Something must have disagreed with me last night,' she said, rubbing at her chest. 'I am sorry to disappoint you, Caroline, but I believe you must prepare yourself for an evening at home.'

'I am very sorry that you are feeling uncomfortable, Aunt,' Caroline said. 'However, Mama is to accompany me. She had already decided on it, and I believe she is looking forward to wearing her new gown.'

'Very well,' her aunt said, looking sour. 'It is all this junketing about I have been doing on your behalf, miss. It does not suit me. Your mama may do her duty by you for once and we must hope that she is not prone upon her bed in the morning.'

'I do sincerely hope she will not be,' Caroline said. 'And I hope that a rest this evening will cure your indigestion, Aunt.'

'If it is merely indigestion,' Lady Taunton said, looking much as a martyr might being led to the stake. 'I think I shall send for my doctor just to be on the safe side.'

However, nothing untoward happened, and Caroline set out with her mother at the appointed time. It was just a small dance, not one of the important affairs of the Season. Julia was greeting her guests, looking delightful in a white dress with spangles embroidered over the skirt. She stood with her mother to welcome everyone, but once Caroline arrived she was released and soon after the dancing began.

Despite it being a small affair, there were several gentlemen present, most of whom Caroline was beginning to know quite well, for she had met them at most of the affairs she had attended. She was, however, a little surprised when she saw Mr Farringdon walk in a little later, and asked Julia about it.

'Mama invited him before George told us that he was in financial difficulty. I wish she had not, for I do not like him. I had hoped that he might not attend, but it seems that he does not know when he is not welcome. I just hope he does not try to get me to go outside with him.'

'If he does, you must simply refuse,' Caroline said. 'Is your card full yet?'

'Almost,' Julia said. 'Oh, look, here comes Sir Frederick. I shall ask him if he will dance with me twice. That will leave no space for Mr Farringdon.'

She smiled beguilingly as Sir Frederick came up to them and offered him her card, asking if he would write his name in the only two spaces available. He did so and returned it to her, turning to bow to Caroline as Julia's next partner came to claim her.

'May I hope that you have a space left for me, Miss Holbrook?'

'Yes, I do have two, as it happens,' Caroline said. She had left them deliberately, but she was not going to admit it. 'One is just about to begin—and the other is just before supper.'

'Then I shall claim them both,' Freddie said and held out his hand to her. 'I hope you found the book you took from the library as enthralling as you hoped?'

'I have managed to read only one chapter as yet,' Caroline said, 'but I am sure I shall enjoy it. Mama says that she wants to read it when I have finished—so you see, I am not the only empty-headed female to be seduced by the delights of Mrs Radcliffe's work.'

'I assure you that I have never thought you empty-headed, Miss Holbrook,' Freddie said, a gleam in his eyes; he knew that she was being deliberately provoking. 'A little reckless, perhaps? Or is that simply a disguise to fool us all?' His manner was decidedly provocative and received the answer it deserved.

'Oh, you are unkind, sir,' Caroline came back at him challengingly. 'What makes you think that I would pretend to be other than I am?'

'It was simply a thought that popped into my head,' he murmured, attempting innocence. 'I dare say I was wrong?' Caroline was silent and he raised his brows. 'Have I offended you, Miss Holbrook?'

'Oh, no, not at all,' she said and looked up at him. 'Please continue what you were saying.'

'I think I meant to ask if you will come driving with me one morning, Miss Holbrook,' Freddie said. 'I was hoping that you might say yes…if you are not otherwise engaged?'

'Oh…' Caroline was a little surprised, for she had not expected it. 'Yes, I do not see why not, sir. I have driven out with Mr Bellingham several times, but, yes, thank you. I should be happy to do so.'

'Perhaps the day after tomorrow?'

'Yes, I believe that will suit. My aunt never makes engagements for the mornings. She prefers to stay in her room until eleven or twelve, but I like to go out early.'

'So I have observed,' Freddie said. 'I shall call for you at ten, if that is not too early?'

'No, not at all,' she said. 'I shall look forward to it.'

Their dance was ending and Sir Frederick escorted her back to Julia, who was to be his next partner. Caroline was momentarily alone, and she saw that Mr Farringdon was making his way towards her. Fortunately, her next partner arrived before he could do so and she was swept back into the throng of dancers.

As the evening progressed, Mr Farringdon made two more attempts to reach her, but Caroline avoided him, and it was not until she stepped outside on the terrace to cool herself for a moment before the supper dance that he succeeded in speaking to her. She had not seen him standing in the shadows, and, as he moved towards her, turned away, intending to return to the ballroom.

'Miss Holbrook,' he said. 'I have been wishing to speak to you. I had hoped that I might be given the honour of a dance with you this evening?'

'Forgive me, but my card was filled almost at once. Excuse me. I must go, for my partner will be waiting.'

'Surely you can spare a moment?' He moved to block her way, sending a little shiver of alarm down her spine.

'No, I must go,' she said and tried to move past him, but he laid his hand on her bare arm, making her jerk away instinctively. His eyes glittered and she thought he was about to say something more, but then his face froze and he took his hand from her arm.

'Miss Holbrook—I believe this is our dance?'

Caroline had never been more relieved in her life as she saw Sir Frederick standing in the doorway. Her face lit up and she moved towards him eagerly, offering him her hand.

'I had not forgotten. I was about to return, sir.'

'Nothing has happened to disturb you?'

'Oh, no,' Caroline said, for she did not wish to make something out of nothing. 'Excuse me, sir.' Farringdon stood back, nodding to Sir Frederick, who was regarding him sternly.

'And that,' Freddie said in a low voice as they went inside, 'was extremely foolish of you, Miss Holbrook. There are some gentlemen you would be safe with on a desert island, but not that one. What made you go outside with him?'

Caroline glanced at him, a hint of temper in her eyes. 'If you imagine that I went to meet him, you are mistaken, sir. I do not like the gentleman and would not even grant him a dance!' The expression on her face hinted that at that moment she did not particularly like Freddie either.

A smile flickered in his eyes as he inclined his head to her. 'I stand corrected, Miss Holbrook, and I am happy to admit it. I jumped to conclusions, but I happen to know that Farringdon is not ideal as an admirer for a young lady like you. Neither is he possessed of a great fortune. I do not imagine your family would think him suitable, for I dare say they expect you to make a good match.'

'Do you, indeed?' Caroline tossed her head at him as he led her into the dance. 'I thank you for your advice, sir. In this instance I believe the advice was not needed, but please do feel free to give me the benefit of your superior knowledge on these matters whenever you wish. As you say, it is imperative that I marry well, and I dare say you may know to a penny what any particular gentleman is worth.' Since he clearly thought her a fortune hunter, she might as well encourage the thought!

Freddie's mouth twitched at the corners, but he made no further remarks on the subject as he led her into the dance. Caroline relaxed as she felt his hand at her waist, and for some reason her anger vanished instantly. She looked up at him a little uncertainly.

'I have distressed you. Forgive me, Miss Holbrook.'

'I think that perhaps I have been rude? I am the one to ask for understanding, Sir Frederick. I was upset and spoke too hastily. Indeed, I was glad to be rescued.'

'No forgiveness is needed,' he assured her. 'I would have you no other way, Miss Holbrook. I prefer that a young lady should speak her mind—and I find you most refreshing.'

Was that another way of saying that she was ill mannered,

but to be forgiven because of her youth? Caroline was not sure if he was mocking her or not, because she was sure that he was laughing inside. She decided that the best thing to do was to retain a dignified silence, which she did for the remainder of their dance, but when he asked if he might escort her into supper she was obliged to smile and thank him.

'And thus might Saint Joan have looked as she was taken to the stake,' he said in a low voice, and as she looked up she saw that his eyes were bright with laughter. 'Am I still to be permitted to take you driving, Miss Holbrook?'

'Do you still wish to?'

'Yes, certainly,' he said. 'I believe…'

What he had been about to say was missed, for they were joined by Julia and a party of young bucks, and after seeing that Caroline had all she needed, Sir Frederick soon left them to the enjoyment of their supper. When she looked for him later, she realised that he must have gone.

She could not help feeling piqued, because she did not know what she had done to give him such a poor opinion of her. It was true that if she married well she might be able to make Mama's life better, and she would like to do something for her brothers too—but she would not wish to marry exclusively for money. Indeed, she could not imagine herself married to most of the gentlemen she knew…

Chapter Three

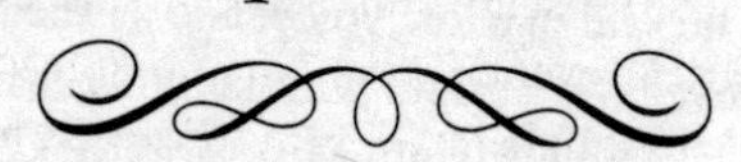

Caroline was thoughtful as she went to bed that evening. She was aware that the evening had been very pleasant, and she was enjoying her stay in town—but for some reason the sparkle had gone out of things after Sir Frederick had left the ball. Now why should that be? She had continued to dance all evening and many of her partners were very personable young men—but somehow none of them made her feel quite as alive as Sir Frederick.

Why had he left early? She wondered if she had offended him by being a little sharp and was sorry that she had been hasty. He'd seemed to imagine that she was interested in making an advantageous marriage and that had made her angry. What had she done to give such an ill opinion of her? Caroline pondered the question, but could not think that she had done anything. It was hardly her fault if she had attracted the attention of several important and wealthy men. She ought not to have said anything about being a duchess, though; the memory made her feel ill at ease with herself.

Sir Frederick had said that he still wished to take her driving, but she was afraid that she might have given him a dislike for her company. She was at heart a very well-behaved young lady despite being sometimes reckless. She decided that the next time they met she would be more careful of her behaviour.

The following day was quite taken up by shopping and appointments with the seamstress, and in the evening they attended a musical event. There was no sign of either Sir Frederick or Mr Bellingham, and Caroline wore a rather fixed smile all evening, and was rebuked by her aunt for being above her company.

'You may be bored, Caroline, but if you show it so plainly you will soon find that you are no longer invited anywhere.'

'I am sorry, Aunt,' Caroline said. 'I did not mean to offend anyone, but I am feeling...' She sighed, because she did not know why her spirits were at a low ebb. She ought not to feel as if the evening were pointless just because her particular friends were not present. 'Perhaps I am a little tired.'

It was merely an excuse, she knew, but she was glad when it was time to leave and she could be alone in her own room. She was a little on edge, and she wondered whether or not Sir Frederick would keep his appointment to take her driving the next morning.

She need not have worried, for he arrived at the appointed time. He looked extremely handsome in his blue coat and pale breeches, his boots having the kind of shine that only a valet of the first order could bestow on them.

'Miss Holbrook,' he said as the footman announced him, showing him into the downstairs parlour where Caroline was pretending to read a news sheet that had just been delivered. 'You look charming this morning, if I may be allowed to say so?'

'Thank you, sir. You are very kind.'

'You are ready?'

'Yes, of course.' Caroline smiled, allowing none of her uncertainty to show as she picked up her gloves and went out into the hall. 'You will not want to keep your horses waiting.'

She was assisted with her pelisse, and, tying the ribbons of her bonnet, followed him outside. The young lad Freddie employed as his tiger was walking the horses and brought the phaeton back to them.

'Thank you, Jim. Up with you now, lad.' Freddie turned to Caroline as the lad obeyed. She had noticed that he was driving a pair of perfectly matched greys.

'Mr Bellingham told me that you had some fine chestnuts, sir. Have you changed your horses recently?'

'No, but I had a chance to purchase these and thought they would be a splendid addition to my stables. One can never have too many horses.'

'Oh, I agree. I should imagine anyone would be pleased to own these.'

'Not all young ladies take such an interest in horses. You are a rarity, Miss Holbrook.'

'Am I?' Caroline looked at him as he handed her up. 'I have loved horses since I was first able to walk down to the stables with my father...dogs, too. Proper dogs, I mean, not the fancy lapdogs that many ladies dote on. At home I like to walk with them, sometimes for hours at a time.' She laughed. 'Indeed, I think I prefer being out with my dogs to talking to some of the people I have met in town.' She drew a sharp breath as she realised what she had said. 'Oh, dear, that was not well said. Now you will think me a country bore and I shall be ruined.'

'Not at all,' Freddie said. 'You have too much intelligence and vivacity to be a bore.'

'I shall take that as a compliment.'

'Well, you may do so, for it was meant as one.'

'Thank you. Do you have a country estate, sir?'

'I have three at the moment,' Freddie said. 'A hunting lodge in Oxfordshire, my family seat in Derbyshire and a shooting box in Scotland, which I seldom use. It was set up by my maternal grandfather and came to me on his death, but I prefer to spend much of my time in London.'

'Oh…yes, I see,' Caroline said. 'I suppose the country does not appeal to everyone, though I believe I prefer it.'

'The countryside can be pleasant enough if one has the right companions. But I do not care to spend too much time alone there when my friends are in town.'

'Yes, of course. Do you have no family, sir?'

'I had an elder sister, but she died of a putrid fever when a child.' His eyes darkened as if the memory still held echoes of pain for him. 'My parents had both died some years earlier, so that meant I was left to the mercy of the servants—and occasional visits from my uncle and grandfather. Grandfather died when I fifteen, but my uncle still lives. As does my godmother, Lady Stroud.'

'I had no idea.' Caroline glanced at him, for she guessed that he must have felt lonely as a child, but his face was a mask that showed no sign of emotion.

'Why should you? It was a long time ago. However, you must not be sorry. If I have few relatives, I have some good friends and many pleasant acquaintances.'

'Oh, yes,' Caroline agreed. 'I believe you are very close with Mr Bellingham, are you not?'

'We have been friends for some time.'

They were entering the park gates now and Caroline saw several ladies and gentlemen she knew. Some were in carriages, but most were on foot.

'Would you count that gentleman as a friend?' Caroline asked after they had been driving for some minutes. She had noticed Mr Farringdon. He was on foot and seemed to be staring fixedly in their direction.

'An acquaintance. I believe his estate is not far distant from my hunting lodge, but I would not count him a friend. We meet at the card tables and at various functions.'

'Yes, I suppose you must play with so many gentlemen at the tables,' Caroline said, looking thoughtful. 'Papa was not lucky at cards. I think it is not always wise to gamble too much.'

'You are very right, though the golden rule is to play only if you can pay.'

'Ah, yes, very true—but I think that gaming has brought more than one gentleman to ruin.'

'I am sure that is so. The devil of it is that one can do nothing to prevent it. When someone has the need for self-destruction, no cautionary words will help.' Freddie was thoughtful for a moment and then he glanced at her. 'But tell me, do you go to Lady Rowe's affair tomorrow?'

'Yes, indeed we shall,' Caroline replied, allowing his wish to change the subject. 'Shall you be there, sir?'

'It was my intention, but I have business that takes me to Oxford, though I hope to return within a few days.'

'Oh...' Caroline knew a pang of disappointment. 'Well, I suppose you must settle your affairs.'

'I must speak to my agent urgently,' Freddie told her. 'There are certain things that must be seen to at my estate and…elsewhere.' He smiled at her. 'Do you intend to stay in town until the end of the Season?'

'I am not sure…' Caroline wrinkled her brow in thought. 'For some weeks yet, I believe, but it depends…on many things.'

'Just so,' Freddie agreed. 'Tell me, Miss Holbrook, have you progressed with your reading?'

They began to discuss the merits of Mrs Radcliffe's writing, passing on to the discussion of literature and poetry. The park was full of people that morning, and, as they made their rounds, they were hailed by Mr Bellingham, who was driving Julia that morning.

Caroline was sorry when they completed their turn of the park and returned to her aunt's house. She smiled and thanked Sir Frederick for his company, and went in feeling oddly out of sorts with herself. She had enjoyed driving with him, but was still uncertain whether, if asked, he would count her as a friend or merely an acquaintance.

Freddie left town that afternoon, his thoughts much exercised by his conversation with Miss Holbrook. She had begun to pop into his mind too often of late, but he had not yet come to a decision concerning his future plans. If he cared to marry, Miss Holbrook was exactly the kind of lively young woman he would wish to make his wife—though he would not wish his offer to be accepted simply for the sake of his wealth and rank. He supposed that in time he must marry, for it was his duty to produce an heir, as his uncle had no children to carry on the family name. However, he would not wish to marry for such a reason.

It would be unfair to the lady and to him. He firmly believed that there must be genuine respect and affection on both sides for a marriage to work—and therein lay the rub, for he could not suppose that he had found much favour in the lady's eyes even if she had caused him a restless night or two. He knew that her careless remark about becoming a duchess had been made out of pique, but it might not be far from the truth. He had noticed that one or two of her suitors were more than a little interested and some were his equal in birth, if not quite in wealth. Was it possible that Miss Holbrook—or her mama—was waiting for the highest bidder? Caroline might be feigning indifference so as to arouse his interest the more.

Freddie had been used to living much as he pleased, and was answerable to no one for his actions. If he were to marry, he would need to make changes to his lifestyle and his various houses. What would do for a bachelor would not do for a lady, particularly one with modern tastes and a lively mind.

Yes, he must consider carefully while he was away. In the meantime, however, he had other more pressing matters on his mind…

It was as well for Caroline that the next few days were too full to allow her time for reflection. It seemed that she went from one affair to the next, sometimes attending more than one event in the same evening. If it was not Almack's, it was a private dance or a card evening, and she met the same people with amazing regularity.

She had begun to realise that there were very few gentlemen she would be happy to see every day of her life. Most of them seemed good mannered and pleasant, but that spark was missing, the vital element that made her feel so much more alive. There were actually no more than two or three in whose company she felt truly able to be herself. Mr Bellingham was perhaps the kindest of her acquaintance and she was usually happiest when with him and Julia Fairchild, who had become a particular friend.

Nearly a week had passed before she saw Sir Frederick again. However, he was with Mr Bellingham and Julia as she entered Mrs Ashton's large drawing room that Saturday evening. Her breath caught in her throat, and all at once her heart began to beat very fast. It was so very pleasant to see him again. She fanned herself delicately, for she believed that her cheeks must be flushed.

Oh, no, this was foolish! She must control her feelings. It would not do for her to show any sign of partiality this early in their acquaintance. He would think she was setting her cap at him! Even though Julia was making signs to her, she would not go to join them just yet.

They had all been invited for the pleasure of having supper, listening to music or playing cards. Some of the gentlemen were already playing cards at tables set up at the far end of the room, but Sir Frederick, Mr Bellingham and Julia were standing near the French windows, which opened on to the terrace, possibly because the room was already warm. She smiled at Julia, and then turned to the elderly lady who had come to greet Lady Taunton, schooling herself to patience. In a little while she would excuse herself and join her own friends.

However, before she could do so, she was joined by three other friends: a young lady by the name of Helen Telford, her brother Henry and her cousin Stephen Rivers. Caroline joined in the animated conversation, for they had all attended a balloon ascension that morning, and there was much to say on the subject. It had truly been a marvellous sight, and Mr Rivers was telling them that he had spoken to one of the balloonists and hoped to take a trip in a balloon himself very soon.

'You will not do so, sir,' Helen said, and looked shocked.

'Oh, you lucky thing,' Caroline said at almost the same moment. 'I should love to go up in a balloon. It looked so exciting. Just think how wonderful it would be to float across the sky and look down on what is happening below.'

'Do you not think that you might fall over the edge?' a voice asked from behind her. She felt a tingle at the nape of her neck and turned to see the person she had somehow expected. 'Or are you so intrepid that you would dare anything, Miss Holbrook?'

Caroline looked into Sir Frederick's dark eyes and saw the mockery there. 'I believe I should like it of all things,' she replied, challenging him. She had a feeling that he was trying to provoke her deliberately and, as before, she was aware that to let herself like him too much might be foolish. 'I think it would be almost impossible to fall out unless one were very stupid, sir—unless it was to crash, of course, but I do not believe that happens so very often.'

'I am certain it would not dare with you on board,' Freddie said, much amused by her answer. He had been watching her from across the room, fascinated by the play of emotions on her expressive face, and he knew he was not the only one to think her exceptional. She was certainly a hit, for you could not go anywhere in society without hearing her name. If her artlessness were real, she was truly a pearl amongst women.

'Now, be truthful, Miss Holbrook,' he said and studied her face, trying to probe beneath the surface. She intrigued him. She must marry well, for she had no fortune, but her manner seemed to say that she would as lief take a nobody as a duke, which had added greatly to her popularity. Was that the real Caroline or just an act? 'Would you truly wish for a balloon flight? I believe I could arrange it if you dare?' His brows rose, answering her challenge with one of his own.

'Do you really mean it?' Caroline was ecstatic, her face alight with pleasure. 'Oh, if only I could. My aunt would not approve, naturally, but perhaps she need not know exactly what I have been doing. We could arrange to drive out to Richmond...Mr Bellingham, too, perhaps?'

'May I be one of this party?' Mr Rivers asked. 'If Helen and Henry came too, it would be quite respectable. A picnic in Richmond Park and a balloon ascension, too. I'm sure your aunt could not object—and she need not know the whole of it, of course.'

Freddie groaned inwardly. He had made the suggestion idly, believing that Caroline would withdraw at the last moment, but from the expression of delight on her face it was clear that she was all for the excursion.

'Oh, I should love that,' Caroline declared with enthusiasm, 'and if we are to go in a party, my aunt will not think it her duty to come with me. When shall you arrange it, sir?'

'For next week,' Freddie said, pulled in by some force stronger than his will. 'On Thursday if it is fine. I shall call for you myself at ten in the morning, Miss Holbrook.'

'Oh, thank you!' Her eyes were glowing. 'You are so kind, sir. I cannot thank you enough.'

'I believe you may change your mind when it comes to it,'

Freddie said. 'But for now, will you do me the honour of becoming my partner at a game of whist?'

'Yes, why not?' Caroline said. She laid her hand on his arm, giving him a brilliant smile. Freddie almost blinked—he had the impression that the sun had just come out and it sent him a little dizzy. She was truly an enchantress, whatever else she might be. 'Tell me, who are we to oppose?'

'George and Julia,' Freddie said. 'She is very modest about her skill, and tells me she plays whist with her grandmother for peppermints.'

'Oh, does she?' Caroline nodded happily. 'I used to play for humbugs with Nicolas. He usually won all the sweets from my jar—but I think he cheated. When I played with Tom I usually won.'

'Ah, yes, your brothers,' Freddie said. 'Do you think either of them will join you in town?'

'I do not think so,' Caroline said wistfully. 'Tom would if he could afford it, I think, but Nicolas is in France at the moment. He was sent as a liaison officer and I have not heard from him for almost a month now.'

'Well, perhaps he will surprise you on his return,' Freddie said. It would be interesting to observe her with her brothers, he imagined. 'Ah, George, you see I have captured Miss Holbrook. I told you I should persuade her to join us.'

'Oh, good,' Julia said and then blushed shyly. 'I should like that of all things, that is if Miss Holbrook chooses.'

'I believe we are to oppose each other, Julia, and I must wish you good fortune, though I dare say you will not need it with Mr Bellingham as your partner.'

'Julia is a demon card player,' George said and laughed.

'Do not be deceived by her modesty, Miss Holbrook. I warn you, at the card table she is ruthless.'

Caroline laughed. She felt fortunate to have been singled out as a fourth at their table, for some of the other company were not likely to be as much fun as her companions.

Someone had begun to play the pianoforte as they settled at their table. As the room was so large they were able to hear the music without losing concentration on their game, or disturbing those who wished to listen to the music. It was a very comfortable, pleasant arrangement.

'It is such a nice large room,' Caroline remarked. 'Of course, not all houses are built so obligingly.'

'Deuced difficult to heat in the winter, I imagine,' Freddie observed. 'I prefer separate rooms if the play is serious, but for an evening like this it could not be bettered.'

'Yes, though it is too warm for my liking. Not like your barn of a place, Freddie. That is cold even in summer,' George remarked.

'You are right, George,' Freddie replied. 'I am thinking of making some changes for the future.'

'You will need to when you marry.'

'If I marry…'

'My dear chap,' George said. 'Your uncle would be damned annoyed if you do not produce an heir, I should imagine. You owe it to the family, you know they are relying on you.' George coughed behind his hand. 'I beg your pardon, ladies, I forgot myself for a moment. Remiss of me. Mixed company, you know.'

'Oh, you need not fear,' Caroline said and dimpled at him. 'You must know that I have heard far worse from my grandfather. When his gout is playing him up the air is like to turn blue. Poor Mama almost fainted one day—the things he said to her!'

'Grandmother is a little like that, though she lowers her voice so that I shouldn't hear,' Julia said. 'But of course I do.'

'I do not believe I know your grandfather,' George said, wrinkling his brow. 'No one has mentioned him in my hearing.'

'Really, George,' Freddie drawled. 'Surely you've heard of the Marquis of Bollingbrook?'

'Good lord!' George looked astonished. 'Everyone knows—or has heard—of the Marquis, of course. I hadn't connected the two.'

'I believe Grandfather was a rake,' Caroline said. 'At least when he was much younger. I know there are some mysteries, secrets in his past, but of course he has never told me anything.'

'No?' Freddie raised his brows. 'You surprise me, Miss Holbrook. I would have imagined quite otherwise. However, perhaps I can unravel at least one of those mysteries for you. I know that your grandfather once took part in a bare-knuckle fight that lasted for twenty rounds. That is one of the few of his escapades that it is permissible to repeat in polite society.'

'How did you know that?' Caroline asked, her mouth quivering as she quizzed him with her eyes. 'Tell me, sir—did he win?'

'Yes, I believe he did.'

'Oh, well done, Grandfather!' Caroline said and calmly laid her trump card, taking the trick. 'I must ask him about it when I next see him…if I ever do.' She sighed.

'Well done,' Freddie said, as she collected her cards and laid a small club. 'A gentleman perhaps paying for his misdeeds. However, there were many other escapades that might not be so admirable as that fight, as I understand it.'

'You must tell us,' Caroline cried, taking the next hand with a nine of clubs. 'I have heard he was a gambler and...well, perhaps I should not say.' She glanced at Julia and then down at her cards.

'No, perhaps not,' Freddie said.

'I think we should change the subject, Freddie,' George observed with amusement. 'It is Julia's birthday dance this weekend. I trust you will be there, Miss Holbrook—and you, Freddie?'

The subject was successfully turned and they applied themselves to the cards. When everyone began to drift into the dining room, several other young people joined them at their table, and the conversation became very animated. Someone mentioned the balloon ascension and somehow the party grew to three carriages, to include Mr Bellingham and his niece Julia.

After supper, Caroline suggested to Julia that they should join forces against the gentlemen at cards, an idea that was taken up with pleasure. Luck must have been with them, for they won two games to one and enjoyed the feeling very much. Despite her shyness, Julia had true character, gathered no doubt from the long hours she had spent playing cards with her formidable grandmother, and she could be ruthless when it came to taking a trick.

Caroline asked Julia if she would care to go shopping with her the next morning. An arrangement was made to meet, and they parted on good terms.

Caroline was feeling very pleased with herself as she joined her mother, who had consented to accompany them that evening. However, her smile faded as Aunt Louisa came up to them, looking very satisfied with herself.

'I am pleased to see that you have taken my advice,' she said, her smug tone making Caroline itch to quarrel with her. 'I observed Sir Frederick's manner towards you this evening. I think he is taken with you. If you continue as you are, I am certain that he will come up to scratch before the Season is done.'

'I am not sure that you are right, Aunt,' Caroline said, containing her irritation with commendable control. Her aunt's comments made her uncomfortable, for she had certainly not set her cap at Sir Frederick. Indeed, until recently she had not been sure that she liked him. She had now revised her opinion and was secretly afraid that she was beginning to like him rather a lot, which only made her cross. She certainly would not wish him to think that she was angling for a proposal! 'We are becoming better acquainted, but there is nothing to show an attachment on either side.'

'You must listen to your aunt, Caroline,' Marianne Holbrook said nervously. She had sensed the friction between them and it made her uneasy, because she knew that her sister would lecture her on her daughter's faults when they were alone. Of course Caroline was a trifle headstrong and wilful, but she was also kind and thoughtful and her mother did not wish to be lectured on the subject. 'I am sure she knows best.'

'Yes, Mama, of course,' Caroline said, though her face was set like thunder. 'I dare say my aunt knows much more than I on a great number of things—but perhaps on this I may be allowed to judge for myself.'

'You are a stubborn, ungrateful girl,' her aunt said. 'Well, I shall not argue with you, Caroline, but you will see that I am right soon enough.'

Caroline's dreams were peaceful enough, though when she woke she did so with a start. She had been dreaming of a room filled with gentlemen playing cards, and a deadly game was taking place between two men, one of whom was Sir Frederick. The reason it had caused her to shiver upon waking was that she knew it was she for whom they were playing.

She laughed as she realised that the dream must have been because of the talk of her grandfather and his reputation last night. What a dreadful rake he must have been in his youth! And by the sound of things, it was not the worst of his escapades by half.

She had always been fond of the old reprobate, though as a child she had seen little of him. He had begun to take more interest in her as she grew up, and on her last visit she had spent some time with him in his library, looking at his books and pictures. However, he had lost patience with her mother and they had left under a cloud. Since then she had heard nothing from him.

She thought about it and then sat down at the writing desk in her bedchamber, deciding to write to him about her visit to London. If he did not wish to read her letter, he could throw it into the fire. However, she thought he must sometimes be lonely, for she knew that his family seldom visited him.

She smiled as she sanded and then sealed her letter with wax and a beautiful gold seal ring that her father had given her as a keepsake shortly before his death. Taking her letter downstairs to be left with the others for franking and posting, she then collected her pelisse and bonnet and, with her maid in attendance, set out for her appointment with Julia Fairchild.

They were to meet at a fashionable milliner's shop and from there would go on to a shop that sold delightful shawls and other pretty trifles. Julia had told her that she had seen a beaded purse that she particularly admired, and Caroline had been thinking of a rather attractive green bonnet she had seen when out with her aunt the previous week. She meant to purchase it if she could, though her aunt had thought it too dark for her.

When she arrived at the shop, she discovered that Mr Bellingham had accompanied his niece, and, as they went in to look at the delightful bonnets on offer, she saw Sir Frederick cross the road. He entered a few moments after them, she thought by prior arrangement with his friend, for Mr Bellingham was not at all surprised to see him.

Caroline was before the mirror, trying on the bonnet she had seen in the window, and Sir Frederick stood behind her, nodding his approval.

'You should wear more green,' he told her. 'I particularly like that on you, Miss Holbrook. You have the colouring for it.'

'You are very kind, sir,' she said and laid it down. 'But I am not sure that it is just what I want.' She wandered away, determined not to let him influence her. Was her aunt right? Was he paying her attention with the notion of asking her to marry him? Mr Bellingham had mentioned that he must marry to oblige his family the previous evening. Did she wish to be married simply for the getting of an heir? She was not sure how she felt about that and she would not allow herself to be rushed into a more intimate acquaintance. She picked up a deep blue velvet hat and perched it on the back of her head. It was becoming but slightly racy, more suited to an older lady, perhaps. She was about to put it down again when she saw Sir Frederick shake his head at her, registering disapproval, and on a spurt of independence, she held it out to the assistant. 'I shall take this if you please,' she said defiantly.

'Do you think you should?' Freddie said, hoping that his expression gave no hint of his satisfaction. She was ravishing in that hat, but he had learned his lesson earlier. 'I think Lady Taunton will not approve. Perhaps you would do better to think about it for a while?'

'I shall mostly certainly buy it,' Caroline said, a militant sparkle in her eye. 'I do not allow anyone to dictate to me if I can prevent it, sir.'

'Very sensible of you, Miss Holbrook,' he said innocently, but she detected a gleam of mockery in his dark eyes. 'But I will wager she forbids you to wear it.'

'What do you wager?' she demanded at once, her eyes bright with challenge.

Sir Freddie thought for an instant before answering. 'If you succeed in wearing it tomorrow when I call for you to go driving, I shall grant you one wish, Miss Holbrook—and if you are forbidden to leave the house with such a wicked thing on your head, you must grant me my wish.'

Caroline was a little taken aback, for she had imagined he would make a small wager of a guinea or some such thing. A wish might mean anything, but, since she had no intention of letting her aunt dictate to her in the matter, she had no hesitation in taking his wager. In her pleasure at thinking of what she would demand from him, she did not realise that she had agreed to drive out with him. It was not until much later that day that she began to wonder just what he had in mind should she lose the wager…

Chapter Four

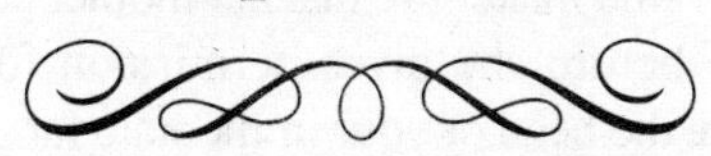

Tom was thoughtful as he took leave of his grandfather and set out for London that morning. He had stayed for ten days, because the contents of the package given to him to examine had taken some serious thought on his behalf, and because he sensed his grandfather was feeling lonely. Lord Bollingbrook had put some propositions to him, which would mean a journey overseas if he accepted them. He had been given time to think them over, and to consider what they might mean to his life. Meanwhile, he was in possession of sufficient funds to pay the most pressing of his debts at home, and the news that both his brother and sister would shortly come into modest fortunes of their own.

Caroline was to have twenty thousand pounds on her wedding day, and she would also be given some rather valuable pieces of jewellery, which were not heirlooms, but had been bought for her grandmother at the time of her wedding. It meant that, far from being almost penniless, his sister was now a considerable heiress. However, Tom had been forbidden to inform her of her good fortune. His grandfather had made that plain as they sat together the previous evening.

'You are to say nothing to the gel or her mother—and certainly not to that aunt of hers, Tom. What you will tell your mother is that I shall not have my gel forced to a marriage she cannot like. I wish to be informed before anything is settled, do you hear me, boy?'

'Yes, sir, of course. May I tell Caroline that, sir?'

'You may tell her to come to me if she is in trouble,' the Marquis said. 'And make sure that her mother understands she must ask me before she gives permission for Caroline to marry. You are the head of your immediate family, Tom—but in this matter I stand on my rights as head of our family. You understand me?'

'Yes, sir, perfectly.' Tom gave him a smile of perfect good humour. 'I can assure you that I have no wish to see Caroline unhappy. Indeed, I should forbid Mama to bully her into something she disliked.'

The Marquis nodded approvingly. He had hopes of this grandson, for there was a wrong done many years ago, a wrong that needed to be put right, and it was too late for him to do it himself. 'And do not forget that I wish to see Caroline when she has the time.'

'No, sir, I shall not forget.'

Leaving the Marquis to the ministrations of his faithful valet, Tom went out to find his groom waiting for him. He took the reins himself, allowing the man to sit beside him as they drove through the estate at a spanking pace.

He had promised his grandfather that he would give him an answer in three weeks. In the meantime, he intended to enjoy himself in London.

'And what, miss, is that on your head?' Lady Taunton looked at her niece in outrage. 'I hope it is not your intention to leave this house wearing such a piece of nonsense? It is far too old for you and it makes you look fast.'

'Oh, no, Aunt, does it?' Caroline wore a face of innocence, her eyes as guileless as a babe's. 'And to think that Sir Frederick encouraged me to buy it—insisted that I wear it for him today. However, if you think I should not, I shall go up and take it off, though I believe he will be disappointed. You know, Aunt, I do not imagine that he would be interested in a milk-and-water miss—perhaps I should be a little bold if I am to capture his interest? But pray tell me if you disagree, ma'am?'

'I imagine you think yourself clever,' her aunt said and scowled at her. 'Very well, my girl, make a show of yourself if you choose. If you get a reputation for being fast, you will ruin yourself, and then no one will offer for you.'

'Oh, Aunt, if only I could believe you,' Caroline said to herself and went quickly down the stairs as she heard the doorknocker.

Her aunt stood at the head of the stairs, watching as Sir Frederick entered and swept off his hat to her niece. He glanced up at her as she stood at the head of the stairs, a flicker of amusement in his eyes, for her annoyed expression told much. He bowed his head to her and then turned to look at Caroline.

'You look beautiful, Miss Holbrook,' Freddie said in a voice that carried to Lady Taunton, who snorted her disgust and walked away as Caroline laid her hand on his arm. 'That hat becomes you well—and I believe I have lost our wager…' He lowered his voice as they went out to the waiting carriage. 'What would you have of me?'

'May I have a little time to think?' Caroline asked, her head to one side. Her eyes were filled with wickedness, making him laugh softly, for he sensed her mood of defiance. She really was enchanting, a girl of spirit! But could he be certain that she liked him for himself—if she liked him at all, that was? 'What would you have demanded of me had I lost?'

'I had thought of something entirely suitable,' Freddie said, 'but I take leave to keep my secret for the moment. I think you have the gambling spirit of your grandfather, Miss Holbrook, and I may win next time.'

Caroline tipped her head to one side, for she saw the mockery in his eyes. 'Perhaps you have already won, sir,' she suggested. 'For you wished me to buy this hat all the time, did you not?'

'I have observed that deep colours become you,' he said. 'I dare say that you are under the influence of others, but I should like to advise you on matters of dress, Miss Holbrook. Be bold in your choice, for it suits you. Do you know that you are considered an original? At this moment you may say and do almost as you wish, for you are the darling of society.'

'No, am I?' Caroline was astonished. She looked at him hard to see if he was quizzing her. 'Are you funning, sir? I know that people have been amazingly kind, but I had not thought to cause a sensation. After all, I have very little fortune.'

'Which matters not a jot in your case,' Freddie said, enjoying himself immensely. He was beginning to accept that she meant what she said, and that artless as her manner was, it was genuine, not assumed. 'I have it on the best authority that there are ten wagers on the books at White's concerning you, Miss Holbrook.'

'No? How terribly shocking,' she said and gave a gurgle of delight. 'Pray do tell me what they are for.'

'No, no,' he said. 'For then you would make up your mind before you were asked and that would prejudice the wager.'

'Oh, that would be even more shocking,' she said, her eyes dancing with merriment as he handed her into her carriage.

'Yes, indeed,' he replied with a straight face. 'Gambling is a serious business, Miss Holbrook. Fortunes have changed hands for a foolish wager when gentlemen have been imbibing recklessly. One gentleman placed a bet that he could shoot the king of spades in the eye when drunk one evening, I recall. He was an excellent shot when sober, but just a trifle off when in his cups. He lost a small estate in Kent that night.'

'How awful,' she said. 'I do not think I should care to gamble so much on such a business.'

'Come, come, Miss Holbrook,' he said. 'Where is your fighting spirit now?'

'Perhaps if I were wealthy,' she said, 'but I should not be able to honour such a bet, for I have no property.' She looked up at him. 'Tell me, have you ever made such a reckless wager?'

'I just told you of it,' Freddie said and laughed. 'But that was when I was much younger and more inclined to wildness. However, I did not much care for the place and I later won something I liked better.'

'Are you usually fortunate at the tables?'

'Oh, yes,' he said carelessly as he drove them through the busy streets. 'Observe that gentleman in the rather odd purple coat there to your left—but do not let him see that you are staring. I won ten thousand guineas from him the other evening. I offered to throw the dice for double or quits, but he would not take it.'

'I dare say he could not afford it, sir.'

'Oh, yes,' Freddie said. 'The fellow has more blunt than he knows what to do with. His uncle recently left him a huge estate—half a million, they say—though he will probably run through it before he has done.'

'Then he is very foolish. I think that gambling for high stakes may be the cause of much suffering amongst the families of those who are addicted, but also unlucky.'

'You are perfectly right, Miss Holbrook,' Freddie said and looked serious for a moment. 'A great friend of mine was ruined that way, and there was nothing I could do about it. Had he gambled only with me, I might have saved him, but he went to low dives where the stakes are sometimes too high. Only the most reckless would play in places like that, I think.'

'You do not?'

'No, no, I am a mild gambler, Miss Holbrook. I usually prefer wagers that are not always for money.'

'Then my forfeit was not to have been monetary?'

'No, indeed.' He arched his brows at her. 'But you will not coax it from me, Miss Holbrook. I am determined that I shall win next time. Have you made up your mind what you would have of me?'

'I think…' Caroline was about to say that she wanted nothing when they were accosted by one of the young bucks walking in the park. He came up to them, sweeping his hat off and smiling at her.

'You look particularly lovely today, Miss Holbrook,' he said. 'But it was Sir Frederick I particularly wanted to address. Have you heard about the mill, sir? It is to take place on the Heath next Tuesday and they say that Gentleman George will win this time. Are you to attend?'

'I imagine I may,' Freddie said and frowned at him. 'However, this is a matter for discussion at another time, Blakeny.'

The younger man looked at him and then flushed. 'Oh, I

see what you mean, Rathbone. But I'm sure Miss Holbrook isn't offended over a small thing like that.'

'No, indeed,' Caroline said, but Freddie merely frowned and flicked the reins, moving on. 'I truly did not mind, sir.' She glanced at him sideways and saw that he was frowning. 'Why are you annoyed?'

'It was not the subject for a young lady's ears. That young idiot should have known better than to speak of it in your presence.'

'Oh, pooh,' Caroline said, and on impulse, 'I should like to see a fight—will you take me to watch it, please?'

'No, indeed I shall not,' Freddie said. 'The scene of a bare-knuckle fight is not the place for a young girl. It is out of the question.'

'But you must,' Caroline said because she was piqued by his attitude. Why did gentlemen always think a lady was too delicate for such things? She had seen her brothers scrap when they were young and had been none the worse for her experience. 'You promised me a forfeit and that is what I want…to come with you to watch the fight.'

Freddie turned his head to look at her in disbelief. Did she know what she was asking? 'You cannot mean it, Miss Holbrook? It would be most improper and your aunt would have a fit if she heard of it.'

'Well, she need not,' Caroline said. 'I shall not tell her, and neither will you—so how will she know?'

'Because everyone would talk of it,' he replied and shook his head at her. 'There would be a terrible scandal and you would be ruined. No, I shall not do such a thing. I do not think you have considered the consequences.' He gave her a severe look. 'This is foolish in the extreme.'

'But you know that paying a gambling debt is a matter of honour,' Caroline said, tipping her head to one side. Her eyes were bright with devilment; though in her heart she did not particularly wish to see the fight, she was determined to get her own way. He could not wriggle out of it, because his sense of fair play would not allow it. 'And there is a solution…if I came dressed in a youth's clothes and hid my hair, everyone would think I was your groom.'

'I do not believe that you dare,' Freddie said, but there was a sudden gleam in his eyes. The plan could just work. Her boldness amused him, and he found the idea appealed to him, against his better nature. Indeed, the idea was so intriguing that he decided to see if she would actually dare to carry it out. 'How would you slip away—and where would you get the clothes?'

'I imagine the fight is to be held early in the morning? I could slip out and perhaps return before my aunt had risen.'

'Yes, I dare say…' Freddie was caught—this was beyond anything he had expected from her and he was tempted to see just how far she would go. 'Of course, I could give a parcel of clothes to your maid, if you truly wish to go through with this—but think carefully. Supposing you were discovered?' He raised his brows at her.

'Both Mama and my aunt scarcely ever rise much before noon. I dare say we might be back home before then.'

Freddie gazed at her doubtfully. It was madness and he knew that he should refuse, but he had always paid his gambling debts… No, no, that was merely an excuse. He could not wrap this in clean linen. In truth he was tempted by the prospect of discovering whether she was really as bold as she claimed.

'If you gave your maid some of your own clothes for me, it might work,' he said. 'You may change back into them after we have left the fight, and then go home as if we have merely been for a drive together…if you truly wish to take the risk?' His eyes were intent on her face.

Caroline was on fire for the idea had appealed to her. It would be an adventure and she had been feeling restricted by her aunt's constant grumbling, the need to behave circumspectly at all times. 'If the clothes are suitable for a groom and I dirty my face, no one will even notice me.'

'How will you slip out of the house?'

'Oh, I shall manage it,' Caroline said. 'I have done it before…at home in the country. It may not be quite as easy in town, but I dare say I can manage it.'

'Very well,' Freddie said. 'We shall make another wager, Miss Holbrook. If you play your part I shall take you to the fight, but if you change your mind you will owe me a forfeit.'

'I think you will owe me yet another forfeit,' Caroline said, her eyes sparkling with mischief. Her head was up, her face alight as she challenged him. He thought her more lovely than he had yet seen her. 'I shall be there—and you must be on time, sir. I do not wish to miss anything.'

Freddie laughed, for she was undoubtedly a temptress. Would it be possible to take her to such an event and return her to her home with no one the wiser? That, of course, was his responsibility and he would certainly find it a challenge.

'I dare say you attend the ball on Monday evening?' She nodded. 'You may oversleep and forget the fight if you wish. I should not blame you.'

'You will not win your forfeit so easily,' she said, her face alight with excitement. 'We shall talk about this again, sir—but now you must pull over, for I see some friends and we must not ignore them.'

Caroline said goodbye to Sir Frederick at the door of her aunt's house. She asked him if he would care to come in for some refreshment, but he refused, saying that he had another appointment. She smiled at him, giving him her hand, which he kissed gallantly before returning to his curricle.

Caroline went into the house. She was still feeling pleased with herself for she had made him give her her own way, and, though she knew the escapade might cause her problems, she was excited at the idea. It was a long time since she had done anything so rebellious and at times had been feeling rather constricted at having to behave in the ladylike manner that was expected of her. Why did ladies always have to be so particular in their behaviour when gentlemen could do much as they pleased? There was so much she would have liked to do that was forbidden her. It was not fair and she was tired of being scolded by her aunt for things that were completely trivial.

'Caroline,' her mother's voice called to her as she walked up the stairs. 'Come here, my love. We have a visitor.'

Mrs Holbrook was standing in the doorway of the parlour she used most while a guest in her sister's house. It suited her because it was small and prettily furnished, and so seldom used for entertaining by her sister that she might think it her own. She looked very pleased with herself, almost excited about something.

'What is it, Mama?' Caroline's heart skipped a beat. 'Is it Nicolas?'

'No, it is your brother Tom,' Mrs Holbrook said, seizing her daughter by the hands and drawing her into the room. 'He is in his chamber changing, for he has just this minute arrived—and with good news. Bollingbrook has settled the most pressing of his debts. There—what do you think of that?'

'I think it wonderful news,' Caroline said, surprised and pleased. 'I am so glad for him, Mama. Do you know why Grandfather decided to do something for him?'

'I have no idea,' Marianne said with a frown. 'After the last time we visited him I thought he would not wish to see any of us again—but Tom says that he has asked particularly for you, Caroline. It would be wonderful if he were to do something for both you and Nicolas.'

'Oh, Mama, why should he?' Caroline said. 'It is quite enough that he has helped Tom to recover from his debts. Besides, Nicolas has found a life for himself and we are well enough as we are, are we not?'

'If your grandfather means to do something, you should visit him,' her mother said, hardly listening to her daughter's disclaimer. 'I know you are engaged for the next three weeks or so, but after that you might go down for a few days. I would stay here, of course, and you could always return. Your brother intends to visit Bollingbrook again in three weeks. He could take you down, and perhaps your grandfather would send you back in his own carriage. Yes, that would be quite acceptable, Caroline.'

'I have no objection to visiting Grandfather,' Caroline said. It would be pleasant to spend a few days with the Marquis. 'But you must not expect anything more, Mama. I dare say Grandfather thought it his duty to help Tom, but I do not need anything. I am quite content as I am.'

'Do not be so foolish,' Mrs Holbrook said and frowned at her. 'Louisa tells me that there are prospects of a marriage between you and a certain gentleman—but nothing is sure, Caroline. I dare say you would receive many more offers if you had a decent dowry.'

'From fortune hunters?' Caroline raised her eyebrows. 'Surely I may find someone who truly cares for me, Mama—and if I should not, it is hardly the end of the world. I may stay at home and be a help to you.'

'Do not be ridiculous,' her mother said and looked cross. 'It is as Louisa told me. You are too stubborn for your own good, my girl. I cannot afford to keep you in a home of my own, and your brother will not want us once he decides to marry. Louisa has offered me a home with her once you are settled; though I am not sure that would serve. However, you must marry, Caroline. Besides, every woman wants a home, husband and children.'

'Do they? Is there truly no other life for a woman, Mama? I have sometimes thought it unfair that we are not allowed to live as men do…' She saw her mother's shocked expression. 'Well, not quite in the way some gentlemen do—but at liberty to please ourselves. Why can we not be lawyers or doctors or some such thing? Why must we limit our expectations to being wives and mothers?'

'Caroline, you are ridiculous,' her mother cried, looking distressed. 'No wonder your aunt complains of you. She says that you might have been engaged by now had you made a push.'

'Mama, it is barely three weeks since we came up,' Caroline said. 'Surely you would not wish me to rush into some misalliance without consideration?'

'No, of course not,' Mrs Holbrook said. 'I did tell Louisa

that I thought it too soon, but she says you will ruin your chances by being too proud—and by speaking too freely. I hope your aunt has no real cause for her fears, Caroline? You have been much indulged at home, but you must understand that you should be careful what you say in society, my dear.'

Caroline felt a pang of remorse as she saw her mother's anxious face. What would her aunt—or her mother—think if they knew of the arrangement she had made with Sir Frederick? She knew that what she had agreed to was very shocking, but she had been driven by a wildness that now seemed very ill advised.

Perhaps it might be better if she allowed Sir Frederick to win his wager—and yet she would dislike having to do so, for she could imagine the mockery in his eyes if she did not go through with the dare.

'Of course, Mama,' she said. 'And now if you will excuse me, I should like to change before nuncheon.'

'Caroline,' Tom accosted his sister as she came downstairs later that day. He looked her over, noting the town bronze she had acquired with approval. She had grown up quickly, and he liked what he saw. 'You look well. Are you enjoying yourself more than you thought?'

'Yes, it has been pleasant,' Caroline told him truthfully. 'I have made so many friends, Tom, and it would be altogether wonderful if…well, you know my aunt. I know I should not complain, for if it were not for her generosity I should not have had a Season at all.'

'Well, I am not so certain of that, and I do know my aunt well enough,' he said and smiled ruefully—he had already fallen foul of Lady Taunton's tongue. 'But the good news is that Grandfather says you are not to be forced into a marriage you cannot like. He will not have it, and he has charged me to make sure that it does not happen, which I should have done anyway. But now we have his blessing. And that means that you cannot be bullied into an alliance just because Aunt Louisa wishes it.'

'That is exceedingly good of him,' Caroline said. 'I would not have thought he would wish to be bothered with such trivial matters.'

'Truth is, we don't know him as we ought,' Tom said and frowned. 'Mama sets his back up, because he thinks her too timid. I believe he blames her for Papa getting into debt the way he did. It is completely unfair, of course, but she irritates him and you know his temper. He has kept himself to himself for too long and now regrets it. If you knew him better, Caroline, I think you would like him.'

'Oh, but I do like him,' she said, surprising him. 'He has always been perfectly pleasant to me—I think it is just Mama he does not care for, which is unkind in him. However, she is a little milk-mannered sometimes and that is what sets him by the teeth, you know. He likes it when you stand up to him, give him back a little of his own mustard.'

'Yes, I see you do know him better than I thought,' Tom said. 'He has been a bit of a dark horse, though…secrets I had never guessed. Nor would have had he not told me himself.'

'Do tell?' Caroline begged, but her brother shook his head. 'Oh, that is not fair. Why am I not to know—because I am a mere female, I suppose?'

'No, certainly that is not the reason. I was told in confidence,' Tom said, 'and I may not break my word, Caroline. You would not expect me to?'

'No, not if it was in confidence,' she admitted with a sigh. 'Are they very dreadful, Tom? Grandfather's dark secrets?'

'Some of them are surprising—but one is rather dreadful,' her brother said. 'At least, some people would find it shocking, though I thought…' He shook his head. 'No, I must not say, forgive me. I ought not to have mentioned it at all, but Grandfather has asked me to do something for him, and if I agree it means that I must go abroad for a while.'

'Go abroad?' Caroline was startled. 'But whatever can you mean?'

'It is just something our grandfather wishes to put right… an old wrong, as he called it.' He laughed and shook his head. 'No, I have told you enough and I shall say no more, tease how you choose. Tell me, where do you go this evening, and shall I be welcome, do you think?'

The conversation was successfully turned, though Caroline's curiosity was merely deflected for a moment. She sensed that there was something very much on her brother's mind, and she had no doubt that she would eventually prise it out of him.

Over the next few days Caroline attended several functions with her aunt and sometimes her brother, at which Sir Frederick was for some reason present. Her determination to accompany him to the prize fight had wavered on several occasions. However, each time she saw him, he asked her if she had changed her mind with a look in his eyes that immediately renewed her courage. She knew that he was expecting her to default and that was the very thing needed to be certain that she did not draw back.

* * *

On the Monday morning, her maid, Mary, brought a bundle to her room, which had been handed to her by Sir Frederick's groom. Caroline had been obliged to take the girl into her confidence, and to give her a handsome shawl, which she had known Mary coveted. It was not the first time she had taken one of the servants into her confidence, and she had no reason to think that Mary would betray her. She had arranged that the girl would open a door at the back of the house and then lock it again, so that Caroline could escape through the mews, to where Sir Frederick would be waiting.

The ball that evening was a serious crush. Caroline was much in demand, dancing twice with Sir Freddie, and twice with Mr Bellingham, also once with her brother as well as many others. However, she took care to keep several of the dances after supper free, and complained frequently to her aunt of the heat, telling her when the clock struck eleven that she had the most dreadful headache and asking if her aunt would mind their leaving early.

'You do look a bit flushed,' Lady Taunton observed. 'You have been racketing around town these past few days. It may be best if you have a lie in tomorrow, Caroline. We do not want you taking sickly.'

'No, Aunt, I am sure I shall not—but I may sleep in if you think it sensible.'

Lady Taunton looked at her suspiciously, for it was not often that Caroline answered her so meekly. However, she put it down to her niece feeling unwell, and, having sent for the carriage, escorted her home an hour sooner than they would normally have left.

'Do you wish for a tisane to help you sleep?' she asked as they parted at the top of the stairs. 'We do not want you taking sickly—that would blight your chances of making a good match.'

'Thank you, but I am sure I shall sleep once I can put my head down.'

Caroline's heart was racing wildly as she went up to her room. Her maid had hidden the youth's clothing in a trunk, but Caroline took it out after locking her door, and tried it on. It fitted her remarkably well. She looked at herself in the mirror, twisting her hair up into a flat pleat that would not be seen beneath the cap, and pulling it tight over her head. She pinned it securely, for she did not want it to come down and betray her. Looking at herself in the mirror, she decided that she made an excellent youth. Anyone looking at her closely might think her features a little fine for a boy, but most people hardly glanced at a groom, and she thought she might get away with it, providing she did not speak.

She decided to keep the clothes on, pulling a light cover over her as she lay down. She was afraid of sleeping late, though Mary had promised to wake her if she did.

In the eventuality, however, she was awake and ready when her maid came to her room with a tray bearing a pastry and a glass of milk.

'I thought you might wish to eat something before you went, miss,' she said. 'If something is bothering you, a full stomach is better than an empty one.'

'Thank you,' Caroline said and took a bite of the pastry and two swallows of milk. 'If anyone should inquire for me, I am sleeping in this morning.'

'Yes, miss,' Mary said, looking at her doubtfully. 'Until

later, when you've gone out driving with Sir Frederick—is that it?'

'Yes, thank you.' Caroline saw the concern in the girl's eyes and pulled a wry face. 'There is not the least need to look like that, Mary. It is just a lark—the same kind of thing as I used to get up to with my brother Nicolas.'

'Begging your pardon, miss, but it ain't the same.'

'No, well, perhaps not,' Caroline agreed. Her stomach was tying itself in knots and she had no idea why she had thought it such a capital notion in the first place. Had it not been for the challenge in Sir Frederick's eyes each time she saw him, she would probably have withdrawn long before this. However, her pride had kept her courage high and even though she was feeling scared at this moment, she was determined to go through with it. After all, she reasoned uneasily, there was nothing so very terrible about going to a prize fight with a gentleman she knew well, was there?

She lifted her head and went out of the room, her maid hurrying after her. Mary unlocked the door for her and then Caroline reminded her to lock it again so that no one would guess that anyone had gone out early. Mary gave her an odd look as she slipped out, and it crossed her mind that the girl might be thinking she was going to meet a lover—which was so foolish it did not bear thinking of! As if she would do such a thing!

Once outside in the cool air of early morning, she hurried through the small garden, out of the gate and into the mews where the horses and carriages were kept. She saw immediately the curricle drawn up just outside the arch, and walked quickly towards it.

'Mornin', milord,' she said in her best mimicry of a stable

lad, which was amusing but would fool no one. 'Was your lordship looking for assistance?'

Freddie looked at her, a gleam of appreciation in his eyes. She made a pretty youth, and he realised that if his friends saw her up beside him they would begin to wonder what he was up to, and his reputation might suffer a blow.

'Good morning, imp,' he said a trifle ruefully. 'Take some dirt from the ground and smear your face a little. You look too clean and sweet for a stable lad.'

'Oh, yes, I forgot,' Caroline said and bent down to scoop up a little mud, smearing her face and neck, also her hands. 'Is that better?'

'A little,' he agreed. 'If we meet any of our acquaintances, keep your head down and do not speak, unless forced.'

'No, milord,' Caroline said.

'Are you ready?' Freddie said. She gave a slight nod of her head. 'You are certain you wish to continue?'

'Yes, quite certain.' Caroline tossed her head, her eyes clear and bright as she gazed up at him. 'I do not know why you are so concerned, sir. It is merely a lark, after all.'

Freddie frowned, for he suspected bravado. Indeed, until this moment he had thought that she would not show, and he was a little taken aback that she seemed so careless of her good name. Surely she must understand what the tabbies would make of it if it ever came out? But of course it was up to him to make sure that it did not!

'Climb in, then,' he said, making no attempt to help her. Unless she could manage it herself they were stumped. He saw that she made nothing of it, seeming as if she obeyed such orders every day of her life. 'Well, then, we shall go—but if you find the sight of blood sickening you must tell me and we shall leave.'

'Blood…' Caroline had hardly thought about the fight until this moment. For her it had all been about adventure, the excitement of doing something she knew was forbidden. 'Yes, well, I suppose there will be some.'

'You may depend upon it,' Freddie said and shot a glance at her. His expression was severe. Caroline, aware that he was expecting her to show some emotion, schooled her features to show none, lifting her chin. 'But we need not stay long if you do not wish it.'

Caroline made no answer. In fact, neither she nor Freddie spoke much for the next hour or so as they made their way to the scene of the fight, which was on Hounslow Heath. It had been scarcely light when they set out, but by the time they had reached their destination the sun had begun to fight its way through the clouds.

Some forty-odd carriages had drawn up at convenient intervals about the spot where the fight would be held. Bare-knuckle fighting wasn't exactly illegal, but it was frowned upon by many and usually took place in secluded locations at an hour when there was least likely to be any interference.

Looking about her, Caroline saw that the carriages belonged mostly to young men, though there were one or two older gentlemen of the sporting persuasion. There were, of course, no ladies of quality present, though she saw a couple of females who could in no way be called ladies. They were dressed in gaudy, revealing gowns and looked as if they might have been out all night, their cheeks painted with rouge. They were laughing loudly with the gentlemen who had brought them, and from their manner looked as if they might be intoxicated.

Caroline had not known what to expect, and she was a little shocked by such free manners, and by some of the language the gentlemen were using. It was the language of the stables, and though she had heard such cant before, somehow she was not prepared for it.

Besides the gentlemen's carriages, there were wagons and men dressed in shabby clothes walking about, at their heels a pack of dogs, some of them hounds and lurchers, also a bull terrier or two with ferocious-looking mouths. The atmosphere was one of excitement and anticipation, and as her eyes travelled round the arena, she saw that men were placing bets and also buying tankards of ale from a stall that had set up some distance away from where they were stationed.

Freddie looked at her speculatively. 'Well, lad, what do you think of it?'

'It is strange,' Caroline said. 'Different...exciting, I think.'

'Exciting?' His smile mocked her. 'A rough place for a lad like you. But it was what you wanted, though we can leave if you wish?'

It was on the tip of Caroline's tongue to tell him that she had seen enough when a voice hailed him, and two gentlemen came over to speak to him. She was thankful that they seemed to have been drinking, and did not glance her way as they talked about the merits of the fight they had come to watch.

The two gentlemen, both of whom were known to Caroline, though only by sight and not by acquaintance, seemed in no hurry to move on. They were making wagers with each other, and drew Sir Frederick into it, asking him his opinion of the outcome.

'I would lay my blunt on Mason,' Freddie told them. 'But I have not seen Gentleman George fight, so I may be mistaken.'

'What will you wager on it?' one of the gentlemen asked.

'Oh, fifty guineas,' Freddie said. 'You may come to me at my club if you should win.'

'Naturally,' the gentleman replied, glancing briefly at Caroline. 'What does the lad say? Who will win, lad?'

'His name is…Sam,' Freddie said, 'and he has no opinion on the matter—do you, Sam?'

'Come, come, let the lad speak for himself, Rathbone. Tell me, lad, what is your opinion?'

Caroline shook her head, keeping her eyes down, aware that she was being studied rather too intently. She averted her gaze. A short distance away she saw that two dogs were squaring up to each other, and in another moment they were at each other's throats, growling fiercely, their fangs bared as they entered a bloody conflict.

It was a horrid sight, and one that Caroline disliked very much, but it diverted attention from her, for instead of trying to separate them, their owners urged them to it and started to make bets on the outcome. The two gentlemen who had come up to Freddie walked off to watch and hazard their blunt in the betting. Freddie glanced at her, raising his brows.

'Do you wish to leave?'

'No, certainly not,' Caroline said, though she had found the dogfight unpleasant, but it was over now and the pugilists were being announced to the crowd. 'I am not so easily distressed, though I do not like to see dogs hurt.'

'Nor I,' Freddie agreed. 'Men have a choice whether to fight or not. Animals are not so fortunate. Personally, I abhor such sports. Well, I dare say we may as well watch the fight since we are here.' Caroline watched as the two men began to square up to each other, thinking that both looked very strong and well matched in size and weight. They began by circling each other, making occasional jabs at each other and ducking. Around them loud voices were raised, urging the men to close with each other and eventually the blows began to land with regularity.

At first Caroline was struck by the excitement and the science of the way the men ducked and weaved, and the skill it took to land a punch on their opponent. However, after some rounds, when they were both reeling from the effect of so many blows, she began to hope that it would soon be over. However, she said nothing, for she was not prepared to let Freddie think her a weakling after all. It was towards the end of the thirteenth round that he turned to look at her.

'I believe I have seen enough. Mason will undoubtedly wear his opponent down,' Freddie said. He began to back his horses and in a few moments they were leaving the Heath. He glanced at Caroline again, noticing her thoughtful expression. 'You did not wish to stay for the end, did you?' he asked after they had driven for a few minutes on the road.

'No,' she admitted, meeting his gaze then, a little flush in her cheeks. 'At the start it was rather fine—two men of equal skill matched in a display of pugilism—but I must admit that it became a little too bloody towards the end—foolish of me to be so squeamish, I know. I am glad to have had the experience, but I do not think I should wish to attend another fist fight.'

'I never expected you to come,' Freddie said. He was unsmiling and Caroline thought that he disapproved of her behaviour. 'You have more pluck than most, Miss Holbrook. I admire you for it, but I should never have allowed you to go through with this mad escapade. Now we must think how to get you home with no one the wiser.'

'I shall have to find somewhere to change my clothes.'

'And wash that dirt off your face,' Freddie said. 'But there is a quiet inn I know of where we may take breakfast in a private parlour and you may retire to the landlord's best chamber to make yourself tidy.'

'You are very thoughtful for my sake,' Caroline told him, a faint flush in her cheeks. 'I have been a little reckless, have I not?'

'My fault, I think,' Freddie told her. 'I should not have provoked you into it.' He raised one eyebrow. 'What of the balloon ascension—shall we call off your part in that?'

'Oh, no, indeed not,' Caroline said instantly. 'I am not so pudding-hearted! You must not think it.'

'I assure you that I do not,' Freddie confided with a smile that lifted her spirits. His smile had set her heart racing rather fast and she knew in that instant that she liked him very much. 'To be honest, I am not particularly enamoured of bare-knuckle fighting. Boxing in a ring with gloves is quite another thing. I doubt very much that I should have bothered to attend this morning if we had not made our little wager. I see no sport in two men hitting each other until one or both can no longer stand up. The sport must have rules and be conducted in a gentlemanly fashion if it is to be watched with any pleasure.'

Caroline made no answer, but she thought a great deal. His behaviour that day had been so considerate, so generous and kind, that she could not help liking him much more than she had thought possible. He seemed to think just as he ought on so many matters that she was inclined to believe him a very sensible and charming man. His mocking air and habit of seeming never to take anything seriously was possibly a mask to hide his true nature, which was perhaps more sensitive than others might realise. However, she naturally kept her thoughts to herself, and, since he seemed to be thoughtful too, they continued in silence until they came to the inn he had spoken of.

He ordered breakfast for them both in the private parlour, and Caroline discovered that she was hungry, eating some cold ham followed by bread and honey, which she washed down with a mug of watered cider. After they had eaten, Caroline took the bundle of clothes Freddie had had from her maid and went up to the bedchamber he had mentioned. She washed her face, tidied her hair and dressed in a green carriage gown and a straw bonnet.

She glanced at herself in a rather grey-looking mirror on the wall, and then went downstairs to the hall, where she saw that Freddie was in conversation with the landlord. He shot a startled glance at her, but then smiled as Freddie pressed some gold coins into his hand.

'I believe he thinks we are eloping,' Caroline said as they went outside. This time Freddie handed her into his curricle, taking care to stop her gown from snagging on the wheel.

'I dare say he may, but we do not need to care for his opinion,' Freddie said as he flicked his reins to give the order to his horses to walk on. 'It seems that we may have brushed through this without much trouble, Miss Holbrook.'

'Oh, do call me Caroline,' she said, as she threw him a speaking glance. 'I do not think we can stand on ceremony now—do you?'

'Perhaps not,' Freddie said. 'Very well, Caroline it shall be, at least when we are alone. And now I shall get you home before your family begin to wonder where you have been.'

Neither of them were aware of a curricle that had just that moment pulled up at the far end of the inn yard. The two young gentlemen, who had come in search of the prize fight, but decided that they would stop for breakfast, glanced at each other in surprise.

'Was that Miss Holbrook with Freddie Rathbone?' Asbury asked of his companion. 'They are somewhat out of the way, are they not?'

'It is a trifle unusual,' Mr Bellows agreed. 'You do not suppose that they have been to…no, no, of course not.'

'To the mill?' Asbury asked and shook his head. 'No, I cannot think it. Not but what she is game enough—but Rathbone has more sense than to take a delicate lady there. Or has he?'

'He has always been a trifle unsteady,' Bellows said. 'At least…he has done some reckless tricks in the past, so I've heard. But surely even he wouldn't do such a thing? Take a lady to a prize fight? No!' He looked shocked, disbelieving, as well he might, for it was unheard of.

'No, I can't think it,' Asbury said. 'But what in the world were they doing here—at an inn like this? I mean, a drive in the park is one thing, but…you don't suppose that…?'

'An assignation?' Bellows said. 'You're off the mark there, Asbury, old fellow. I know she is free in her talk, but she ain't fast. I admire her. I won't believe there was anything havey-cavey about it.'

'I am sure you are right,' Asbury said, but frowned. He wouldn't care to think anything unkind of Miss Holbrook, for he liked the spirited beauty very well, but it had put some doubt in his mind concerning her character. He had wondered if he should make her an offer, but now he thought that perhaps he would not. A gentle, biddable girl might be more suitable as the mother of his children. 'There must be some perfectly reasonable explanation for them having just come from that inn…though I am damned if I know what it might be.'

Chapter Five

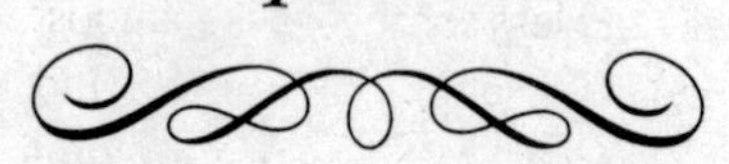

It was not to be hoped that she would escape her aunt's eagle eye when she returned to the house—it was past noon and Lady Taunton had already been to her niece's room to ask how she was feeling that morning. Having been met by a maid who stumbled over her words of explanation and looked guilty, her suspicions had been aroused, though Caroline's appearance was just as it ought to be and, when questioned, she answered innocently enough.

'Oh, I had quite forgot an appointment to go driving with Sir Frederick when I said that I might rest,' Caroline said, feeling guilty as she lied. She knew herself to be in the wrong, for she had indeed been foolish. 'Besides, my headache had completely gone this morning, Aunt.'

Louisa Taunton looked at her with dislike. 'I think you enjoy flouting me, Caroline,' she said, her mouth twisting. 'I do not know what mischief you have been up to, but I should warn you that it will come to my ears eventually, miss. You can do nothing in society that remains a secret for long, and if you have acted unwisely it will rebound on you. I have told you often enough that you are too free in your manners. You believe that you may do as you like, but go too far and you will discover that I was right.'

'I must be such a trial to you, Aunt,' Caroline said. 'Why did you agree to bring me out this Season if you so heartily disapprove of me?'

'For your mother's sake. She has no more idea of control than a nodcock, and less sense than a peagoose. You have been much indulged as a child, Caroline. Had you been my daughter, I should have taken a cane to you long ago.'

'Perhaps it was as well for me that you are not my mother,' Caroline replied. She lifted her head, meeting her aunt's angry gaze. 'If you will excuse me, I shall go up and change my gown. Mama wishes to attend an exhibition of art this afternoon and I have promised to accompany her.'

Lady Taunton snorted her disgust and turned away as Caroline walked up the stairs. The stubborn girl would go her own way, it seemed. She was heading for a fall, but there was no telling her, and her aunt sustained some satisfaction in thinking of how much she would enjoy dealing with Caroline's eventual disgrace.

Caroline entered her room, shutting the door and locking it behind her. She put her hands to her heated cheeks, for her aunt's criticism had struck home more deeply than usual. She was aware that she had behaved badly that morning, though she seemed to have brushed through it with little more than a scolding. Her spirit was not crushed, nor her determination to take part in the balloon flight on that Thursday, but she admitted now that there were some things she ought not to dare, and she told herself that she would be more sensible in future. She did not care what her aunt thought of her, but she would not like to bring shame and distress to her mother. And she could not help wondering if perhaps her reckless behaviour had lowered her in Sir Freddie's estimation. That would indeed be a heavy price to pay.

She washed her face in cold water, and then changed into a pretty walking gown of patterned green muslin before going downstairs to partake of a simple nuncheon that had been prepared for them in the dining room. Her mother and aunt were already seated, Marianne looking up with a smile as she entered.

'You are better this morning, my dear,' she said. 'I do hope you will not be like me, Caroline. I suffer with dreadful heads from time to time.'

'Oh, I think it was just the heat last night,' Caroline replied and dropped a kiss on top of her neatly dressed head. Her mother was wearing a fetching cap of Brussels lace and in truth looked much younger than her years. 'I am perfectly well, dearest Mama—and looking forward to attending the gallery with you this afternoon.'

'Yes, I am looking forward to it, too,' her mother said, giving her a look of affection. 'I was speaking to Mr Herbert Milbank about it last week. He told me that there were some fine watercolours to be seen, as well as oils, and you know that I paint a little, dearest—though of course nothing I produce could ever be thought good enough to be shown.'

'But of course they are,' Caroline told her. 'It is just that you are too shy to allow it. I think you have a good eye for landscapes and some of the portraits you have done are so like the subject it is unreal.'

'You flatter me, dearest,' her mother said, but looked pleased. 'Sit down and have something to eat, my love. This ham is very good and I think you missed your breakfast, did you not?'

'Oh, Mary brought me a pastry,' Caroline said with a little flush. She had eaten heartily at the inn with Sir Frederick, for the cold air had given her an appetite. 'I am not very hungry just now.'

'Eat something to please me,' her mother urged. 'This cold chicken is very good.'

Caroline helped herself to a small piece of the meat and some green peas, but pushed them around her plate, feeling unable to swallow even this small morsel. However, she drank a cup of tea, and then went upstairs to put on her pelisse and bonnet.

'Is everything all right, miss?' Mary asked as she helped her to find the gloves she needed to complete her ensemble. 'Lady Taunton was that suspicious earlier, I was sure she guessed something was wrong.'

'She knows nothing,' Caroline said. 'It is mere speculation.'

'No, miss, but if it were to happen again...'

'Do not worry, Mary, it shall not.' She smiled at the girl, picked up her reticule and went along the hall to her mother's bedchamber.

Mrs Holbrook was looking doubtfully at herself in the mirror. She had put on a green velvet bonnet trimmed with black ribbons and turned to her daughter as she entered. 'Do you think this is wrong for me, dearest? Ought I to stick to black entirely?'

'No, indeed, Mama, you should not,' Caroline said at once. 'You look very nice, very respectable—and it is two years since we lost Papa.'

'Your poor father,' Marianne said and sighed. She blinked hard and then turned back to the mirror. 'Well, I think it is quite suitable, and Papa would not have wanted me to mourn for ever. Besides, he could not expect it in the circumstances.'

Caroline wondered what her mother meant, but forbore to ask. She felt a little tingle at the nape of her neck. It was unusual for her mother to say anything of the kind, and the green bonnet was new—something that made her wonder.

The carriage was waiting for them when they went downstairs. Jeremy the coachman helped first Mrs Holbrook and then her daughter inside. Caroline glanced sideways at her mother's face—she had sensed that she was oddly nervous and wondered why that should be.

The art gallery was not overcrowded, though several ladies and gentlemen were walking about the large room, looking at the pictures, most of which were reasonably priced works of art. The artist was a newcomer to the scene, and giving his first show, but already his work had aroused considerable interest and Caroline had noticed that several of the pictures had been marked as being sold.

'This is rather nice, isn't it, Mama?' Caroline stopped in front of a portrait in oils of a young girl playing with a hoop. 'Isn't she pretty?'

Her mother did not reply immediately, and, glancing at her, Caroline saw that her cheeks were quite pink. And then she saw that a gentleman was staring at them. She recognised him at once, though she had not spoken to him for some weeks.

In his middle years and of medium height, he was still an impressive man. He came towards them, raising his beaver hat to reveal a head of thick dark hair. He was stoutish though not fat, his impressive moustache flourishing under a patrician nose, his eyes grey and just now smiling at...her mother.

'Ah, Mrs Holbrook,' he said. 'How very pleasant to see you

here. I had hoped that you might attend today.' He inclined his head politely towards Caroline, but it was obvious that her mother was the object of his interest.

'Mr Milbank. I remembered it most particularly,' Marianne told him, blushing like a young girl. 'For you told me you were the young man's patron, did you not?'

'Yes, indeed. I saw some of his work when I visited Lancashire a few months back. Not in an exhibition, you know, but hanging on the wall of a modest home. I've had the devil of a time persuading him to show his work, but I managed it at the last, and it seems to be a success. It was that portrait of a young girl that took my eye, you see—she is older now, for I met her, but just as beautiful, I assure you.'

'The picture has no price tag,' Mrs Holbrook remarked.

'No, for he does not wish to sell it,' he told her. 'But there are many pretty pictures that are for sale—if you care to see them?'

Mrs Holbrook said that she did, taking his arm. Caroline remained looking at the picture for a while—there was something in the girl's smile that intrigued her. She did not notice the gentleman approach until he spoke to her.

'Charming,' Freddie said, 'and a little like you in some ways, Miss Holbrook.'

'Oh…' Caroline was startled, a blush coming to her cheeks as she glanced at him. 'Do you think so? I was not expecting to see you here this afternoon, sir.'

'Were you not?' His eyes quizzed her. 'Did you imagine that I had no interest in such things?'

'Oh…well, I would not have expected you to attend the show of an unknown artist, though I am sure you have many valuable works of art.'

'Perhaps…' Freddie smiled oddly. 'But it is amazing what one finds at these affairs. I think I shall buy this picture.'

'Mr Milbank says that the artist does not wish to sell.'

'Does he not?' Freddie smiled. 'Well, then, I may have to persuade him, for I am determined to have it.'

'And do you always get your own way?' Caroline met his gaze boldly, a hint of challenge in her eyes.

'Usually,' he said. 'When I truly want something I am not often denied. Ah, here are George and Julia—shall we join them, for it was to meet them that I came this afternoon?'

Caroline suddenly felt a little disheartened at the thought that Sir Frederick had not come to the gallery with the sole intention of seeing her, but brushed the feeling aside. 'Yes, I knew they might come,' Caroline said, 'but you must excuse me, sir. I believe my mother needs me…'

'Then I shall not keep you, but do not forget that we are engaged to each other on Thursday, Miss Holbrook. I am looking forward to our excursion very much.' Caroline met his challenging look, her cheeks a little warm, for she knew that she was being mocked.

'As I am, sir,' she said. 'Please excuse me for the moment.'

She walked away, conscious that his eyes were on her, wondering why her heart was beating so very fast. Was she imagining it, or had his manner become just that little bit more reserved towards her?

Caroline looked at her mother with approval that evening. Marianne was dressed in a simple grey gown, but had a spangled shawl draped over her arms, and was wearing the pearls she had been given as a wedding present when she had married Mr Holbrook. Her hair had been dressed in a new, becoming style that was swept softly off her face and finished in an attractive coronet on her head, which had been dressed with a scrap of exquisite lace.

'Mama, you do look lovely,' Caroline said. 'I can see that I shall have a rival this evening.'

'Do not talk such nonsense,' Marianne said. 'I thought that perhaps it was time I began to wear something other than black.'

'More than time,' her daughter agreed, but when they went downstairs together, Lady Taunton's expression was one of disapproval. She gave her sister a speaking glance, but said nothing as she led the way out to the carriage. Her silence spoke more than words could have done, and mother and daughter were aware of her displeasure.

It was clear from her manner that she did not approve of her sister's new touch, but Caroline thought that her mother looked happy for the first time in an age. However, once they were at the dance, her usual court soon surrounded her and it was a while before she noticed that her mother was talking animatedly to Mr Milbank. She smiled inwardly, believing that she understood the change in her mother's manner of late, and feeling pleased by it. If her mother were to find happiness with that gentleman, she would be delighted.

It was not until quite late in the evening that Caroline realised Mr Asbury was present. He had not asked her to dance, which was unusual, and she noticed that he was paying a great deal of attention to Julia, who was looking very pretty in her pale pink gown. Caroline wondered whether she might have done something to offend him. However, when Julia brought him over to join her and Mr Bellingham just before supper, he seemed as polite as ever—but he still did not ask her to dance.

Caroline was not concerned enough to be troubled by his neglect for she already had more than her share of partners. However, she wondered why Sir Frederick was not in attendance, for he had said that he would see her later that evening.

'Oh, Freddie was called suddenly to his uncle,' George said when she asked. 'However, he says that he shall return tomorrow evening so you need not worry over the excursion on Thursday.'

'What excursion is that?' Caroline turned in surprise as she heard her brother's voice. 'Where are you off to?'

'Sir Frederick has arranged for us to watch a balloon ascension on Thursday,' Julia said. 'There is a party of us going, Mr Holbrook, and we shall have our nuncheon in the park at Richmond if the weather is fine.' She smiled at him shyly. 'Why do you not accompany us, sir? I am sure there is room for one more.'

'Yes, I should think I might,' he said, looking pleased to have been invited. 'I was going to take a look in at Manton's, you know; had an appointment to discuss what might suit me, but I can do that another day. It was just a little matter of purchasing a pair of pistols and there is not the least hurry.'

'Are you sure you wish to come?' Caroline asked her brother with a little frown. 'Will you not find it rather tedious? I imagined you were busy with your friends.'

Since his arrival, some gentlemen who were generally considered to be rakish young bucks had taken Tom into their circle.

'Oh, lord, no,' Tom said with an ingenuity that immediately endeared him to every one but his sister. 'I can visit my clubs any day, but a balloon flight sounds the greatest fun—and I shall be with you and Miss Fairchild, and that will be exceedingly pleasant.' He bestowed an admiring glance on Julia, which made her blush with pleasure.

Caroline knew that she could do no more to dissuade him without appearing churlish. It was an unfortunate occurrence—he would be sure to frown on the idea of her going up in the balloon, more from a point of safety than anything else. She smiled and said that she was glad he had nothing better to do, smothering a sigh. She still meant to take her chance in the balloon, but it would probably earn her a scolding.

She danced with her brother next, for he had asked her to reserve a space for him, and tried not to feel disappointed that Sir Frederick had had to leave town so suddenly. However, if his uncle had sent for him, it was probably important and she must not mind that he had not found a way of letting her know. Still, she could not help wondering if her fast behaviour had earned his disapproval. If he had been thinking her a suitable wife, he had quite possibly changed his mind.

Later that night, as she sat brushing her hair before she went to bed, she was thoughtful. Sir Frederick's absence had brought one fact home to her—without him her evening had seemed less enjoyable. Was it only that he had not been there, she wondered, or was she beginning to tire of attending so many society affairs?

She wondered why Mr Asbury had been a little reserved with her too. She had seen him looking at her oddly once or twice, but could not imagine what she had done to offend him. He had been one of the acquaintances she liked best apart from Mr Bellingham and Sir Frederick—and his desertion was perhaps a little hurtful. However, the rest of her court was as attentive as ever, and she had received two proposals that evening. One from a young gentleman she thought far too intoxicated to know what he was doing, and another from a gentleman she completely disliked.

She had been relieved to escape from both of them, and wished fervently that she had not granted them even one dance each—which she might not have done had Freddie been there. There was only one more day before she saw him again, but it seemed an age away. She knew that he had been attentive to her, but they struck sparks from each other more often than not, and, unlike her aunt, she did not believe that he was looking to take a wife just yet. At least if he were, he had given her no indication that she might be his chosen bride.

Still holding her pretty silver-backed hairbrush, Caroline gazed at her reflection. When she had first arrived in London she had believed that she preferred Mr Bellingham and had almost made up her mind to it that she would accept him if he offered for her. But now she seemed to have crossed some sort of line and felt much closer in spirit to Sir Freddie than she had… Yes, Sir Freddie was the way in which she thought of him now, she realised, a smile on her lips. He was no longer merely an acquaintance, but a close friend. She liked it that he had not mocked her for her foolish insistence on being taken to the fight, confiding in her that he did not much care for bare-knuckle fighting himself. It might have been said simply to please her, but he had made her feel better and she was grateful to him. And yet after that he had seemed to become more distant and Caroline struggled to understand why.

She was not sure exactly what her feelings were towards him at this minute, but she knew that the evening had seemed flat without him. She was sighing as she put down her hairbrush and went to bed. What was so important that it had taken Sir Freddie from town at such short notice?

* * *

'What was it that made you send for me so urgently?' Freddie asked of his uncle that evening after they had dined. 'I half-expected to see you taken ill and I was very relieved to find you as hale as ever, sir.'

'I'm not about to give up the ghost just yet, my boy,' his uncle told him with a wry grimace. 'I know you ain't exactly short of the readies, so I've no hold over you, and no doubt you would resent any suggestion from me about your marriage.'

'It depends what kind of a suggestion you meant to make,' Freddie said, looking at him guardedly. He was his uncle's heir only because the Marquis had lost two sons to a hereditary weakness that had come to them through their mother's family. As for fortune, he had sufficient of his own and was not hanging on for his uncle to shuffle off this mortal coil. However, he was too much his own man not to feel his hackles rise as he saw the expression in his uncle's eyes. 'I am aware that as your heir I owe you a duty, sir. My mother was fond of you, and you may have considered that she married beneath her. However…'

'Selina married on the rebound,' the Marquis said and frowned again. 'She was in love with someone I did not approve of and I told her that she would be letting the family down if she married him. He was on the catch for his second wife and I believe she turned him down after I gave her my opinion. I never knew all of it, but she was very distressed for some months—and then she married your father.'

'I knew there was someone else,' Freddie said, looking thoughtful. 'She told me once that she had loved someone, but was unable to marry him. She came to love my father in time, but not in the way she had loved her first choice.'

'I may have been wrong to interfere, but she was my sister,' Southmoor said and grunted. 'I realised later that I might have wronged her. It made us enemies, which was a shame, for I always liked him, even though I thought him unsuitable for your mother. However, he had three wives and managed to kill 'em all off…though I think he cared for his last. She was a gel of spirit. Almost half his age she was when he married her, but they were happy until she died. I think her death almost killed him…'

'Forgive me, sir, but I do not quite follow you. Of whom are we speaking—and what has it to do with my marriage?'

'Bollingbrook, of course. You've been squiring his granddaughter about town, so I've been told. I wanted to know what your intentions were towards her.'

'Indeed?' Freddie's tone became reserved, slightly chilling. His eyes narrowed menacingly, for he did not allow anyone to question him on matters of a private nature. 'And where did you obtain this information, sir?'

'It hardly matters who told me,' his uncle said. 'Don't give me that top-lofty stare, Freddie, for it won't wash. I'm merely asking whether or not you intend to make Bollingbrook's girl an offer?'

'And what if I do so intend?' Freddie asked, a glint in his eye that would have made anyone else shudder and retreat.

'Bollingbrook was once a friend of mine,' Southmoor said. 'I dare say he was a bit of a loose screw at times, but we were close at one period. I warned your mother against marrying him because I thought he would make her unhappy. I thought you should be aware that he is unlikely to welcome an offer from you. I am happy enough for you to marry the gel if she's the one you want, but you may get short shrift from Bollingbrook.'

'I see—then perhaps I should thank you for the warning,' Freddie said, a glint in his eyes. 'I do not say that I should wish to marry her, but if I did I should not care too much for Bollingbrook's objections—or yours, sir.'

Southmoor stared at him for a moment and then laughed. 'No, sir, I do not suppose that you would. But if you are determined on her, then there is something else I think you should know…'

'Very well, I shall listen if it is important,' Freddie said. 'Though I doubt it will weigh much in the scale of things.'

Caroline woke to the excitement of knowing that she would see Sir Freddie later that morning. She ran to the window to look out, feeling relieved when she saw that the sky was a clear blue and it promised to be a beautiful day—just right for the balloon ascension. She decided to dress at once and was already struggling into her gown when Mary came in with her tray.

'Miss Caroline, what are you about?' the girl asked. 'You'll never fasten them hooks like that, miss. Stand still and let me do them for you.'

'Oh, Mary, I am so excited,' Caroline said, her eyes bright. She turned her back so that the maid could fasten the row of hooks at the nape of her tailored gown, which had a slender skirt and small puffed sleeves and would be ideal for climbing in and out of the basket of a balloon. 'It is such a lovely day, isn't it?'

'And what mischief are you about today then, miss?' Mary looked at her doubtfully, for she had seen her mistress like this before. 'You ain't excited for nothing and that's a fact.'

'I am going to a balloon ascension,' Caroline said. 'It will be so thrilling…' She laughed in delight. 'You will never guess…but I am going to go up in one if everything turns out as it should.'

'You never will, miss!' Mary was shocked. Her mistress was too reckless in her opinion and would, she felt sure, land in trouble one of these days. 'Them things is mighty dangerous. You might fall out and break your head.'

Caroline's laughter pealed out. 'Oh, Mary, of course I shan't fall out—but you won't mention this to anyone?'

'You know I wouldn't, miss. I shan't betray you, though they might put me to the rack and torture me with hot irons.'

Caroline was too well bred to laugh at the girl's solemn avowal, though she was very much pleased by Mary's show of loyalty.

She was downstairs waiting by the time the knocker was raised and the footman admitted Sir Frederick. Her brother Tom had arranged to drive to the meeting in his own carriage, though she knew he was hoping that he might have a passenger on the return—and it was not his sister. She had seen a certain look in his eye as he addressed Julia, and she rather thought her friend preferred him to many of her suitors.

'Miss Holbrook,' Freddie said, his eyes going over her appreciatively as he saw the stylish gown she was wearing. It was fashioned of a pale grey, soft material and she was wearing the infamous blue hat on her head. She was quite magnificent, a vivacious woman and very much in her own style, he acknowledged and noted the bright sparkle in her eye. 'I see that you are ready and waiting.'

'Yes, sir. I was up early, for I am eager not to miss a moment of the treat you have promised us.'

'You are still of the same mind, then?' His eyes seemed to challenge her and she raised her head defiantly.

'Yes, sir. Did you imagine that I would change my mind?' She tipped her head on one side.

'No…' Freddie looked at her thoughtfully. 'I believe you to be as brave as you are beautiful, Caroline. Shall we go?'

'Yes, please.'

Caroline happily accepted his hand as he helped her into the seat of his new phaeton. It was extremely racy with high wheels and painted in yellow and black. The pair of horses drawing it were coal black and, if anything, more spirited than his greys; they were, he confided, a new acquisition.

'I think I may have to part with my chestnuts soon,' he told her. 'Having heard of these, I decided to buy them…just in case.'

'They are adorable,' Caroline said. 'Somewhat of a task to handle, I dare say, though you make nothing of it, sir. I have noticed before that you have exceptional hands. I thought no one could rival Nicolas, but I believe you would be a match for him.' She shot a mischievous glance at him. 'My brother allows me to drive his phaeton occasionally, did you know that?'

'Oh, no, miss!' Freddie said swiftly. 'You won't wheedle round me with that one, so don't think it. These brutes are too strong for you. It takes me all my time to handle them.'

'Which you do beautifully,' she said and laughed as she saw the expression in his eyes. She was feeling on top of the world—she had discovered that it was very amusing to tease him as he teased her. 'We shall just have to have another wager, sir.'

'None that concerns these horses,' he replied, a flicker of amusement in his eyes. 'However, should we discover a wager that pleased us both, I would not be averse to letting you drive me—though I think with the greys, not these devils.'

'That would indeed be a good beginning,' she murmured, a husky gurgle in her throat as she saw the little nerve flick at his temple. 'But first things first, sir. Today will provide quite enough excitement—and you know, next time we wager, you may very well win.'

'I am not sure that I should ever best you, minx,' he said with a mock scowl. 'However, it may be amusing to try.'

'Just so, sir.' Caroline's air of innocence was patently false, bringing a little snort from the gentleman beside her.

'At least you might call me something other than sir,' he said in assumed outrage. 'You said that we were friends—or do you wish me to return to calling you Miss Holbrook?'

'Only when my aunt or one of the old tabbies is by,' Caroline said. 'To be honest, I think of you as Sir Freddie—if you would not mind me using your name in that way?'

'As you wish,' he said, a gleam in his eyes. 'What happened when you returned home the other morning? Did you escape detection?'

'My aunt was as cross as crabs,' Caroline said. 'She suspected something, for she had questioned my maid—who assures me that hot irons would not make her betray me! However, there is nothing Aunt Louisa can do, for she has no idea of what happened.'

Freddie looked thoughtful and said, 'I dare say we got away with that little escapade—but you know that it will be different today, do you not? Your friends will see you enter the basket and it will not long remain a secret.'

'Oh, but there is nothing so very shocking in it,' Caroline said. 'Mama might be anxious if she knew that I intended it, for she is of a nervous disposition, you know—but I dare say I shall not be the first lady to go up in a balloon.'

'No, there have been others, but the flights took place at private estates. I think your aunt may censure you, Caroline.'

'I do not mind that so very much,' she said and looked at him, her expression serious now. 'But I should not like to incur your ill opinion, sir. Do you think it very fast of me?'

'Good lord, no,' Freddie said. 'A little reckless, perhaps—but I do not censure you. What made you think I might?'

'Oh, I do not know…' She considered telling him that Mr Asbury had seemingly turned against her, but decided that she would keep it to herself. It was her problem, not his, and she might find that she was mistaken another day.

'Well, you may forget any such foolish notions,' he said and smiled at her in a way that made her heart jerk. 'I do not think that anything could make me think ill of you, Caroline.'

'Oh…' She blushed slightly and looked down at her gloves, which were a fine York tan leather, smoothing at the fingers for a moment. 'I trust you found your uncle well, Sir Freddie? Mr Bellingham told me you were called away unexpectedly.'

'Yes, I broke my word to you, did I not?' Freddie said and frowned. 'I thought he might be unwell, but it was just a small matter of business—nothing important at all.'

'Oh, I am pleased to hear that,' she said. 'I was a little anxious for your sake. It is awful to lose someone of whom you are fond.'

'I suppose I am fond of the old reprobate in a way,' Freddie said. 'I must admit that we sometimes have words, but it usually blows over. Neither of us is one to hold a grudge.'

'Oh…' She looked at him inquiringly, but no further information was forthcoming. 'My grandfather wishes me to visit him soon. I think my brother intends to go down at the end of next week. Mama thinks that I should go with him, and return after a few days. She says she shall make my excuses to everyone.'

'She does not go with you?'

'Grandfather does not care for her. They fell out some years ago. She is terrified of him and I think that annoys him somewhat—and he suffers greatly from gout, which does not sweeten his temper.'

'Ah, yes, the curse of many a rake at the end of his days, I think,' Freddie said. 'I dare say he likes his port too well.'

'I am sure he does,' Caroline said. 'No, Mama does not go with me—though I think she may have other reasons for remaining in town.' She smiled as he arched his brows at her. 'I believe she has a beau…'

'Indeed, that must be a happy turn out for her,' Freddie said.

'Yes…if I am not mistaken, which I think I am not.' Caroline began to recount the story of her first meeting with her mother's admirer, her conversation lively and entertaining. In this way their journey was accomplished and they were soon meeting up with their friends as arranged.

Freddie steadied his horses as they approached the park and smiled at her. 'Do you know, I think we are almost there.'

Chapter Six

Caroline was a little shocked to see how large the company had grown by the time they arrived. It had been meant to be a private affair, but somehow the secret had got out and at least thirty of their acquaintance had turned up in their carriages to watch. Not only were so many of their friends there, a small crowd of interested onlookers had arrived to watch as the balloon was being made airworthy by the appliance of hot air into the great canopy. Indeed, so many people were crowded around it that it was difficult to actually see it when they first arrived.

'Oh, there is quite a crowd,' Caroline said as Freddie drew his phaeton to a standstill, and assisted her down. 'It is very exciting, isn't it?'

'Yes, very,' he said, amused by the bright look in her face. He wondered when she would realise that it was impossible to go through with her avowed intention, but said nothing to discourage her. He had no doubt that she would dare to do it, for he thought that she was afraid of nothing, but she must see that it would come to her aunt's ears in no time at all. 'Ah, here is your brother.'

Caroline looked at Tom as he came up to them. He looked excited and she suspected what he was about to say before he spoke.

'I am told you mean to go up, Caroline—and there is one more place available in the basket. I should very much like to go with you. It would look much more the thing if I accompanied you.' He glanced at Sir Freddie a trifle uncertainly. 'I think perhaps you may have wished to take that place, sir—but it would wash better if it were me, do you not agree?'

'Yes, I do, as it happens,' Freddie said. He saw by Caroline's expression that she was disappointed, but believed that if anything could get her through this without too much censure, it would be her brother's presence in the basket. 'You are very welcome to take my place, for I have been up before—several times, as it happens.'

'Oh, you did not tell me,' Caroline said, gazing at him in surprise. 'But I suppose that is why you were able to arrange this…' She saw something in his eyes. 'Why, it is your balloon, is that not so?'

'I must confess that you have found me out,' Freddie said, amused. 'I am fascinated by the idea of flight, Miss Holbrook. I believe that this is just the forerunner and that one day we shall have a much more controllable method of flying.'

'No, do you, sir?' Tom looked at him with unconcealed enthusiasm. 'I have heard talk of it, but I thought it was all a hum. We must discuss this another day, when you have time, of course. I am very interested in anything scientific.'

'You must dine with me at my club one day,' Freddie said and frowned. In taking an interest in Miss Holbrook, he seemed to have landed himself with very much more than he had intended. 'We shall arrange it. And now I think the balloon is almost ready. You should make your way through the crush if you do not wish to keep the balloon master waiting.' He looked at Caroline, eyebrows raised, but did not ask again if she were sure. Now that her brother had agreed to accompany her, it should cause no more than a few raised eyebrows from all but the high sticklers. She might find herself less popular in some drawing rooms than before, but that might be repaired.

'Oh, yes, Tom, do let's go,' Caroline said and started off a little ahead of him. She knew that word of her adventure would reach her aunt swiftly, but she was determined to go through with it. Even her brother's presence would not make it all right in her aunt's opinion, though she thought that her mother might accept it as just another of her naughty tricks.

Caroline was helped into the basket by her brother. She had a feeling of tremendous excitement as she looked at the man who was preparing to take them up. He introduced himself as Mr Jackson, smiling at her as he began to explain the principles of hot-air ballooning, which she listened to with interest.

'Oh, this is so exciting,' she cried as there was a roaring sound above her head and the balloon began to lift off from the ground. For the moment they were still attached to the anchor ropes, because they were not quite ready to cast off. 'How high shall we go, sir?'

'It depends on the currents of air,' Mr Jackson was explaining to her when all of a sudden there was the sound of something snapping and one of the ropes gave way. Because they still had another rope tethering them to the ground it made the balloon shudder and tip to one side, and then go crashing downwards.

Caroline screamed as she felt herself falling. The shock of a hard landing sent the basket lurching over to one side and she stumbled, but recovered her balance quickly. She realised immediately that there could be a danger of fire and scrambled quickly over the sides of the basket. She saw Mr Jackson do the same and called to him. All around them there was noise and confusion, and it was only when Caroline felt strong hands pulling her clear of the ropes and debris that had fallen on top of them that she realised she wasn't badly hurt. Shaken and bruised, she looked into the face of the man who had pulled her clear.

'Caroline!' Freddie cried. 'My God! You could have been killed! Are you in pain? Where does it hurt?'

'I'm all right,' Caroline said, shrugging off the shock as if it were nothing. 'Just a little bruised I think…but where is Tom?' She looked around for her brother and saw that he was lying on the ground a short distance away. It looked as if he had been thrown clear before they crashed, and he was lying very still. 'Tom! Is he dead?' she cried and now there was fear in her eyes as she ran to him. 'Tom…' She fell to her knees beside him on the ground, looking at him anxiously. 'Tom! Tom, my dearest…' she cried, horrified by the turn of events that had ruined their happy day. 'Oh, Tom, speak to me…'

'Let me have him.' Freddie was by her side almost at once, laying her brother down carefully and making an examination of him. 'He is still breathing,' he said after a moment. 'I think he may have broken his arm, and he must have hit his head, for he is unconscious.' Caroline had remained on her knees, watching him handle her brother with an expertise that spoke of his having done such a thing before. How sure and gentle he was, so reassuring in a crisis. Now his eyes met hers as Tom gave a moan of pain. 'It is as I thought, but I believe it might have been much worse. I think we may safely move him to somewhere more comfortable.'

'He will do better in my curricle than your phaeton.' George Bellingham had come up to them unobserved. 'Let us get him into it. I will engage to take him home and you must come after in your own rig.'

Behind them, shouting warned of fire and Caroline glanced back to see that the canopy was blazing. Mr Jackson was leading the efforts to put out the flames before they got out of hand, but it was certain that the balloon was ruined.

'Oh, Freddie, your balloon…' Caroline cried.

'It is of no consequence. I am grateful that none of you was hurt more. As for Tom, I think we should get him to an inn,' Freddie said, frowning. 'The sooner a doctor sees to him the better.' He glanced at George.

'As you say. I know of a small discreet place near by. The Henderson Arms. You may follow me if you wish.' He glanced at Caroline. 'I dare say you would wish to accompany your brother?'

'Yes, please.' She glanced at Freddie. 'You will forgive me? I must go with Tom.'

'Of course.'

Freddie bent over the half-unconscious Tom, lifting him in his arms and carrying him, with some slight assistance from George. Tom moaned and seemed to come to himself for a moment, his features registering extreme pain as they moved him. They laid him down in the curricle, Julia having vacated it for the greater ease of his comfort. She was white with distress, tears hovering on her thick lashes.

'It is too awful,' she said to Caroline. 'I know you wish to go with him, but I shall follow with Sir Frederick, if I may?'

'Yes, of course,' Caroline said. 'Oh, poor Tom. He was so looking forward to this trip—and to many other things, I imagine. This will quite ruin his visit.'

She climbed into the curricle, taking her brother's head upon her lap, and soothing his head with her fingers. She glanced round to see what Freddie was doing, but he seemed to be making arrangements with his tiger. He looked round just as the curricle began to move off, catching sight of her pale face, though by then she had turned her attention to her brother and was whispering words of encouragement. She was not sure that Tom knew she was there, for he seemed to have fainted again, but she continued to stroke his head and talk to him, believing that Freddie knew what he was saying when he said that it might have been much worse.

It seemed an age until they reached the hotel, though it was in truth only a short distance from where they had gathered in the park. George Bellingham jumped down, giving his reins to a groom who came running.

'Stay with Tom, Miss Holbrook,' he told her. 'I shall arrange for a room and a doctor, and then return. We shall have him carried to a chamber and then his hurts can be tended.'

'You are so kind,' Caroline said, her face pale and anxious. 'If anything happens to Tom, I shall never forgive myself. He only went up in the basket because he thought it would protect my reputation.'

'You must not blame yourself,' George said. ' No one could have known that a rope would give way like that…it was most odd.' He shook his head. 'Excuse me, I must waste no time in arranging all.'

Caroline watched as he strode towards the inn and disappeared inside. She continued to stroke her brother's head and counted the seconds until her friend returned. It seemed an age, but he brought several men with him, and, within moments, Tom was being carried inside the inn and up the stairs to a room where he was carefully deposited on clean sheets. Caroline hovered nearby, wondering what she might do for the best, but she had hardly had time to think of taking off his boots before she heard voices behind her and turned to see Freddie and another gentleman, who she realised was a doctor.

'We were lucky enough to find a doctor at the site of the ascension,' Freddie told her with a grim nod. 'We shall need to cut his coat off, Caroline—and Julia is waiting downstairs alone in the parlour. I think you should keep her company—it will not do either her or your reputation the slightest good to be seen in an inn parlour alone. You may be able to stand it, but she ought not to be exposed to undeserved censure.'

'Yes, of course,' Caroline said in a small voice. His tone had been harsh. He was clearly very angry and she felt that he was blaming her for her part in this affair. Indeed, it was all her fault and he was right to censure her! 'I shall do as you say, sir.'

He did not seem to have heard her, for he paid her no attention as he went to the bed and, with the assistance of the physician, began to cut away Tom's tightly fitting coat. Caroline threw an unhappy glance at the bed where her brother was just beginning to moan once more, clearly roused from his stupor by the pain their ministrations had caused him.

'Bear up, old chap,' Freddie said encouragingly. 'You will

be right and tight in a while. Doctor Fortescue has had practice enough at binding the wounds of soldiers. He will make short work of this.'

Caroline went down to the parlour. Sir Freddie's tone to her brother had been kind, which told her that he was angry at her alone. Her spirits had fallen to nothing, for she had taken the blame of Tom's injury upon herself and was distressed by his pain. There was no denying that he would not have been there had she not teased Sir Freddie into arranging the whole thing. It was no wonder Sir Freddie had lost his good opinion of her! She had behaved shamelessly in demanding to be taken to the mill and insisting on being taken up in a balloon.

Julia was the picture of dejection when Caroline entered the private parlour that their host had provided, but she was not alone, for George was with her. She jumped to her feet as soon as she saw Caroline, running towards her, her face wet with tears.

'How is he?' she asked. 'Please tell me that he is not dead—I do not think I could bear it.'

'Julia, do not be foolish, my dear,' George expostulated with a gentle smile for her. 'I do assure you that Freddie knows about these things. Tom may feel groggy for a few days, but I dare say he will come about and be none the worse for it.'

'The doctor is with him now,' Caroline said, taking Julia's hands and holding them tightly. She lifted her head, summoning her courage. 'I dare say he will soon have him patched up.'

'Do you think so?' Julia blushed for she realised that she must have betrayed herself. 'I was so distressed…it was a dreadful thing to happen. Sir Frederick says that Mr Jackson has examined the rope and it had been tampered with, but I am not sure what he meant…'

'Tampered with? In what way?' Caroline was bewildered.

'I thought it odd that it should just snap like that,' George said, nodding to himself. 'Freddie is always meticulous about things like that, as is Jackson. The rope had been frayed by a knife or some such thing.'

'Then it was deliberate…not an accident?'

Julia gave a cry of distress. 'Who would do such a wicked thing?'

'I do not know,' Caroline said, putting an arm about the girl and drawing her to a wooden settle to sit down. She could feel Julia trembling and sensed that the girl had been much affected by the accident, perhaps the more so because it was Tom. 'I did not truly see what happened, because it was all so fast. There was no time to think about anything.'

'It was quite deliberate.' George looked at her above the head of his niece, who was hanging her head and on the verge of more tears. 'Whoever the rogue was, he meant to cause a dreadful accident, though why I cannot say.'

'Why should anyone wish to harm poor Tom?' Caroline said, and turned as she heard an indrawn breath behind her. 'You startled me, Sir Freddie. Please do not tell me that it is bad news about Tom?'

'Nothing of the sort,' he said. 'It is as I thought. He has a broken bone in his arm, but the injury is not life threatening. We can only be grateful that no one else was badly hurt. It does not bear thinking of. You could all have been killed.'

'But who could have done such a terrible thing?' Caroline asked.

'Jackson did not see it happen, but there were so many people crowding about the canopy that it is not surprising. It is unlikely that we shall be able to trace the culprit, though I shall see what can be done.'

'You are sure that it could not simply have been an accident?' Caroline asked.

'Quite certain. It was the first thing that Jackson checked. He is meticulous in all his preparations—and the more so because he knew that you were to go up in the basket. I particularly stressed that all care must be taken.' His look was so severe that Caroline felt sick—he was clearly very angry.

'Oh, dear…' Julia swooned. George was just in time to catch her as she fell forwards and lowered her to the settle with gentle care. 'I am so sorry…' she whispered as her eyelids fluttered open. 'What a silly goose I am.'

'This has all been too much for you,' George said. 'I must get you home, for you are not well, Julia.'

She made a faint protest, looking apologetically at Caroline. 'I ought to stay with you,' she said, 'but in truth I do not feel well.'

'You must go home,' Caroline said. 'I shall stay with my brother for the time being.' She looked at Sir Freddie. 'Would you mind fetching my mother? I think she would want to be here and I cannot leave him.'

Freddie hesitated, giving her a hard stare. She was wondering if he meant to refuse her, when someone came into the parlour.

'The young gentleman is conscious now,' the physician announced. 'He is in some pain and will need nursing of the kind that I do not think may be procured here, for such injuries can sometimes turn infectious. Perhaps some arrangement could be made to convey him to his home?'

'Yes, I shall fetch his mother and a suitable vehicle,' Freddie said. 'You get Julia off, George. We don't want her fainting again…' His gaze turned to Caroline, seeming to her to become colder. 'Go upstairs to your brother and stay there until I bring Mrs Holbrook. It would only start a deal of pointless gossip if someone were to see you here. I shall be no longer than need be and until then you must stay with Tom. Do you hear me, Caroline? You are not to leave the bedchamber for anything!'

'Yes, yes, of course.' She left the room immediately, feeling chastened. It was obvious that Sir Freddie thought that the blame for this débâcle lay squarely in her court. But did he really need to be so harsh to her? She felt tears prick her eyes, but blinked them away.

She knocked softly at the door and then entered her brother's bedchamber. He was lying propped up against a pile of pillows, but opened his eyes and looked at her as she approached, attempting a weak smile.

'I'm sorry, Caroline,' he apologised in a faint voice. 'Seems I made a mess of the whole thing, ruined your day.'

'How could you think that? Besides, it was hardly your fault!' Caroline's throat was tight with emotion, for it was like him to think of her. 'I am merely distressed for your sake, dearest.'

'What happened?' Tom looked puzzled. 'There was an odd sound and then we just fell like a stone.'

'One of the ropes gave way. Sir Freddie says the rope had been tampered with deliberately.'

'Good grief! What fool would do a thing like that?'

Caroline agreed, giving a little shudder as she realised how close they had all been to a terrible death. 'Why should anyone want to harm you, Tom, or me? I do not understand…' A soft moan broke from him and she hastened to his side. 'Is the pain very bad?'

'I should like a drink of water, if you wouldn't mind,' Tom said. 'I think there may be some in that jug over there, on the washstand.'

Caroline went to investigate, but it was empty. She picked it up and turned to look at him. 'I am afraid there is none left, Tom. The doctor must have used it to wash his hands. I shall go and fetch some more.'

Tom seemed not to have heard her. He was lying with his eyes closed, clearly in some pain. She went softly from the room and down the stairs, wondering how best to discover her host, but as she hesitated at the bottom of the stairs he came out of a door to her left and saw her hovering uncertainly.

'Ah, there you are, miss,' he said. 'I was about to send the chambermaid up with a jug of fresh water. Is there anything else you would like for the poor gentleman?'

'Yes, please,' Caroline replied. 'I think a little brandy might not come amiss, sir, if you please.'

'Right you are, miss. You go up to him and I shall send it immediately.'

Caroline turned and ran up the stairs. As she did so, she heard a burst of laughter and some gentlemen came out into the hall behind her. She paused on the landing at the top of the stairs to glance back for a moment and then hurried down the hall to her brother's room, unaware that she had been recognised by one of the party.

Tom was looking for her as she came in, and she explained that the landlord was sending up water and brandy.

'It might help with the pain if it is very bad,' she told him.

'Yes, it might,' he agreed with a grimace. 'But you ought

to have rung for the maid, Caroline. It won't do for you to be seen here alone, love. You know what Aunt Louisa is like and the rest of the tabbies with her—they will put two and two together and make six.'

'I was only a moment,' Caroline said. 'Besides, you are my brother. Only a mean spirit could find fault with my being here with you, I believe?'

'Yes, well, most people would understand once they knew,' Tom said. 'But whispers can do a lot of harm, and people always think that there must be some truth in these rumours.'

'No smoke without fire?' Caroline said and smiled at him. 'I dare say you are right, but I shall not let it weigh too heavily, for truth to tell I do not care if some think ill of me.' Though in her heart she knew that she cared very much for the opinion of one person in particular.

Caroline sat with her brother for two hours before she heard voices at the door and then her mother came in, looking upset and anxious. Marianne had clearly shed a few tears on the way here and Caroline got up to go to her and embrace her as soon as she entered.

'It is all right, Mama,' she said. 'Tom is just sleeping. He was in some pain, but after he drank a little brandy he fell asleep and seems to be resting easily.'

'Is there any fever?' his anxious mother asked, and laid a gentle hand on his brow. A look of relief came over her face as she realised that he was resting quite peacefully. 'Thank God! We owe his safety to Sir Frederick, I am sure.'

'I believe it is merely a slight break,' Caroline reassured her. 'However, he will be better at home. Have you brought our own coach?'

'Yes, I have,' Mrs Holbrook said. 'I was out when Sir Frederick first came for me, but he found me on my way home from the lending library. I hope you appreciate how much he has done for us today, Caroline?'

'Yes, of course, Mama,' Caroline said, her manner a little reserved—she could not help thinking of Freddie's coldness to her earlier. 'It was very kind of him to help us as he did. Did he return with you?'

'No. He asked if he should, but I refused—I am sure he had something on his mind, though he would undoubtedly have come had I needed him. However, I have my coachman and two grooms, and I am sure we can manage well enough without him.'

A slight moan from the patient brought her head round to him at once, and for the next few minutes all her attention was for her son. She fussed over him, but, receiving a request not to do so, laughed in relief. Clearly Tom was feeling much better and when asked if he felt up to making the journey home was quick to say that he would do so if she could arrange for him to be helped down the stairs.

Mrs Holbrook rang for the maid and gave instructions. A chair was duly produced and Tom helped into it. Two strong men then carried him from the room and down the stairs. Caroline went ahead to alert the coachman, and her mother followed, urging the men to be careful and not to drop their precious burden. Her fretting possibly made their task that much harder, but it was accomplished without too much pain for the invalid, and within some ten minutes or so Tom was settled in his mother's carriage as comfortably as could be arranged.

Mrs Holbrook, inquiring what she owed for the care of her

son, was told that Sir Frederick had already paid for everything, including the doctor's fee, and she was overcome with gratitude, which she continued to pour into her daughter's ear all the way home.

'He is the perfect gentleman,' she told Caroline twenty times. 'Everything that is kind I am sure. He will make some fortunate lady a very satisfactory husband.'

Although she stopped short of saying that Caroline should make a push to gain his affections, as her aunt had many times, it was clear to her daughter that she thought it a perfect match. Caroline did not protest as she would have to her aunt's bullying, for there was little that she could say. It was perfectly true that Sir Frederick had done all that could have been asked of him, but his generosity was not a reason for marriage. Caroline liked him very well, had counted him one of her best friends. Indeed, she had wondered if she might like to be married to him, but she was not sure after that morning if he liked her as well as she had thought.

She was subdued on their return to the house, and followed the servants who carried her brother up to his own room. His arm had begun to hurt again, and Mrs Holbrook shooed her from his room, while retaining the services of the butler to help her settle her son as comfortably as possible. She then went down to the stillroom and made up a tisane to her own prescription, which she allowed Caroline to take up for him.

'It will help him to sleep,' she said to Caroline. 'I shall not go out this evening, for I could not bear to leave him in this condition, but you must go with your aunt to the soirée as arranged, dearest.'

'Do you think I could cry off for once?' Caroline asked. 'I would much rather not go this evening, for although I was not harmed I was a little shaken by the accident—and I could help you to sit with Tom.'

'Very well, my love,' Marianne said and looked at her with approval. 'Yes, it must have been a shock for you when the balloon fell, and I dare say it will not matter in the least if you miss one evening's pleasure. And it would be a help to me to have you here—just in case he should take a turn for the worse.'

Caroline did not believe that anything of the kind would happen, but she was pleased that she did not need to go to the musical evening with her aunt. Lady Taunton had not been pleased when they returned to the house, and Caroline could only think that she had done something to annoy her.

The next morning Aunt Louisa was still in a foul mood and her annoyance with both Caroline and her sister was not alleviated when she informed them that she had learned that rumours had begun to circulate concerning her niece.

'But you know the truth of it, Aunt,' Caroline said when she was subsequently questioned by the older woman. 'Tom was hurt in the accident, and that was the reason I was at the inn. It is unfortunate that someone saw me there, but you may easily scotch such tales by telling the truth.'

'Which I did, as you would expect,' Lady Taunton said with a scathing glance. 'I dare say we shall brush through this easily enough, but had you been a little more circumspect in your behaviour, miss, it might never have been thought possible in the first place. I have warned you. If you gain a reputation for being fast, you will lose more than you bargain for!'

'I do not think I have done anything particularly wicked,' Caroline said, crossing her fingers behind her back. Had anyone seen her dressed as a youth, she might have been in serious trouble. 'When our friends hear the tale and put their side of the story about, people will soon forget this nonsense.'

'Well, it is to be hoped so,' her aunt said. 'But once this kind of thing happens, the tales often linger. You must be particularly careful in future that you do nothing that could cause further gossip.'

They were in the small back parlour, to which her aunt had summoned her, and neither of them heard the knocker, so it was with some surprise when a visitor was announced. Caroline turned to look at the young man standing in the doorway and ran to him with a cry of delight. 'Nicolas dearest! It is so good to see you. I had hoped you might get leave while we were here, but I thought it unlikely.'

'Well, here I am, puss,' Nicolas said and embraced her in a bear hug. Looking up at him, she thought that he had grown since she had seen him, and he looked wonderful in his scarlet uniform. 'Now tell me, what is this I hear about Tom?'

'Oh, do come up and see him,' Caroline said, linking her arm through his. 'It will cheer him up immensely to talk to you. He is very annoyed that Mama has forbidden him to get up again for at least two days.'

Nicolas inclined his head to his aunt. 'I hope you are well, ma'am? I shall greet you properly later, but I am eager to see my brother—if you will excuse us?'

Caroline drew him from the room, hugging his arm. 'You arrived in the nick of time,' she confided. 'Aunt Louisa was giving me a fearful scold! I know it was my fault that Tom was hurt, for he wouldn't have been in the basket if it hadn't been for me, but I couldn't be blamed for being in that inn.'

'I suggest that you start at the beginning, puss,' Nicolas said, grinning at her. 'Then I might have a hope of understanding.'

'Oh, you!' Caroline said, but obliged him with the full story, which took them up to the landing where Tom's bedchamber was situated. 'So you see, she was quite unfair!'

'Yes, she was, but you should learn to dissemble, puss. You are defiant and it puts her in the right of it. Bite your tongue and think before you answer. There is no point in antagonising her. After all, she did stump up the blunt for this trip.'

'Yes, I know, and I am behaving very ungratefully,' Caroline said, feeling a little ashamed. 'I shouldn't wrangle with her, for no doubt she means well—but I cannot like her.'

'As to that, she is not my favourite person by any means.' He grinned at her. 'But let us see what Tom has to say, shall we?'

Caroline nodded, following her brother into Tom's bedchamber. He had been sitting up and reading a book, but he threw it down with a joyful cry as he saw Nicolas.

'Thank goodness you are here,' he said. 'Perhaps you can convince Mama that I am not on my deathbed, Nicolas. It is true that I have a little pain still, and my arm feels awkward in this splint, but I shall expire of boredom if I am forced to stay here for two days. I am promised to Bollingbrook next weekend and that only gives me a few days to enjoy myself.'

'Indulge her for one day,' Nicolas advised. 'By what I hear, you were lucky to escape so easily and will need to rest for a while, otherwise you may find yourself fainting. And that, dear brother, would cause our much-loved mama to go into a decline herself.'

'No, I do not think so,' Caroline said, eyes sparkling. Her mood of despondence had been lifted by Nicolas's arrival.

'She has seemed much better of late, brighter in herself and happier. I think she has a secret admirer…'

'Mama—an admirer?' the brothers exclaimed in unison. 'You are roasting us, Caroline!'

'No, indeed I am not,' she said. 'Please say nothing to her yet, for she has not told me anything, but I have met him once or twice now…and she likes him. I think he likes her very much, but I do not know how far they have progressed.'

'I thought it was you who came here to catch a husband,' Nicolas said and laughed in delight. 'Well, if I ever heard such a blessed thing! I should be much pleased if she were to take him. I think she and Papa went on tolerably well, but it wasn't all April and May with them, and she has been down in the dumps since he died. Yes, it would be a good thing for her.'

'That is how I feel,' Caroline said, 'but I am not sure there is anything to celebrate yet. It may all fall through.'

'Good for her,' Tom said. 'You may not know this, either of you—but Aunt Louisa has been bullying her into making a home with her when I marry or before that if she can persuade her to it.'

'Good grief,' Nicolas said and looked revolted. 'Poor Mama would be truly under the cat's paw. We must save her from that at all costs.'

'I think she would not like it at all,' Caroline said. 'She spoke wistfully of living in a cottage so that she might live as she pleased, but I think Mr Milbank is wealthy enough to provide her with a decent home of her own.'

'I can see you have been busy, little puss,' Nicolas said. 'Now tell me, how did you come to be in town, Tom—and why do you have to visit Grandfather next weekend?'

'Grandfather stumped up the readies to settle most of my

debts and allow me a short visit to town,' Tom said. 'He has asked me to do something for him in return, and I think I shall, though it means I shall have to go abroad for a while.'

'Shall you like that?' Caroline asked, recalling how upset Julia had been when he was hurt. 'Would it not affect plans for—?' She broke off because she had no idea whether or not her brother returned Miss Fairchild's affections.

'I have no immediate plans for the future, except to put the estate into good heart,' Tom said with a slight frown. 'I could not think of marriage until I could support a wife, if that is what you were wondering, Caroline. Mama has no need to rush into anything, though I would be happy to see her settled if she wished it—but I am not on the catch for a rich wife, or a wife at all for the moment.'

'Oh, I see,' Caroline said and felt sorry for her friend, because it was obvious that her brother was too proud to ask Julia to be his wife, at least until he had something more than a rundown estate to offer her. 'Well, you must do as you please, of course.'

As she finished speaking, their mother came into the room. She was delighted to see all her family together, and immediately charged Nicolas with taking his sister to the ball that evening.

'Tom was to have come with us, you see,' she said, 'but I am sure Lady Jersey will be only too happy to accept you in his place. I shall stay here, of course, in case my son needs me, but Louisa will go.'

'Why do you not let me stay with you, Mama?' Caroline asked. 'I am sure Nicolas may find his own amusement for one night.'

'No, dearest,' her mother said. 'It is a matter of choice, and I shall not be entirely alone. A friend has promised to call, just for a few minutes. We shall have a quiet supper together, and talk…'

'Mama, do tell,' Caroline said, mischief in her eyes. 'Is it Mr Milbank?'

Marianne flushed and then smiled. 'I can see you have guessed it, Caroline, and since we are all together, I must confess that Herbert has asked me if I will consent to be his wife. I have asked him here this evening to give him his answer—and now, perhaps you will all have your say?'

'You should marry him, Mama,' Caroline said. 'He seems a pleasant gentleman and likes you very well.'

'Take the fellow,' Nicolas said and grinned wickedly. 'You are too young to wear the weeds for ever, Ma.'

'Marry him if you wish,' Tom said, 'but there will always be a home for you with me, Mama, whatever happens.'

'Bless you, dearest,' Marianne said, looking at Tom. 'But I must tell you that I feel happier now than I have for a long time. Papa and I did well enough together, and I was fond of him until he died—I would not want any of you to think that I had entirely forgot your father.'

'We should not have thought anything of the sort,' Caroline said. 'I hope you will take Mr Milbank, Mama.'

'Well, it is you it will affect most,' Marianne told her daughter. 'If you do not form an attachment this time, you will be obliged to live under his roof, which he is very happy for you to do—so you must not think you are forced to accept an offer you cannot like. I think you would be well suited with a certain gentleman if he should offer, but there is no saying he will.'

'What is this?' Nicolas asked, mischief in his eyes. 'You did not tell me this, Caroline!'

'Well, there was too much else to say,' she replied. 'But if you would like to take me driving this afternoon, I shall tell you all there is to know.'

Chapter Seven

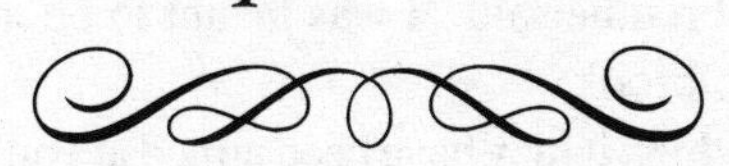

'George, a moment if you please!' Freddie hailed his friend as he saw him leaving the premises of a gentleman's hat shop in Brook Street. He ran across the road, dodging between the traffic to catch him. 'How is Julia today? I trust she took no harm yesterday?'

'No, no, I do not think it,' George said with a little frown. 'She was merely distressed. It was a shocking thing to happen. You do not know any more concerning the incident, I suppose?'

'I have made further inquiries and it is quite certain that the rope had been tampered with, as we suspected. It must have happened under our noses, for Jackson swears that it was sound when he began to set up the balloon and I trust him completely. However, with so many people milling around before the flight, it might have been anyone. I do not imagine we shall discover the culprit, for we have nothing to go on. It was fortunate that things were no worse. Despite her denials, I am sure that Caroline was much shaken, and bruised, and Tom must think himself lucky he is no worse.'

'Miss Holbrook was very brave and acted with calm good sense. But why should anyone want to hurt her—or her brother, for that matter?' George looked puzzled.

'I have no idea,' Freddie said with a frown. 'However, I intend to make inquiries into this affair. It will not stop here.'

'No, it cannot,' George agreed. 'I don't suppose it was aimed at someone else…?' He lifted his brows.

'Exactly,' Freddie said. 'I was meant to be in that balloon with Miss Holbrook.'

'Then you think it may have been aimed at you?' George was shocked and stared at him incredulously. 'Although she could easily have been killed—both of you might have died, to say nothing of Jackson. If that is the case, you have a dangerous enemy, Freddie. He is ruthless and cares not who he harms.'

'Yes, unless it was merely a malicious act from a mindless idiot who did not understand what he did.'

'You think it might be simply that?' George raised his brows. 'But why would anyone do such a thing?'

'At this moment I have no idea, but I intend to discover the truth. We want no more *accidents*, George. I shall set an agent to work to discover what he may and I think I may take a trip out of town myself.'

'Were you thinking of going immediately?'

'Why do you ask?' Freddie saw something in his friend's eyes. 'Spit it out, man. It clearly bothers you.'

'There are some spiteful rumours circulating, Freddie—about Miss Holbrook…'

'You mean because of that business with the balloon, I suppose? I know it was a little bold of her, but surely nothing that could cause her to be censured?'

'That and other things…' George frowned. 'Apparently,

she was seen alone at the inn, coming from the bedchamber. Obviously, she had been with her brother, so that may be set to rights easily enough, but it seems that she was also seen leaving an inn early one morning quite recently…with you.'

'Damn!' Freddie glared at him so fiercely that George was taken aback.

'Didn't mean to offend you, old fellow. Dare say it is all lies?'

'That is the devil of it,' Freddie said. 'I did take her to an inn—and that's not the worst of it, George. I took her to a mill and she was dressed as a youth.'

'That was somewhat reckless of you, Freddie.'

'I know it,' he said with a rueful smile. 'She demanded it of me in settlement of a wager, George—but that is no excuse. I admit that I was at fault. I wanted to see if she would dare and she did! Sneaked out in borrowed clothes, as game as anything. We left before the fight finished, as it happens—but she would have seen it out if I'd let her.'

'She is very spirited,' George said, 'but quite innocent, you know. It would be a sad thing if she were to lose her reputation for a lark, Freddie.'

'Yes, you are right, of course,' Freddie replied. 'This other business must wait for the moment. There is something I must do first…'

'That was no accident,' Nicolas said and frowned as he looked at his brother when they were alone. 'Caro told me the rope had been deliberately frayed. It must have been done in the hope of causing harm—either to you or Caroline.'

'But it was a last-minute decision,' Tom said, wrinkling his brow. 'That I should go up with her, I mean. It was to have been Sir Frederick.'

'Damn it!' Nicolas was concerned, angry. 'She might have been killed! I cannot think that Caroline has an enemy…but it might have been intended for Rathbone. Besides, he is to blame for risking her safety in that ridiculous thing!'

'No, no,' Tom said. 'I do not think you can blame him for this, Nicolas. Caroline teased him into letting her go up and he would have been with her had I not intervened.'

'Then the intended victim must have been Sir Frederick…' Nicolas frowned. 'Though I cannot think why anyone might want to harm our sister in the process.'

'It might have something to do with the money…' Tom mused thoughtfully. 'Grandfather has decided to leave a large chunk of his fortune to us—not the entail, of course, but it is a sizeable amount as I understand it.'

'You mean to suspect our uncles—cousins?' Nicolas looked dubious. 'I know they are not exactly fond—but murder?'

'No, of course not. Uncle Sebastian will get what is his, naturally. The entail cannot be broken, nor should it. Uncle Claude will also get something—the London house and a small estate in Cornwall, which came to Bollingbrook through his second wife, I believe. However, there is someone else who might stand to gain if we were not around when Grandfather dies.'

'I don't understand you,' Nicolas said. 'Who could possibly benefit?'

'I dare say Grandfather won't mind me telling you this much in the circumstances,' Tom said. 'There is a fellow in Jamaica who might benefit if the named heirs were dead. I suppose he *is* an uncle of sorts, though illegitimate. Grandfather wants me to sell the plantation out there and I'm to do something for this uncle fellow.'

'You mean the old gentleman had another son in Jamaica?' Nicolas was fascinated, his eyes bright with amusement. 'He hasn't been out to the plantation since before he married our grandmother. I understood he had left the management of his property there to his overseer…'

'It is a wonder that there is anything left to sell, for it has been shamefully neglected,' Tom observed. 'But it seems that the man was entirely trustworthy. Now he has died and Grandfather says it is time to sell. Whatever I get for it will come to me, and that may be very little. Apparently Grandfather had property elsewhere, which did not come to him through the estate. It was sold some years ago and the money invested safely. Caroline is to have something and you, I imagine—but there should be a couple of hundred thousand pounds, and Grandfather is determined that his elder sons shall not touch a penny of it. I think he intends to divide it between us and the fellow in Jamaica.'

'Good grief!' Nicolas ejaculated, feeling astonished at the size of the bequest. 'Now that alters things somewhat. As lazy as he undoubtedly is, even Uncle Sebastian might consider stirring himself for that kind of money.'

'No, you cannot think it? His wife was an heiress and both daughters married well. Come to think of it, Uncle Claude married to advantage and he has but one daughter. Grandfather gave her ten thousand when she married.' Tom frowned. 'I cannot say with any certainty that it was truly an attempt on Caroline's life or mine. Besides, Uncle Sebastian has no sons at present and the Bollingbrook estate may well come to me in the end—or you, if I die.'

'But if it were the bastard…surely he is in Jamaica? And surely you would be his intended victim, not Caroline!'

'He may not be in Jamaica. Apparently, he wrote to Grandfather a while back and told him that he intended to visit England and that he would call on him.'

'Do you think his letter was intended as a threat of some kind? I dare say he might think himself ill used if nothing has been done for him.'

'Yes, that was in my mind,' Tom said.

Nicolas frowned. 'Shall you risk going out to Jamaica?'

'I think I must. The overseer's daughter is to marry, and she wants to know if her future husband may purchase the estate. An offer has been made, but it is paltry. I must see what can be done elsewhere.'

'You will need someone to watch your back.'

'Any ideas?'

'I might have. I shall ask around and see if I can find a suitable man for you. You need an old soldier, Tom. A man you can trust in a fight.' Nicolas was thoughtful. 'Meanwhile, you must take more care—you and Caroline.'

'I trust I may rely on you to behave yourself this evening?' Lady Taunton looked at Caroline with something not far from dislike. 'We can only hope that the rumours circulating town have not become so strong that we shall be asked to leave. The patronesses of Almack's are extremely strict, as you very well know, and if you are treated with some coolness you have only yourself to blame. The very idea of going up in a balloon! It is not the behaviour expected of a respectable young lady, I can tell you. And as for being seen coming from the bedchamber of an inn alone…' She clicked her tongue in disgust. 'It is no wonder if people are talking.'

'I promise you that I shall be circumspect this evening,' Caroline replied, feeling unusually chastened.

'We must hope that that is an end to it,' Lady Taunton replied with a sour look. 'All I ask is that you do not disgrace me, Caroline.'

It was not to be expected that Caroline went with a light heart to the assembly that evening. Her mother had declined to accompany them, because she was worried about Tom, who seemed a little less well that day, but she would not hear of Caroline staying at home.

'You must go, my dear,' she insisted. 'Especially if there are silly rumours circulating. To stay at home might cause people to think they were true.'

Caroline knew that her mother was right. To stay away when she had been given vouchers would look as if she had something to hide. It was usually a very insipid evening, for she knew that Sir Frederick would not be there. Mr Bellingham had told her that Sir Frederick had never attended these gatherings, had not done so since he was first on the town. The most that she could hope for was to dance twice with Mr Bellingham and perhaps stand up for a waltz or two with others of her friends, for there was often more ladies than gentlemen present.

She wished that she might have seen Sir Frederick—she was afraid that he was still angry with her and that had left her feeling rather low. Since the incident at the balloon ascension, he had seemed to change towards her—what could have happened? And why did she mind so much?

Caroline was aware of something different as she went into the ballroom with her aunt. People turned their heads to look at her and she heard a little buzz of noise, as if they were whispering. For a minute or two she and her aunt stood alone, and then Mr Bellingham brought Julia across to speak to them.

Caroline's cheeks were a little warm, for her friends usually surrounded her as soon as she entered a room; she felt wretched, for clearly her aunt had been right. After a moment, one or two others drifted over to join them and she began to feel better. However, she was aware of an odd atmosphere, and even when Sally Jersey came over to speak to her, she felt that there was something a little chilly in that lady's manner.

Caroline lifted her head and danced with George, determined to brave the evening out whatever happened. He, of course, was just as usual, making her laugh and complimenting her on her gown so that she began to relax a little and wonder if she had imagined that she was being given the cold shoulder by some of the older ladies. It was just as their dance was drawing to a close that she heard a little gasp of surprise that seemed to echo from the assembled company as one. And then, turning her head towards the door, she saw that a gentleman had entered, accompanied by an elderly lady.

'Good grief!' Bellingham said, clearly startled. 'I never thought I would see the day. Freddie here and his godmother too! He intends business…'

'What do you mean?' Caroline asked, looking at him.

'Lady Stroud hardly ever attends this sort of affair these days,' George said. 'She was one of the leading hostesses of her day, of course—a stickler in all matters of propriety. Clever devil!' A look of appreciation had entered his eyes.

'I do not understand…' Caroline said, her voice fading as he nodded at her encouragingly, a flicker of amusement in his eyes. She began to see what he was getting at. 'Oh…'

'Trust Freddie to see you right, m'dear,' George said and smiled at her. 'Knows he got you into it, up to him to see you safe.'

'No, please...' Caroline said, her cheeks becoming hot. This was dreadful! George was suggesting that it was up to Freddie to make her an offer because he had compromised her, and that wasn't right at all. 'It was all my fault. He mustn't—'

'Freddie might be a bit reckless, careless, even, at times,' George said, still smiling rather oddly at her. 'But he knows what is expected of a gentleman—and he is fond of you, m'dear. He'll see you right and tight.'

Caroline knew that he was leading her towards Sir Frederick and Lady Stroud. She wanted to break away from him and seek a place to hide, but his hold on her arm was quite firm and it was clear that there was no escape for her.

'Lady Stroud,' George said. 'May I say that I am delighted to see you here this evening, ma'am. It is too seldom that we see you in company these days.' He looked at Caroline. 'May I present you to a young lady I admire, ma'am? This is Miss Caroline Holbrook.'

'I am aware of the gel's name,' Lady Stroud said a little testily, her steely gaze fixed on Caroline's face as she addressed her godson. 'Pretty enough, I'll grant you that, Freddie. I dare say you'll know how to steady her.' She fixed Caroline with a bayonet look. 'A spirited gel, so my godson says. He often talks a great deal of nonsense, but in this instance I have been prepared to listen to him. Miss Holbrook, I believe they are about to play a waltz. I give you permission to dance with Rathbone. Off you go, now, and try to look as if it pleases you.'

'Thank you, ma'am.' For once in her life Caroline did as

she was bid without demur. 'Sir, you are very kind.' She lifted her head, meeting his eyes without flinching.

'Caroline, my privilege,' Freddie said, taking her by the hand and leading her towards the floor. 'Do not look so scared. I promise you that her bark is much worse than her bite. She is actually on your side, though you may not think it.'

'Lady Stroud is very good,' Caroline said, a trifle pale though her head was up, her smile in place. 'But it was not necessary to ride to my rescue like a white knight, sir. I am quite able to manage for myself.'

'Caroline, do you not know what people are whispering—what they are thinking? You were seen leaving the inn with me on the morning of the fight.'

'Oh…' Caroline glanced up at him, her eyes wide. 'I thought it was just that I was alone at the inn when Tom was hurt.'

'No,' Freddie said. 'You might have ridden that out, but this is more serious—and it is my fault. Therefore I must do my best to see you clear of it. Lady Stroud still has significant influence in society and if she is seen to approve of you…'

'Yes, I see,' Caroline said and swallowed hard. 'I thought…Mr Bellingham said…thank you for thinking of it, sir. I know this is all my own fault, though I do not see that I have committed a terrible crime.' Her eyes were suddenly filled with defiance as her pride took over and she threw off her subdued mood. 'You did not seduce me, sir, and are therefore blameless.'

'No, not blameless,' he said honestly. His expression was serious, a little harsh. 'I have a way of teasing, Caroline—a provoking manner that sometimes leads others to recklessness that they would not otherwise think of, and I believe this is what happened in your case. Therefore, I must do what I can to—'

'No!' Caroline said quickly. 'I am not sure what you mean to say, sir, but I must tell you that I shall soon be leaving London on a visit to my grandfather. I think that it would be better if you waited until I return...if you have anything you wish to say to me.' Her cheeks were flushed and she concentrated very hard on the second button of his pristine shirt.

'Very well, if that is your wish,' he said. 'My own feeling is that Lady Stroud may do all that is necessary. I do have something to say to you, Caroline, but it may easily wait for a few weeks.'

'Thank you,' she said and smiled up at him. Her smile at that moment was so brave and so beautiful that Freddie was momentarily dazzled. 'You are very kind, sir, and I am glad that you are not cross with me.'

'Have I done something to make you think that I might be?' He raised his brows at her.

She took a deep breath. 'You seemed angry after Tom was hurt...at the inn.'

'I was angry at what had happened,' he said. 'You made light of the accident, Caroline, but you could have been badly hurt. And it is for this reason that I must leave town for a few days. If someone is trying to harm one of us, I think it needs investigating.'

'You are very kind to take an interest.'

'Anything that concerns you, concerns me, Caroline. Besides, whoever tampered with that rope may have had another victim in mind altogether.'

'Do you have an enemy, sir?'

'I dare say I have more than one,' Freddie said, looking

grim. 'He may do his damnedest as far as I am concerned, but when the safety of others—your safety, Caroline—is concerned, that is another matter.'

There was such sincerity, such anger in his eyes that her heart caught. She knew in that moment that there was a special feeling between them, but the dance was ending and she was unable to say more as Sally Jersey came up to them at that moment. She gave Freddie a look of pure mischief.

'Sir Frederick, this is indeed an honour. I had long given up hope of seeing you here, my friend.'

'As well you might,' he said. 'It took a great deal to bring me here, Sally—but I imagine I have no need to elaborate? I believe that my godmother will do all that is necessary.'

'Of course,' the lady replied and threw Caroline a speaking look. 'You are a fortunate young lady, Miss Holbrook. I believe I may not say more for the time being, but now that I understand you were visiting Lady Stroud that morning, there cannot be the least need for censure. It seemed a little odd that you should be seen leaving an inn with Sir Frederick at such an hour, but I understand that he was forced to stop because his horses had some trouble with their harness. It is all explained and shall be forgotten. Come along, Caroline. I want you to take pity on a young gentleman who is newly come to town. He is very shy and may tread on your toes, but I know that you will be kind to him.'

Freddie watched as Lady Jersey bore Caroline off with her. He smiled a little as George came up to him.

'The chestnuts are yours, my dear friend. I believe that was our bet—that when you saw me here I should have met my match?'

'You had no choice but to come in the circumstances,'

George said. 'The bet was a matter of marriage. You have until Christmas, Freddie…'

'Very well,' Freddie replied, frowning slightly. He gave his friend a quizzical look. 'You know, I am not sure that a few months will be long enough. I'm damned if I know if she will have me.'

Caroline sat staring out of her bedroom window. It was a wet day and the streets of London were unappealing. Her thoughts were running in a direction she did not like. She was almost certain that Sir Frederick meant to make her an offer of marriage. An offer he felt obliged to make because of the scandalous gossip that had been circulating about her.

He had left Almack's soon after his dance with her, though Lady Stroud had stayed on for two hours, keeping Caroline by her side most of the time and introducing her to everyone who came near as her new friend.

'My godson brought her to visit me early one morning recently,' Lady Stroud lied stoutly, 'and we took to each other like ducks to water. She's a gel after me own heart. I like a gel with spirit. Can't stand these milk-and-water manners today!'

Her sally had attracted polite laughter, which meant an end to the threat of scandal. Caroline had watched and listened, for it was soon clear to her that Lady Stroud was a martinet in the matter of proper manners and much respected. When she took her leave, she instructed Caroline to visit her soon, and told her that she expected them to become good friends in the future.

Caroline had thanked her for coming to her rescue and received a stern look in return. 'I don't make a habit of lying, young lady. Make sure that you give me no cause to regret this evening. I happen to be very fond of Freddie. He owes a duty to his family. He will be expected to provide the family with an heir soon, and his wife must be above reproach.'

Caroline had mumbled something appropriate. She was very grateful to the elderly lady for helping her, and even though she was forced to endure another lecture from her aunt on the way home, she knew that Lady Taunton was impressed.

'Of course you know what this means,' she told Caroline before they parted. 'I shall say no more—but I was right all the time.'

Caroline had not answered her, because she was very much afraid that Sir Freddie did intend to make her an offer. Not because he loved her, but because he thought it was the proper thing to do—and people would expect it after what had happened at Almack's. His coming there just to dance with her—when he had never done so before—was sure to be taken as a sign that he meant to marry her. She knew from Lady Stroud that he was looking to settle and she had been warned that his wife must be beyond reproach. Surely he could not truly wish to marry Caroline! Her reckless behaviour had aroused gossip, and she had nothing to offer him. It could only be a misplaced sense of honour that had prompted him to think of it.

She had prevented him from speaking that night, and perhaps once the gossip had died down he would reconsider. After all, it was not truly necessary—and she did not want to be married for the sake of her reputation.

She would miss seeing him over the course of the next few days, and she thought that she might not be in London when he returned. She was to visit her grandfather at the end of the next week, and Mrs Holbrook was talking of leaving London soon. She had spoken to Caroline of it the day after Mr Milbank came to supper.

'It may not be necessary for you to come back to town after your visit to Bollingbrook,' she had told her daughter. 'I am thinking of going down to Bath. Mr Milbank believes it would suit me better than racketing around London, and I think he may be right. I should naturally wish you to join me there. I am sure that you will make new acquaintances in Bath, Caroline, and anyone who wishes to see you will take the trouble of travelling there, I am certain.'

'Will Aunt Louisa accompany you to Bath, Mama?'

'No, I do not think so,' Marianne said. 'I have a little money of my own, Caroline. I have been reserving it for the future, but I think I shall not need it now. I have decided to accept Mr Milbank's offer. It is so that we may see each other comfortably, and make what arrangements we wish, that I have decided to go down to Bath. I am afraid that your aunt is not pleased by my decision.'

'But you will not let her displeasure change your mind, Mama?' Caroline looked at her anxiously, for in the past months her mother had been much influenced by Lady Taunton.

'No, I shall not,' Marianne said with more determination than her daughter had seen from her. 'I shall tell you now, Caroline. My first marriage was not all that it might have been—but I think that this time I am truly loved. I should be foolish to turn down this chance of happiness.'

'I am sorry that you were not happy with Papa.'

'It was only after my illness,' her mother said. 'Until then I think he cared for me as much as most men care for their wives. But I was ill and things were not right between us. He formed another attachment—a relationship that lasted until his death.' She lifted her head proudly. 'I did not know it, though I suspected it—and then, after his death, I received a very unkind letter. I showed it to Bollingbrook, but he told me not to make a fuss about it, and that was one of the reasons we disagreed. He was inclined to think me foolish. However, I did not think that an affair of long standing was something I could simply forget as if it had never happened.' She shook her head. 'It does not serve to dwell on these things. I shall forget it now, because it no longer matters.'

'I am sorry you were hurt,' Caroline said, understanding now why her mother had seemed to fade away after her father's death. It was not just a matter of grief, but also of hurt and disappointment. 'But I think you will be happy with Mr Milbank.'

'Yes, I am perfectly sure of it,' Marianne said. 'I did not think that I could ever feel anything for anyone again, other than my children—but it has happened and I feel young once more.'

'You look young,' Caroline assured her mother and hugged her. 'Yes, let us go down to Bath, dearest Mama. I believe it will suit both of us much better than London.'

'Yes, my dear, we shall do so. We must attend the masked ball at Lady Mannering's house, but after that we shall go.'

The ball had begun with Caroline being surrounded by eager partners as always, for it seemed that society had decided to think the best of her and her popularity was restored. Mr Bellingham had written his name in three spaces, her brother Nicolas in another two. Although everyone wore masks, it was easy enough to guess who most of the guests were, though one or two eluded Caroline.

The room became very warm as the evening wore on and the French windows were opened on to the garden to allow some air to circulate. Caroline felt the heat a little before supper and decided to slip outside to the garden rather than go into the dining parlour. She was not in the least hungry and she did feel very sticky, for it was an airless night.

It was not so much better on the terrace, but at least the air was fresh out here, and the gardens looked enticing in the moonlight. She thought that she could smell some kind of night-blooming flower and was about to go in search of it when someone came out onto the terrace.

'Ah, I thought I saw you come out,' George said. He removed his mask and Caroline did likewise, for she thought it was in part due to the silken mask that she felt uncomfortable. 'Were you thinking of taking a stroll in the grounds?'

'Yes,' Caroline said, welcoming him with a smile 'I was not in the least hungry and thought it would be pleasant out here.'

'The air has been heavy all day,' George said and offered her his arm. 'May I walk with you, Miss Holbrook?'

'Yes, that would be nice,' Caroline replied with a smile. 'Have you heard from Sir Freddie? Do you know when he will be returning?'

'I fear not. Has he said nothing to you?'

'He had some business out of town, I believe, but I do not know when he may return.' She was torn between wanting to see him again and dreading it—she was afraid that his sense of honour would make him offer for her even if he did not truly wish her to be his wife.

They had strolled some distance from the lights of the ballroom. George was struck by the look on her face, for he sensed that she was deeply troubled. Could it be that she did not wish to marry Freddie? He hesitated for a moment, then, 'If there is anything I can do for you, Miss Holbrook, you have only to ask. You must know that I...have a great admiration for you.' Caroline's head came up and he smiled oddly. 'I do not think that it can be a surprise to you.'

'Oh, Mr Bellingham,' Caroline said, her breath catching in her throat. 'I have appreciated our friendship greatly but...'

'You care for someone else?' he asked gently. 'You may speak plainly. I shall not be offended, my dear, for I have suspected it, but I know that you are leaving town for a while and that nothing is settled. Indeed, you seem a little unhappy—and I wished to speak. I have never thought of marriage. I am set in my ways, and I had thought that Julia would be my heir, for I have no title to consider. However, if you need me, I am at your service.'

'How kind you are, sir, but you must not concern yourself for me.' Caroline reached out to touch his hand. He had not quite proposed to her, but she knew that he might have done if she had given him encouragement.

'I think so well of you, sir. And I like you more than any other gentleman of my acquaintance except—' She stopped and blushed. 'I am not perfectly sure...'

'I understand perfectly, more than you imagine, I dare say,' he said. 'I should be happy if our friendship were to continue, my dear.'

'What a generous man you are,' Caroline said. 'I think myself very fortunate to have such a friend.'

'Thank you. I am glad to have your good opinion, Miss Holbrook.' George smiled at her. 'I think perhaps we ought to go in for your aunt will be looking for you.' Hardly had he finished speaking when they saw her brother Nicolas walking towards them across the smooth lawns.

'It was our dance, Caroline. Ah, I see you are with Mr Bellingham,' he said. 'Then all is well. I merely came to see if you had wandered out here alone, puss.' He grinned at her and nodded to George. 'Warm this evening, isn't it?'

'Yes. We came out to take some air, but we are about to return to the ballroom. I believe you are to go out of town in a few days?'

'Yes, that is perfectly right. My brother has to visit Bollingbrook and Caroline is to go with him. Tom isn't fit to drive yet, of course, though he is much recovered in himself, so I shall take them down.'

'I am thinking of travelling to Bath this coming weekend,' George told him. 'The road follows the same direction you must take for a while, I dare say. We may see each other on the way.'

'Indeed we may,' Nicolas said. 'My mother goes to Bath in a few days I believe. You will surely see her there, and us too after our visit to Bollingbrook. I have agreed to drive Caroline there before I return to my regiment.'

'Yes, I had heard of Mrs Holbrook's intention,' George said with a smile. 'My estate is on the way, not too distant from your grandfather's. I shall stay there for a few nights on my journey, I believe. I have a little business to attend to before I go on.'

'Then you must visit us at Bollingbrook,' Nicolas said. 'I dare say the old gentleman may like to give a dinner for his neighbours while we are there.'

'Perhaps. We shall see,' replied George, who knew Bollingbrook's reputation as a recluse these past years. 'And now I must bid you both good evening as I am engaged for the next dance...'

He went on ahead of them, leaving the brother and sister together in the garden. Nicolas looked at his sister thoughtfully.

'Bellingham is a decent chap,' he said. 'You might think yourself fortunate if he asked for you, puss.'

'He is very kind,' Caroline told him a trifle wistfully. 'And I do like him, but I am not sure who I wish to marry just yet.'

'It's this other fellow you've got your mind set on,' Nicolas said and frowned, for he had heard some gossip. 'I don't say as there's anything wrong with that, Caroline—but if he ain't come up to scratch yet, he may not.'

'I know,' Caroline said. 'I am not sure I wish to marry him if he does, Nicolas. Sometimes I have thought…and yet I do not know. This marrying business is more difficult than I had imagined. I had always believed Mama happy with Papa, but it seems that it was not so…and that upsets me a little.' It had made her wonder if there was such a thing as true love, and she was not certain that she could trust her own feelings. Was the most she could sensibly hope for a marriage of convenience with someone she liked?

'Well, I dare say there is time enough for you to find someone you can like.' Nicolas glanced over his shoulder as he heard a rustling noise behind him. He was not carrying his pistol, though it was in the pocket of his topcoat. 'I believe we should go in, puss—and I should tell you that I think it would not be sensible of you to venture out alone while you are in town.'

'Are you thinking of what happened the other morning?' Caroline saw the concern in his face. 'I know Sir Frederick thinks someone deliberately caused that accident to the balloon, though I cannot imagine why anyone would want to do such a thing.'

'It is difficult to know the reasoning behind it,' Nicolas agreed. 'But Tom and I think that you should take care, Caroline—just in case you were the intended victim.'

'I know that I might have been killed, but why should someone want me dead? As far as I know I have no enemies and my dowry is virtually nothing.'

'It may not be as insignificant as you think,' Nicolas told her. 'Grandfather may do something for all of us if he chooses.'

'Grandfather has a lot of secrets, doesn't he?' Caroline said. 'He hinted as much to me once, but when I asked him what he meant he became cross and told me to run away to my mother.'

'He certainly does—more than we could ever know!' Nicolas said and laughed. 'Well, puss, I think we have probably lost our dance, for here comes your next partner, if I do not mistake his look. I shall leave you now—I have an appointment elsewhere, but do not forget what I told you…the garden is out of bounds for you without someone to protect you.'

'Then I shall not venture out even if it is hot,' Caroline said. She glanced over her shoulder, for she had felt for the past few minutes that she was being watched…

'I shall miss you when you leave London,' Julia said, looking a little wistful. 'I am happier with you than any of my other friends, Caroline. I do hope we shall not lose touch?'

'Oh, no, I am sure we shall not,' Caroline said. 'I shall write to you and tell you all what is happening. Have I told you that Tom has to go abroad for a while?'

'Go abroad?' Julia looked surprised and then upset. 'Oh, I did not know. Will he be gone long, do you think?'

'I would not think it,' Caroline answered, for she could see that Julia had been greatly affected by the news.

'Mr Asbury has made me an offer of marriage,' Julia said. 'Please, do not mention it to anyone, for I have asked him for a little time. I am not sure, you see. I like him very well, and he is the only gentleman to have offered for me—other than Mr Farringdon.'

'Oh, yes,' Caroline agreed. 'You would not wish to marry Mr Farringdon…' She frowned as she realised something. 'He has not been in town for a week or more now, I think. At least I have not seen him.'

'George said he has been obliged to leave town in a hurry. His tailor had heard rumours of him being near to ruin and he was pressing for settlement.'

'Oh, that is unfortunate for him,' Caroline said, for even though she did not like the gentleman, she would not wish such a fate on anyone. 'However, I must admit that he had a way of looking at one that was most uncomfortable.'

'Oh, yes,' Julia said. 'It is strange how some gentlemen make one feel happy in their company—and others do not.'

'Yes, isn't it?' Caroline agreed. 'It is not easy to know one's own heart sometimes, is it?'

'I know my own heart,' Julia replied with a frown. 'But Mama wishes me to marry quite soon and she likes Mr Asbury…'

Caroline looked at her, feeling sorry because she knew that it was useless for her friend to have hopes of Tom. However much he might be attracted to Julia, he would not offer for her until he could afford to support her. She wished that she might say something to ease Julia's uncertainty, but she could not, for Tom had said nothing of his intentions to her and it would be wrong to arouse false hopes.

'Well, perhaps things will turn out as they ought,' she said and smiled at Julia. 'Oh, dear, sometimes I think it would have been very much easier to have been born a man, don't you?'

'Oh, yes,' Julia agreed. 'At least one could have asked the person one liked instead of having to wait to be asked.'

'Yes, that is unfair,' Caroline said, 'though I think that if I truly wanted to marry a gentleman who did not speak, I might just give him a hint.'

Julia looked at her and sighed. 'You are so much braver than I,' she said. 'All I can do is smile and hope…'

'Will you allow me to drive for a while?' Caroline asked her brother. They had been driving for some distance and the busy streets of London were left far behind them now. 'It is ages since you taught me to drive, Nicolas, and I have had no opportunity since you left to join the army, and I should be glad of some practice.'

'Very well,' Nicolas said and handed the reins to her. 'The road is quiet enough. Do you see that phaeton up ahead of us, puss? Let us try to overtake him before we come to the cross-roads. Do not be anxious—I am here to take over if you cannot manage it.'

'Oh, yes,' Caroline said, much amused. She was sitting up beside him, but she glanced over her shoulder at Tom, who was resting with his head back, his eyes closed. 'Wake up, Tom!' she cried. 'We're going to race that phaeton ahead of us.'

'God save us!' Tom said wryly. 'You were supposed to be saving me from more injury, brother—not exposing me to certain death.'

'Never fear, Tom,' he said with a grin. 'I am here and I shall take the reins if Caroline cannot manage it.'

Caroline's face was vivid with excitement. She could feel the wind in her hair as her bonnet blew off, hanging by its ribbons, and she cried out to her brother as they caught up with the vehicle in front of them.

'Go on, Caroline,' Nicolas urged. 'Pull out and pass him now. It is easy enough for we are at the crossroads and you have plenty of room.'

'Do you think I ought?' Caroline asked, knowing a moment of doubt. It had been fun catching the phaeton ahead of them, but she had recognised it and would have slowed up had Nicolas allowed it.

Seeing her hesitation, Nicholas snatched the reins back from her and flicked his whip over the horses' heads so that they sprang forward. The other carriage had increased its own speed and for a moment they were wheel to wheel. It was only when Nicolas saw the farm wagon coming from the right of the crossroads that he became aware of danger. It would have been wiser to drop back and let the phaeton have right of way but instead, he shot through and cut across to the left, causing the driver of the phaeton to curse and rein his horses in sharply.

Nicolas squeezed ahead, though it was only the skill of the other driver that saved them from an accident. Nicolas looked back with glee as he saw that they had left the phaeton far behind.

'It was a pity it was over so quickly,' he said regretfully. 'I should have liked to race him for longer. He is no mean whip, Caroline.' Realising that she was silent, he turned his head to look at her. 'Did I scare you, puss?'

'No, I was not frightened,' she said. 'But...that was Sir Freddie. I wasn't sure until we caught up with him, for there are other phaetons painted in those colours, but those were his horses and I caught a glimpse of his face as we shot past. He was very angry, Nicolas.'

'He came off all right,' Nicolas said, slightly shocked to discover who he had almost overset.

'By his judgement, not yours,' Tom said from behind them. 'You are completely mad, Nicolas. You should not have encouraged Caroline to drive like that on the open road. And you were reckless to pass him that way. I do not think I should want to be in your shoes when Sir Frederick catches up to us.'

'Well, I dare say he will not, unless I wish him too,' Nicolas said. 'I shall let them have their head for a while yet.'

'You will have to rest them eventually or change them,' Tom said and sat back, closing his eyes again. 'Besides, it is almost time we stopped for nuncheon. There is an inn no more than five miles ahead of us. I stopped there on my way up and it serves tolerable food.'

Nicolas glanced back over his shoulder. 'There is no sign of him. I dare say we shall reach the inn and eat our nuncheon before he catches up to us.'

Caroline was silent. She did not think that Sir Freddie would allow the incident to go without rebuke, and she was not at all surprised when a few moments later Tom called out that the phaeton was behind them. The driver caught up to them easily, keeping pace whatever Nicolas did in an effort to lose him, but did not attempt to pass. Though there were places that would have allowed it easily had Sir Frederick wished it, for even Nicolas was aware that Sir Freddie's blacks had the beating of him if their master chose.

When he turned into the inn yard at Tom's insistence, the phaeton followed. Nicolas jumped down, assisting his sister and then his brother, who was still not as nimble as usual. Sir Freddie was attending to his horses, speaking to the ostler who had come running. One of the grooms had attended to Nicolas's curricle, but it was clear that the preferred attention was being given to Sir Freddie.

'You go ahead,' Nicolas told Caroline and Tom. 'I had best have a word first. It will not do to come to blows in the inn itself. If we are to quarrel, it may be done out here.'

'But it was my fault in part…' Caroline began, only to find herself being firmly propelled towards the inn.

'Leave him to it,' Tom said, a firm hand at her elbow. 'Nicolas can handle himself, and it is his own fault if Sir Frederick gives him a set down.'

'Oh, but…' Caroline glanced back unhappily as she saw that the two men were closing on each other purposefully. 'I do hope they won't fight, Tom.'

'Well, I know who will feel sorry for himself if they do,' Tom said. 'Sir Frederick trains at Cribbs's Parlour. Nicolas is all pluck, but I think Rathbone is heavier, and has more science, I dare say. He is sure to give Nicolas a bloody nose if it comes to a mill.'

As they entered the inn, their host greeted them by beaming and welcoming them to his establishment. Tom asked for the private parlour, saying that there would be three of them for nuncheon. However, they had not been seated long before they heard voices and then the parlour door was flung open and Nicolas came in, followed by Sir Freddie. Caroline threw a scared glance at her brother, but was relieved to see that he did not have a bloody nose. He was slightly chastened, but did not seem resentful as he told them that he had invited Freddie to join them.

'I have apologised for stealing the road,' Nicolas said and grinned, a little shamefaced. 'But Sir Frederick has been dashed obliging about it.'

'No harm was done, though that was more luck than judgement,' Sir Freddie said and his eyes glinted as he looked at Caroline. 'However, it was not a fair race, for I had no idea of what you meant to do. Had I been aware that you meant to overtake me if you could, I should not have allowed you close enough and it would not have happened.'

'Oh, come on,' Nicolas exclaimed. 'That is doing it a dashed sight too brown. I shall not believe that you were not aware of me coming up behind you.'

'I did not think that you would be fool enough to try to pass at the crossroads,' Freddie said with a lift of his brow. 'If I were to meet you on the road another time, I should be more prepared.'

'Let us make a race of it,' Nicolas said. 'We are on our way to Bollingbrook—do you go that way?'

'Yes, as a matter of fact, that is exactly my intention. I have something I wish to discuss with Bollingbrook. I shall be staying at an inn nearby and will call on your grandfather in a day or so. If you are serious about this race, Nicolas, we shall come to terms. Besides, it will be best to rest the horses. I dare say yours are almost blown after the way you pushed them.'

'You are the most complete hand,' Nicolas said, for he had taken to Sir Freddie at once, despite being given a tongue-lashing in the yard for having risked the health of his sister and brother. He had loyally refrained from telling Sir Frederick that Caroline had been driving until the overtaking manoeuvre, perhaps because he sensed that it would have brought a further tongue-lashing. 'Yes, I agree. We shall make a wager when you come to Bollingbrook. Here's my hand on it.'

He offered his hand, which Sir Freddie took with a wry twist of his lips. He then sat down on the settle next to Caroline and looked at her, his brows lifted.

'Nicolas informs me that you were not in the least scared?'

'No, not of the race,' she said, 'but I thought you would be angry because of the way he cut you up at the crossroads.' She looked at him uncertainly.

'Had he been anyone else, I might have wrung his neck,' Freddie said lightly, though with a look that seemed to say he meant it. 'However, I shall hold my hand this time. I suppose that you will want to be a part of this race?'

'Yes, please,' Caroline said instantly. She was surprised, for she had thought he would forbid it. 'Indeed, I should!'

'Then we shall have the same wager as before?'

'Yes!' Her eyes sparkled—she suddenly felt much better than she had since the morning of the balloon ascension.

'Very well, Miss Holbrook,' Freddie said, a gleam in his eye. 'If I win, I gain my wish, and, if Nicolas wins, you shall have what you desire of me—but there is one condition to this race.'

'And what is that, sir?'

'You will be my passenger and not your brother's. At least then I shall be certain of you ending in one piece. And you will not be allowed to drive!' He fixed her with a piercing stare, which told her that he was not ignorant of the truth concerning her behaviour earlier that morning.

'Dash it all, sir!' Nicolas exclaimed. 'That's a deal too much! Caroline is my sister, after all, and I would never do anything to harm her.'

'Sir Freddie is in the right of it,' Tom agreed. 'You are both too headstrong by half! And I'll wager fifty guineas he beats you, Nicolas.'

'Fine brother you are,' Nicolas said with a wrathful eye. 'I'll take your fifty guineas, Tom! But as for whose passenger she shall be—that must be Caroline's choice.'

'Oh, I shall go with Sir Freddie,' Caroline said happily. 'For if I win my wager, he must teach me to drive his blacks—'

'The greys,' Freddie said, 'and it's a deal.'

Chapter Eight

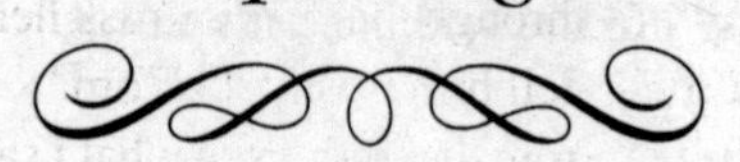

Freddie had refused to accompany Caroline and her brothers, promising to meet with them again within a day or so. He had no intention of encouraging Nicolas to race him again while Caroline was his passenger. Instead, he put his feet up and thought about the girl he had made up his mind to marry.

He had been slow to come to his decision, but his mind was set now. She had seemed natural enough and pleased to see him—once she realised he was not going to quarrel with her brother—but he sensed it would not be easy to gain her consent to the marriage. Because of all the gossip in town she had taken it into her head that he meant to make her an offer as a matter of honour, whereas nothing could be further from the truth.

He would have to think of a way to persuade her… Thinking about the various methods of persuasion that he might use brought a smile to his lips. Some of them would, he was sure, prove extremely pleasurable.

'Well, girl, let me look at you,' Bollingbrook said as Caroline ran to kiss his cheek. His eyes dwelled intently on her face for a moment. 'You have become an elegant lady, Caroline. I think you must have all the young bucks by the ears.'

'Oh, Grandfather!' Caroline cried, her eyes bright with laughter. 'Of course I have not.'

'She has, sir,' Nicolas said. 'They were falling over themselves to dance with her when I accompanied her to a ball. I had to fight my way through the crowd to ask her for a dance.'

'That isn't true—tell him it isn't so, Tom.'

'Well, it ain't far from the truth from what I saw,' Tom said, smiling at his sister affectionately. He looked at his grandfather. 'And how are you, sir? Feeling a little better, I hope?'

'As a matter of fact, I am,' the Marquis said. 'Got myself a new quack. Heard of him by chance and sent for him to call. He prescribed a new mixture, which seems to have helped for the time being at least. But we shan't talk of me. I've had my day. I want to know what you young people have been up to. Caroline, come and sit by me and tell me if you have settled on a beau yet.'

Caroline moved one of the pretty gilt chairs nearer to his large wing chair and sat down. She proceeded to chatter about what she had been doing in town, which made her grandfather laugh. Seeing that he was in a good humour, Nicolas joined in, telling him about army life, and Tom watched in his own quiet way, letting them have their sway until his grandfather looked at him.

'What of you, sir?' The Marquis' eyes narrowed. 'You don't look as hale as you did when you were here last. Been overdoing it, have you? What's the matter with your arm?'

'Tom was hurt,' Caroline said defensively, for she would not have her brother criticised unfairly. 'There was an accident with a balloon and Tom's arm was broken.' She did not mention her part in the affair, for she thought it best that he should not be told it all. Fortunately, it did not occur to him that she might also have been involved.

'Lucky to be alive, are you?' Bollingbrook beetled his brows. 'Damn stupid thing to do. Any fool knows those contraptions aren't safe. Well, we shall talk later, Tom. Go and rest for a while before dinner. The journey must have done you up.'

'Yes, I think it has to a certain extent,' Tom agreed and got to his feet. 'If you will excuse me.'

'Humph,' the Marquis said as he went out. 'I didn't know he had the gumption. Why anyone would want to fly I can't imagine. Don't know what the world is coming to!'

Bollingbrook sighed before looking at Nicolas. 'Nicolas, get off and find something to do before dinner. I want a few minutes alone with my girl.'

'Yes, sir, as you wish,' Nicolas said and grinned at his sister. 'I shall see you later, puss.' He winked at her as he went out.

'Impudent pup,' the Marquis grumbled, but in a mild manner that told Caroline he wasn't truly annoyed. 'Now then, girl, tell me the truth—have you seen someone that you fancy? If you have, I shall want to look him over. I want to make sure he is good enough for you.'

'I think there may be someone, Grandfather,' she said, 'but he hasn't spoken yet and I am not certain that he will.'

'What's the matter with the fellow? Ain't he got eyes?'

'Oh, yes,' Caroline said and laughed. 'He is very handsome and a little arrogant at times, I think—but he is also kind and funny and…' Her words tailed off. 'I think I may be in love with him, but I don't want to be if he doesn't love me.'

'Can't dictate something like that,' her grandfather told her. 'Either you are or you ain't. I only ever loved one woman, and that was your grandmother. The moment I set eyes on her I knew I had to have her. There was opposition to our marriage from her family, but I wasn't going to be beaten. I couldn't have cared less what anyone said or did, she was mine from the moment I saw her.'

'She was very beautiful,' Caroline said, thinking of Angelica Bollingbrook's portrait. 'I wish I had known her, Grandfather.'

'I wish you had too. You are very like her—and you would have loved each other.' He sighed deeply. 'Yes, I have wished that she could have known you, all of you.'

'I wish that she might,' Caroline said.

'Well, well, it can't be helped,' the Marquis said. 'I've shut myself off from the world too long, but there's time enough to repair things. You and your brothers shall not be forgotten, miss, and there's my promise to you. Run along, now. I shall see you later.'

Caroline was glad that she had come down to visit her grandfather. It was good to be in the country again, and though she had enjoyed the whirl of social activities in London, she thought that perhaps she preferred a quieter life.

The weather had settled into warm, balmy days and she spent much of her time either walking or riding with her brothers. She had persuaded Nicolas to take her driving in the park and they had enjoyed themselves letting the spirited horses have their head. It was on the morning of the second day after their arrival at Bollingbrook Place that she pulled Nicolas's phaeton to a standstill in front of the house just as a visitor arrived. She knew at once that it was Sir Freddie, and that he had seen her.

'Well done,' he said as he handed his reins to his tiger and came to help her down. 'I see that you have been practising, and perhaps we shall make a whip of you yet.'

His words of praise brought a flush to Caroline's cheeks and she gave him a shy smile, looking away quickly as his eyes seemed to penetrate her thoughts. She must not let him see that she was head over heels in love with him!

'Do not encourage her, sir,' Nicolas begged, grinning broadly. 'Given the opportunity, I think she would set up her own rig and then we should none of us know what she was up to!'

'Well, I dare say a suitable vehicle would not be so very dangerous,' Freddie said. 'Miss Holbrook would not be the only female whip; there are one or two notables, such as Lady Cheshire and Selma Hamilton.'

'Now you've done it,' Nicolas said with a look of mock despair. 'We shall have no peace now until she has set up her own curricle.'

'Oh, I want a phaeton,' Caroline said, giving her brother a challenging look. 'Something a little racy with a high-stepping pair to give me a certain touch.' She peeped under her lashes at Sir Freddie, but he had not risen to the challenge.

'What did I tell you?' Nicolas shook his head. 'There will be no dealing with her now!'

Freddie laughed, but made no further comment as he accompanied the pair into the house. Tom had been reading in the front parlour, but, having seen them through the window, came out to greet Sir Freddie and invite him to nuncheon.

'That is very kind of you,' Freddie said. 'But perhaps I ought to speak with your grandfather first?'

'I should leave it until later if I were you,' Tom advised with a wry grimace. 'He has his quack with him now and I think there is a little matter of a new dressing. In an hour or two he will no doubt be restored and feeling rather better.'

'Very well, I shall take your advice,' Freddie said, and glanced at Caroline. 'When do you intend to go down to Bath?'

'The day after tomorrow,' Caroline told him. 'Grandfather wants me to stay longer with him next time, but my mother will be expecting me—and, as she may be planning her wedding, I do not wish to keep her waiting.'

'Shall we arrange our race for then, Nicolas?' Freddie turned to him with a lift of his brows. 'We may meet at the Waverly Arms, which is just five miles from Bath, and race to the Abbey. After Caroline has transferred to my phaeton, of course.'

'Yes, a capital notion,' Nicolas said and grinned at him. 'But we have not decided a wager, though you have one with Caroline.'

'The race is enough in itself,' Freddie said, 'but if you wish for a wager—shall we say twenty guineas to the winner?'

Nicolas agreed. 'Twenty guineas it is!'

The details settled, they repaired to the dining room.

They spent the next hour or so very pleasantly eating and drinking. The conversation veered from prize fighting to horse racing and the likelihood of Bonaparte staying put on Elba for long, and then back to town gossip. The time passed so pleasantly that it was almost three in the afternoon before they rose from the table.

'Will you walk with me for a while?' Freddie asked

Caroline as they went out into the hall. 'I am sure your brothers have other things to do…'

'I can take a hint,' Nicolas said and grinned at his brother. 'Come along, Tom. I dare say we know when we are not wanted. I'll give you a game of billiards if you're up to it.'

'What do you mean if I'm up to it?' his brother demanded. 'Tell you what, we'll settle on the best of three…'

'How are you feeling now?' Freddie asked as they left the house and began to stroll across the lawns towards the rose arbour. His eyes moved over her with some concern. 'I know the accident was an unpleasant shock for you the other day, though you claimed you were not hurt—and of course you were denied your trip in that balloon.' He said nothing of the affair at Almack's, for he knew she would shy away from it like a young filly being put to its first fence.

'As if I cared for that,' Caroline said. 'I should still like to go up one day, but my only concern was for Tom. I think we were lucky that more serious harm did not result from such an accident.' She stopped walking for a moment to look at him. 'For myself, I cannot understand why anyone would do such a thing as to tamper with that rope. Why should anyone wish to harm Tom or me? Or you, sir, for that matter?'

'Indeed, it was more likely so, for the change was made only at the last moment, and I think the damage must have been done earlier that morning.'

'Yes, perhaps,' she said, looking at him doubtfully. 'Have you any idea who it might have been, sir?'

'None at all,' Freddie said. 'But I have not been idle, Caroline. I shall discover the truth in the end, I promise you.'

Caroline nodded. 'I think that you would always do what you set out to do, sir.' She blushed and dropped her gaze as she saw the expression in his eyes.

'Miss Holbrook…Caroline,' he said and looked down at her face. 'You do not have to answer me now unless you wish, but I—'

He was interrupted by a shout from the house and then Nicolas came sprinting across the lawns towards them.

'I am sorry to interrupt you,' he said, 'but Caroline must come at once. Grandfather has had some kind of a seizure and he is asking for her.'

'Oh, no,' Caroline said and looked at Freddie anxiously. 'You must forgive me, sir. May we speak again another time?'

'Yes, of course,' he said. 'Go to your grandfather, Caroline. I shall come tomorrow to inquire how he is—perhaps we may speak then?'

'Yes, thank you,' she said. 'Please excuse me…'

She fled across the lawn towards the house, her heart racing. These past couple of days her grandfather had shown his true affection for her, and she had felt happy that at last she was getting to know him. It would be a sad thing if he were to die just as they were truly becoming acquainted.

'Forgive me for disturbing you,' Nicolas said to Sir Freddie after his sister had left them. 'But I had no choice.'

'Obviously my meeting with Lord Bollingbrook must wait for another time,' Freddie said. 'It is unfortunate, for there were one or two matters I wished to discuss with him. I shall return tomorrow and in the meantime I hope that your grandfather is not seriously stricken.'

'He is as tough as old boots,' Nicolas said with a grimace that hid his affection. 'At least he has been, apart from the gout—but of course there is always a first time. But please do feel free to call whenever you wish.'

'Thank you. I shall,' Freddie said and nodded. 'I trust we shall not have to postpone our race. Good day to you now, Nicolas.' He tipped his hat and set out for the stables to have his phaeton made ready.

Nicolas turned and walked back to the house. He was almost certain that Sir Frederick had been about to make Caroline an offer, and he wished it might have happened before he had interrupted them. It would have secured his sister's future.

Tom was talking about making arrangements for his journey to Jamaica and Nicolas would need to return to his regiment in just over a week's time—which meant that Caroline would have no one to look out for her. If Tom was right and the attempts on his life were down to money, she might also be in some danger.

The doctor was still with Bollingbrook when Caroline arrived. He turned his head as she entered, smiling and beckoning her closer, though he had a finger to his lips, warning her to speak softly.

'The Marquis is resting, Miss Holbrook. I have given him something that will help him to sleep for a while.'

'Will he be all right?' Caroline looked at him anxiously. 'He isn't going to die—is he?'

'It was fortunate that I was here,' Dr Harris told her with a frown. 'I believe that it was merely a slight seizure and he should be well enough in a few days. However, the next few hours are all important. He must rest—and he should not be upset in any way. However, you must be aware that it could happen again, and if it does…'

'Yes, I see,' Caroline said and looked at her grandfather, who was now sleeping soundly. 'It is odd, but I have never considered him old. He is always so full of pepper that we take him for granted.'

Doctor Harris looked at her kindly. 'Do not despair, Miss Holbrook. He may yet be spared to you for some years to come.' He took his large silver watch from the pocket of his waistcoat and glanced at it. 'I have another call to make—but if you should need me at any time, please do not hesitate to send for me.'

'Thank you, sir. You are very kind.'

Caroline brought a chair to the side of her grandfather's bed and sat down beside him. His right hand was lying on the cover and she reached out to touch it with her own, wondering what he had wanted to say to her so urgently. The doctor's medication had obviously worked before he could communicate with her, and so she would sit quietly with him until he woke from his sleep.

She let her thoughts return to the few minutes she had spent alone with Sir Freddie. She had sensed that he was about to ask her to marry him—but did he truly care for her or was he merely offering out of a feeling of responsibility?

She had tried to deny her feelings for Sir Freddie, but, as her grandfather had said, you either loved or you did not; if she admitted what was in her heart, she had loved Freddie from the very beginning. There was something about him that had drawn her to him as a moth to the flame, a certain look, his smile and the way his ready wit matched hers. Whenever he was with her she felt alive and happy. She had not wanted to admit it, but now she could no longer pretend to herself that she was not head over heels in love with him.

But she must not reflect on her own feelings now. She glanced towards the bed as her grandfather stirred restlessly in his sleep, and she thought she heard him murmur a name.

'Angelica…' The words were slurred, indistinct, but had a desperate ring to them. 'My beloved…do not leave me…'

He was calling for the young wife he had loved and lost, Caroline thought. None of them had truly understood his grief, she realised now, or the loneliness he had imposed on himself after Angelica's death. Why had he done that? Was it grief or for some other reason that he had punished himself? Feeling her heart twist with pity, she stood up and bent over him, kissing the papery softness of his cheek.

'I am here, dearest,' she said. 'Rest now. There is nothing to fret for. I am here…'

He murmured something, but the frown faded from his forehead and he seemed to rest easier. Caroline stroked his brow for a moment and then resumed her seat until he seemed to settle. She sat with him, watching as he slept peacefully until Jenkins came to tell her that her brothers wished her to go downstairs and eat dinner with them.

'I shall watch over him, miss,' the valet said, nodding at her encouragingly. 'He speaks of you often to me, Miss Holbrook. If there is any change, I shall send one of the maids to fetch you at once.'

'Yes, perhaps…' Caroline got to her feet. She bent to kiss her grandfather's cheek once more. 'I know he is safe in your hands, Mr Jenkins. I shall come again for an hour or so later this evening.'

She went down to the dining parlour, answering her brothers' anxious inquiries as they sat down to dine together. As children, they had found the Marquis daunting, a figure of awe, but of late they had begun to know him and a shadow of anxiety hung over them all. He had been a dominating figure in their lives, and it would seem odd if he were no longer there.

It was just as Caroline and her brothers were about to rise from a rather sombre meal that one of the maids came to tell her that her grandfather was awake and asking to see her.

'Oh, thank goodness!' she cried, feeling the relief sweep over her. 'I shall come at once.'

She went quickly up the stairs and hurried to her grandfather's bedchamber. She tapped the door and went in as she was bid, halting as she looked towards the bed, hardly knowing what she would find. However, the Marquis was sitting up against a pile of pillows, taking a little refreshment from a cup that his valet held for him. He waved Jenkins away as he saw her.

'Enough for now, thank you.' Lifting his hand, he motioned to Caroline to come forward. She did so, thinking that he looked a little weary, but seemed to be otherwise much himself. As far as she could see he had not been paralysed and it appeared that his doctor had been right in saying that the seizure had been slight. 'Well, there you are, Caroline. Jenkins told me you were anxious, so I thought it best to have you up to see for yourself that I am as right as ninepence. It was just a little unpleasantness, nothing to worry about at all.'

'I am glad to see you recovered, Grandfather,' Caroline said with a smile. He was clearly not as well as he claimed, but he was not at death's door, for which she was heartily grateful. 'We have all been a little anxious, you know.'

'Humph,' the Marquis grunted. 'I hope you had the sense not to send for the rest of the family?'

'We thought it best to wait, sir.'

'Good. I don't want Sebastian or Claude troubling themselves to come all the way down here. I've nothing to say to either of 'em!'

'Grandfather! You should not say such things.'

'No, you shall not pull caps with me, Caroline. I don't mince my words. Never have done and it's too late to begin now. There's no wrapping it up in clean linen. I don't give a fig for either of 'em and they care less for me. I ain't saying it ain't my fault, but that's the way of it.'

'I am sorry for it, sir.'

'Well, I ain't and we'll say no more of it. You and your brothers are here and that's enough.' He sighed and closed his eyes for a moment, but opened them again as she moved away from the bed. 'No, don't go yet, girl. I have something to tell you. It concerns you more than your brothers.'

She saw that his hand was trembling and she reached for it, holding it gently in her own. 'You should not distress yourself, Grandfather. Surely it may wait until you are feeling better?'

'I've been lucky this time,' the Marquis told her and grimaced, rubbing at his chest as if he felt some discomfort. 'It would be easy to put off what must be done, but if I do you may have grief of it one day.'

'I do not understand,' Caroline said and held his hand a little tighter as she felt him quiver. 'How does your secret concern me?'

'It is time that you knew the whole story. It may shock you, but I would not have you live in ignorance of the truth. You see, it concerns my Angelica. You will have heard stories of her, I dare say?'

'I know that you loved her very much, sir.'

'She was my whole world,' the Marquis said, his voice ragged with remembered grief. 'I loved her more than my life. Her happiness was my only concern and I would have done anything to please her—though I know that what I did was wrong. I make no bones about it. Guilt for my sin has haunted me through the years, but I did it because I loved her and I could not bear to deny her anything.'

Caroline sat on the edge of the bed, looking at him in pity as she saw his anguish. 'You do not have to tell me this now, sir. I see that it affects you deeply. Whatever it is, it may wait.'

'No, child, let me speak,' her grandfather said. ' I have told you that Angelica's family did not wish her to marry me?' Caroline nodded, wondering what was troubling him so much. 'She defied them and ran away with me because she loved me. She was brave, if reckless…'

'She loved you as you loved her, Grandfather.'

'It was her dearest wish to have a child,' the Marquis said. 'But I was older and I ought to have been wiser for her sake…it was my fault that she died.'

'What do you mean? I do not understand you, sir. I thought Grandmother died of a fever?'

'It is a long story and began the first time I saw her. My Angelica. She was so beautiful that I could not resist her. Even when her brother told me…' His voice faded to a harsh whisper and he closed his eyes as if it were almost too much for him.

'Tell me, sir. It may ease your pain.'

'I knew that she was delicate,' the Marquis said. 'Her brother did not wish her to marry at all. He warned me that she must never have a child…that the strain of it would be too much for her heart.'

'How could he know that for certain?'

'He claimed it was a hereditary weakness. I did not care for such things. I only knew that I wanted her…loved her. I had my heirs. I did not need or want more children, but Angelica did. I tried to avoid giving her a child, but she guessed what I did and she begged me to give her a baby. I gave in to her pleas and by doing so I killed her. I adored her and I killed her. She was not strong enough, you see, and caught a chill that finished her off. Before she died she begged me to love our son and I did love him more than any other. When he married your mama, I thought that he could have married better. I have not been fair to your mama—or to you and your brothers, Caroline. Now I would make recompense. I cannot make up for what I did to Angelica, but I shall do what I can for her grandchildren.'

Caroline was silent for some minutes after he had done. 'But you were not to blame for her death,' she said at last. 'Angelica wanted a child and you gave in to her pleas…that does not make you a murderer.'

'Her brother called me that and he was right,' the Marquis said. 'I was warned that she was not strong enough, but I stole her from her family. I married her and I gave her a child…a child that ultimately killed her. Her brother hated me for it, and I have hated myself…'

'I am sorry that you have suffered so much, Grandfather,' Caroline told him. 'But why do you feel that this concerns me?'

'Angelica's weakness was hereditary, Caroline. They told me that it does not pass to the male line, but only to the female…' His eyes were sad as they rested on her face. 'You are so very like her that I fear for you.'

'You think that I might carry Angelica's weakness?' Caroline glanced up at him, her eyes wide with shock. 'But that is foolish, Grandfather. I am as healthy as can be. You need not concern yourself on my account.'

'It did not show in Angelica until she caught a fever after giving birth…it might not come out in you until later.'

'It will not affect me,' Caroline said quickly. 'I know that it has worried you for my sake, sir—but I am quite well.'

'I do not say that you should never marry, child,' the Marquis said. 'But you must be aware that you might never be able to give your husband a child.'

'You cannot know that,' Caroline cried. The idea suddenly distressed her more than it should. She had been told by more than one person that it was imperative that Sir Freddie's wife gave him an heir for the sake of the family name. Now Caroline was confronted with the thought that she might not be able to marry the man she loved. 'No one can know such a thing. I am perfectly well.' Her voice rose as she tried to deny what he was telling her. It could not be true! It must not…

'Do not be angry with me, Caroline,' the Marquis begged. 'Angelica's death has weighed on me all these years and of late I have begun to fear for you.'

'I am not angry,' Caroline told him, but her thoughts were whirling in confusion. 'You must rest now, sir. You have told me what you think I should know, and I am grateful—but there is no need for you to worry for my sake.'

Caroline's heart was heavy as she left her grandfather and went to her room. If she did carry this mysterious illness in her blood, she could not in all honesty marry Freddie. He needed an heir and she might simply be too delicate to give him one.

Chapter Nine

After spending a restless night, during which she slept little, Caroline visited her grandfather's room to see how he was. Jenkins was with him, and she could see that it was not a good time to call, but at least she was able to reassure herself that he had taken no further harm.

She went downstairs, but did not join her brothers in the breakfast parlour. Instead, she walked down to the stables and asked the groom to saddle a suitable horse for her. He asked if he should accompany her, but she shook her head, allowing him to help her mount, and setting out at a good canter, which soon developed into a headlong gallop.

The wind in her hair and the exhilaration of riding helped to blow away the confusion of her thoughts. She covered much of the estate, passing two tenanted farms and a lake, and returning at a slower pace an hour or so later. It was as she was passing the Home Woods that something caught her eye, and instinct made her duck her head over her horse's neck. Her instinctive reaction may have saved her, for she heard the shot whistle harmlessly by as she raced on, her heart hammering wildly in her breast.

Arriving back at the stables at a fierce canter, she flung herself down and left the horse standing for the groom, while she ran up to the house. Her brother Nicolas was coming from the front door and he frowned as he saw her.

'Why didn't you ask me to accompany you if you meant to ride?' he asked, and then, seeing her white face, 'What happened, Caroline?'

'Someone took a shot at me as I passed the Home Woods. I caught a glimpse of him in the trees and ducked forwards over my horse.'

'Go into the house and stay there!' Nicolas commanded, his face like thunder. 'This thing wants sorting once and for all.'

Caroline did not stay to argue. She found Tom in the back parlour he favoured. He was reading a news sheet delivered from the Receiving Office with some letters. She related her story to him breathlessly. Tom shot up from his chair immediately, his expression a mirror image of his brother's.

'Where are you going?' she asked. 'You are still recovering from that damage to your arm, Tom.'

'I can walk and I can shoot if need be. I am going to help Nicolas look for this rogue,' her brother said. 'We'll take some of the men with us. It is time this fellow was stopped or we shall none of us be safe.'

'Oh, Tom...' she said but there was nothing she could do to stop him for he was clearly determined.

After he had gone, she tried to find something to occupy herself, but ended by pacing up and down in an agitated manner, until one of the maids came in to announce a visitor.

'Sir Frederick Rathbone to see you, Miss Holbrook.'

'Sir Freddie!' Caroline ran to him, her hands outstretched. She was so relieved to see him and it showed in her expressive face. He took her hands, his strong fingers closing round hers in a way that instantly calmed her. 'I am so glad you have come! My brothers have gone to look for a rogue who fired on me as I rode past the Home Woods, and I am afraid that something will happen to them.'

'Someone fired at you?' Freddie's expression darkened, becoming one of outrage.

'Yes, when I was out riding this morning.'

'You were alone?' Freddie swore beneath his breath. He had thought her brothers had more sense than to allow it, and yet he knew her well enough to be sure that if she wished to ride alone nothing would stop her. 'This becomes serious, Caroline. I think I shall go in search of your brothers and see if they have had any luck in finding this rogue.'

'Oh, please take care,' she said. 'Must you go? I dare say it was merely a poacher misfiring.'

'If we discover that it was so, I shall be relieved. I think there must be a more sinister reason behind these attempts and I must ask you to remain in the house for the moment. Please excuse me, Caroline. I came here for another purpose entirely, but that must wait for the moment. I shall return with your brothers…' He gave her a rueful smile and left.

Caroline stared after him as he walked from the room. It was almost more than she could bear to be cooped up in the house when everyone else was out searching for the rogue who had fired at her, but she knew that she must obey her brothers and Sir Freddie. They were risking their lives for her sake and she could not make things more difficult for them by flouting their wishes.

After a while, a maid came to ask if she would step up to visit her grandfather for a few minutes. She did so, finding him looking much refreshed after his valet had finished ministering to him.

'What is this I hear, miss?' he asked, frowning. 'Jenkins has it that someone fired at you from the Home Woods—is that true?'

'Yes, sir, though I wish he had not told you. The doctor said that you were not to be upset.'

'I should be more upset if I were not told something like that,' Bollingbrook said. 'I trust you were not hurt, girl?'

'Only frightened for a moment,' Caroline said. 'But it is odd that this has started happening now, is it not? It seems that someone wishes me ill, though I do not know why.'

'I dare say it is a matter of money,' her grandfather told her, looking angry. 'I have recently changed my will. You and your brothers will benefit substantially when I die, Caroline—and you are to have something when you marry.'

'But surely…' She looked thoughtful. 'Who would know that you had changed your will, sir?'

'No one ought to know anything,' he growled, 'and I shall have something to say to my lawyer if it turns out that this is at the bottom of it. Someone in his office must have spoken of it—and I shall want to know to whom he betrayed what should have remained secret!'

'But who would want us dead? Not my uncles or cousins?'

'I do not think it for the estate is entailed and they must have expected I might leave you something from my private fortune—but I have not always lived as I ought, Caroline. There is another: a child I fathered on a trip to Jamaica before I met my Angelica. I went there to see the property left me by my second wife, and had what most would call a shameful affair. Later, when I returned home, I learned there was a child, a son—but I was married to Angelica by then and I told my overseer to take care of it. I believe a good family adopted the child, and I know little more.'

'I see…' Caroline bit her lip. She had always known there were secrets in her grandfather's past, though she was shocked at this revelation. 'It is unpleasant, sir. To think that someone wishes to kill us for the sake of money—but, of course, we cannot be sure of anything.'

The Marquis looked thoughtful. 'A man makes mistakes in his life and there may be others with a grudge against me. Well, we must just hope that the rogue is found, whoever it is, and an end made to this affair.'

'Yes, Grandfather.' Caroline sighed. 'I must own I do not find it comfortable to be the target of someone's malice.'

The Marquis gave a shout of harsh laughter. 'I dare say you do not, girl. If I were younger I should be out there looking for the rogue now, but I imagine I may leave it to your brothers.'

'And Sir Freddie,' Caroline said. 'He has gone to help them.'

'Who the devil is he?'

'Someone I like very well, sir.'

'Ah, the wind is in that quarter, is it? Send him up to see me when he returns to the house.' The Marquis frowned. 'Do not forget what I told you, Caroline. He will have to be a certain kind of man to accept that you should not have a child.'

'You do not know that for sure, sir.' Caroline wrinkled her brow in thought. 'He wished to speak to you yesterday, sir—but was prevented by your discomposure.'

'Well, I am much recovered now, girl. I shall see him at his convenience. Give him my compliments and ask him to step up and see me if he will when he returns.'

'Yes, Grandfather, I shall do so—though I am not sure when that will be.'

His eyes narrowed as he looked at her. 'Caroline, Caroline,

you are so like your grandmother. You have her reckless spirit, her certainty…' His eyes shadowed with doubt.

'I am glad to be like my grandmother in so many ways,' Caroline told him. 'But please do not worry for my sake, sir.' She smiled at him as she prepared to take her leave. 'Is there anything I may do for you?'

'No, I am well cared for. Jenkins is a good man and I rely on him completely—but you will come and see me again before you leave?'

'Yes, of course.' She hesitated, and then, 'I had thought perhaps you might wish me to stay until you are on your feet again?'

'No, though I thank you for the kind thought. You must go to your mother, Caroline. I shall speak to Tom about this incident. I think he should put off his visit to Jamaica until this business is settled.'

'You must do as you think best, sir.'

'Yes, yes, I think I shall rest now. You may leave me, for I am sure you have plenty to do.'

Caroline left her grandfather to go downstairs again, and it was not long before she heard voices in the hall and then her brothers and Sir Freddie came into the parlour where she was sitting. She got to her feet, looking at their faces, sensing that they were pleased about something.

'Did you catch him?'

'Not quite,' Nicolas said, 'but Sir Freddie winged him as he went by on his horse. One of the grooms had spotted him in the woods and we went after him. We thought we had him cornered, but he got away after firing a shot in our direction—though I think he will not be bothering any of us for a while.'

'I merely clipped him in the arm,' Freddie said. 'But it may be enough to quieten him for a while—and in the meantime we must take what precautions we can to prevent something like this happening again.'

'But how can you do that?' Caroline asked.

'In London, I had you followed for the last few days you were there. I had made no similar arrangements for your grandfather's estate, but with his permission I shall do so—and in Bath something similar will be put in place.'

'You had me watched in London?' Caroline stared at him for a moment, and then laughed. 'Yes, I see…I thought that someone was watching me that night in the gardens. Do you remember, Nicolas? When I was speaking to George Bellingham and you came out to look for me? I thought then that someone was there, spying on us.'

Nicolas nodded. 'I went to search for her, because Tom and I had decided that she might be in some danger if she wandered off alone, but she was safe enough with George Bellingham. We thought all this bother might be down to the business in Jamaica…for the inheritance, you know.'

'You mean the son Grandfather had whilst in Jamaica,' Caroline said. 'He told me that you knew about that, Tom. I dare say it might cause a scandal if it came out—but that is nothing compared to what is happening now. If this person is trying to kill me…you and Nicolas may not be safe from his spite.'

'Good grief,' Nicolas said. 'Heaven knows what more scandals the old man has up his sleeve.'

Freddie smiled, lifting his brows. 'I dare say there are skeletons in the closets of a good many families, some of the very highest distinction. However, I agree that we must see that this remains a family secret.'

'A family…ah, I see,' Nicolas said and grinned. 'I think I

will go up and have a word with Grandfather before supper. The old reprobate has plenty to answer for, though I shall not make a fuss for he is not up to it. Tom, will you come with me? I have something particular to say to you.'

'Oh, very well,' Tom said. 'I shall speak to you later, sir. You will stay to dine with us, I hope?'

'Certainly, I should be very happy to do so.'

Freddie smiled and inclined his head as Nicolas steered his brother from the room. It was obvious that the younger brother had realised what was going on and would no doubt explain to Tom as they went upstairs.

Caroline had taken a seat by the window. She sat resolutely looking out into the garden, her cheeks a little pink, her hands clasped in her lap until she sensed that Freddie was beside her. As she turned her head to look at him, he went down on one knee.

'Oh, no, you must not,' she said, a little flustered. 'At least, there is no need… I am sure that the last thing you truly wish is to make me an offer, sir. Only think of the scandal it might bring to your family if this Jamaican connection were to come out.'

Freddie rose and fetched a chair so that he might sit next to her. He reached out and took her hand, looking into her eyes as she gazed at him, clearly anxious. 'What is this foolishness, Caroline? You must know that I care for you—that it has been my intention to ask you to marry me for a little while now?'

'I have thought perhaps…' She stopped and blushed. 'I had hoped you might…but this must alter things. I feel that you have been caught up in something that is not of your making, sir. If you felt obliged to make me an offer, this must set you free.'

'If I wished to be free.'

'Do you not?' she asked, looking at him uncertainly. 'Only think of the scandal, sir.'

'Was it so wicked, Caroline?' He raised his brows. 'Your grandfather is not the first gentleman to get himself a bastard son.'

'There is more…' Caroline hung her head. 'Grandfather told me last night.'

'Another skeleton in his closet?' Freddie smiled oddly.

'This one concerned his third wife—my grandmother…' Caroline hesitated, suddenly knowing that she could not bear to tell him and see the light fade from his eyes. 'It is something that I believe you should hear from him. I do not regard it myself, but it must be for you to make up your own mind.'

'Is it so very terrible?'

'No, perhaps not—but only consider, I have been reckless.' Caroline hung her head. 'I teased you into taking me to that prize fight and I would have gone up in the balloon if the rope had not snapped. And I fully intend to be with you when you race Nicolas tomorrow…' Her eyes were dark with emotion. 'Do you think that—considering what you now know of my family—I should make the right kind of wife for you, sir? What would your uncle say?'

'If I told him, he would probably say that it was a deuced coil but all for the best, Caroline. He told me that he and your grandfather had quarrelled years ago, but that he was prepared to make it up if Bollingbrook would agree.'

'Was that why you hesitated to speak?' Caroline asked, her eyes intent on his face.

'No, it was not. If I seemed reserved with you at any time, it was because I was not perfectly sure I wished to marry. I had become accustomed to living in my own way and knew that if I married I must make changes.'

'And are you sure that you wish to marry now? You must not think yourself obliged in any way, sir. I know why you came to Almack's that evening, but it cannot signify. I need never go back to London unless I wish, and in the country no one will bother about what I did there.'

He smiled at her. 'Believe me, I should not allow the gossips to drive me into making an offer I did not choose to make, Caroline. I do truly wish to marry you.'

Caroline felt a weight lift from her shoulders, but persisted. 'You must speak to Grandfather, listen to what he has to tell you about my grandmother and then ask me again if you still wish it.'

'Nothing he or anyone else could say would change my mind.'

'But—'

Before she could finish, she felt Freddie's hands on her shoulders. He turned her round to face him, and she trembled as she saw the look in his eyes. The next moment, he bent his head, taking her lips with a kiss that was soft and gentle at the start, but became more intense, hungry, as he felt her response. Swept away on a tide of feeling she had never experienced before, Caroline melted into his body, wanting this wonderful feeling to go on and on. It seemed to her that the kiss was endless, but when at last he withdrew, she felt herself sway and might have fallen had he not held her.

'Oh…' she said in a bewildered tone. 'I did not expect to feel like that…'

'No?' Freddie laughed huskily. 'You are a sweet innocent, my dear one, and I adore you for it—but I must admit I have not felt quite this way before.' His eyes quizzed her. 'So what are we to do, Caroline, my love? You are reluctant to marry me because your family may become the centre of a scandal—and yet we clearly have an uncontrollable passion for one another. Will it suit you better to become my mistress?'

'Sir! You are outrageous,' she said, stung by the suggestion. As she saw the laughter in his eyes, she realised that he had merely been teasing her. 'Oh, Freddie, I do love you. I think I should die if anything came between us…but is it really fair to you?'

'What is this foolishness, my love?' He questioned with his eyes.

'You must speak to Grandfather. I am not sure it would be right if I accepted your very generous offer. I wish you to think very carefully about what he has to say to you—and then ask me again.'

'This is very mysterious. Do you think I care for a little scandal? I have not been exactly without blame in my life, Caroline. Some would think that you were the one who had cause for complaint, not I.'

'It is not just the Jamaican business…though there is that, too.'

'Surely it cannot be so very terrible?'

'Oh, Freddie, it might be worse than you imagine,' she said, her mouth soft with love. She longed to accept his offer, but her sense of fairness held her back.

He took her hand, caressing the palm with his finger. The stroking movement was delicate but it brought her close to swooning with what she knew must be desire. She melted against him as he put his arms about her, gazing up at him longingly. 'I feel so strange and not at all as I ought. I think if you do not marry me, I might end by taking up your very disobliging offer to become your mistress…'

'Well, it must be one or the other,' he told her as he stroked her cheek with the tips of his fingers, making her shiver with excitement. 'I confess that I cannot live without you, my darling. If you refuse me, I may very well—'

They were interrupted by a knock at the door, which opened as they moved apart, to allow Jenkins to enter. 'Excuse me, Miss Holbrook—Sir Frederick. My master requests that you visit him for a moment or two before dinner, sir.'

'Very well, I shall come in one moment,' Freddie said, and as the door closed behind him, 'You know that I adore you, Caroline. What is your answer, before I speak to Lord Bollingbrook?'

'You know that it must be yes—if you feel the same,' she said, swept away on a tide of recklessness. 'I would marry you even if I had to elope with you, Freddie. My hesitation was for your sake, not mine—I shall be happy to be your wife.'

'Very well, that is settled,' Freddie said and there was laughter in his eyes as he looked down at her. 'We shall marry against all opposition and be damned to the tabbies!'

'Oh, Freddie!' Caroline cried, laughing as he dropped a light kiss on her forehead. 'I am so glad that we met.'

Freddie kissed his fingers to her as he left the room. Jenkins was waiting for him at the top of the main staircase and he was conducted along the passage to the Marquis' suite of rooms.

'Please go in, sir,' Jenkins said. 'His lordship is waiting for you.'

'Thank you,' Freddie said. 'Is his lordship well?'

'Yes, sir, better than might have been expected. The doctor said that he was not to be upset, but I have no fear that you will come to blows.'

Freddie smiled and nodded, going into the room that was indicated. He discovered that Lord Bollingbrook was sitting in a wing chair next to the fireplace, where a small blaze cheered the room. He was a man of some seventy years, his hair silvery white, as were his brows, but there was strength in his features, and he was clearly in possession of his wits, for his eyes blazed with a fierce vitality.

'Good evening, sir,' Freddie said. 'I am Sir Frederick Rathbone. I believe you asked to see me?'

The Marquis looked at him through narrowed eyes. 'Humph,' he said in a tone that boded very little good will. 'So you're the one, are you? What have you to say to me?'

'I hope you are feeling better, sir,' Freddie said. 'There is much I would wish to say to you at another time, but this may not be the right occasion.'

'Don't pass me off with that flummery,' Bollingbrook muttered sourly. 'What are your intentions towards my girl?'

'Ah…' Freddie nodded pleasantly. 'It is my intention to make Caroline my wife quite soon.'

'Not without my permission you won't,' Bollingbrook said and glared at him. 'I shall want to know a lot more about you before I give it. Who are you and what are your prospects?'

'My fortune is adequate, I believe—and in the fullness of time I shall inherit my uncle's title and at least as much of the estate as is entailed. For although we have our disagreements, he cannot avoid it.'

'Damned entails!' Bollingbrook growled. 'I'm in the same

boat meself—bound to leave this place to me eldest son, but he won't get a penny more, I can tell you. I'll leave most of the money where I please.'

'That is your prerogative, sir.'

'Well, go on then, sir—who is this uncle you mentioned?'

'The Marquis of Southmoor. He knows you very well, I believe?'

'Southmoor? I thought the fellow was dead—as he ought to be by rights! We fell out years ago over your mother. Selina would have married me had he not forbidden her. He had no right to do it, for I cared for her and should have treated her well. I married badly that time—and that was his fault.' Bollingbrook glared at Freddie. 'I demanded satisfaction when Selina turned me down, and we fought a duel. Not that it gave me much satisfaction.' He looked at Freddie, his expression harsh with dislike. 'Well, that's it then, sir. You can take yourself off and never darken my door again. I shan't give you my girl—not if you went down on your knees and begged for it. I won't have Southmoor's breed in my family! You can forget Caroline.'

'That I shall not do for you or any man,' Freddie said. 'Pray tell me why a quarrel between you and my uncle should prevent my marriage to Caroline? Surely it happened too long ago to matter now?'

'Insolent pup,' Bollingbrook snapped. 'This conversation is at an end. Please have the goodness to leave.'

'Certainly, sir. This is your house and I shall not enter it again without an invitation, but my intention remains the same. You are the head of the family, but not Caroline's guardian. There are others I might apply to for permission, and you may be sure that I shall do so.'

'I am the head of this family…'

'As you say,' Freddie said, a glint of steel in his eyes. 'I shall not say more at this time, but Caroline has a mother and brother who may think differently.' Bowing his head, he turned and walked to the door.

'Damn you, sir! What do you mean by that?'

Freddie glanced back at him, a slight smile on his lips. 'If you should reconsider, please feel free to let me know that you would like me to visit you again.'

'Never! Damn you!'

Freddie looked grim as the curse was flung after him. He walked along the hall and down the main staircase. At the bottom Nicolas was standing speaking to one of the footmen. He turned as Freddie came up to him, extending his hand.

'I believe I am to wish you happy?'

'You may do so, for I intend to be,' Freddie said and took his hand in a firm grip. 'However, you should know that Lord Bollingbrook has forbidden me to marry Caroline.'

'Why in God's name should he do that?'

'He once wished to marry my mother, but my uncle forbade it and they fought a duel over it,' Freddie said, his tone dangerous. 'I believe there is no love lost on either side, for my uncle tried to dissuade me from making Caroline an offer—but I have and Bollingbrook shall not stop me. I think I have your blessing and Tom's—and I shall apply to Mrs Holbrook.'

'Tom would not deny you, though he has recently had reason to be grateful to Bollingbrook.'

'Whether I have Tom's blessing or not, I intend to marry her.'

'Good for you!' Nicolas said. 'You may count on me, and as for the rest…I leave the details to you.' Nicolas frowned as Freddie picked up his hat, gloves and driving whip from the hallstand. 'You are leaving?'

'Your grandfather threw me out, figuratively speaking.'

'But what shall I say to Caroline?'

'Say that I was called away, but shall see her tomorrow.'

'Nothing else?'

'Only if the subject is causing her distress. If Lord Bollingbrook should upset her—then you may tell her that nothing is changed between us.'

'Oh...' Nicolas grinned. 'Like that is it? He will kick up a fine dust, I dare say. He's had his own way for years. It may do him good to discover that at last he has met his match.'

'He would already have discovered it had he not been so recently ill,' Freddie replied grimly. 'But one thing you may be certain of, Nicolas—I do not intend to give her up.'

Nicolas inclined his head. Had he been wearing a hat, he would have taken it off to the man he was beginning to like very much. Freddie nodded in return and then went out, leaving Nicolas to stare thoughtfully after him.

'But why did he leave?' Caroline asked. 'It seems strange that Freddie should go without a word to me.' Her eyes narrowed as she looked at her brother. 'You're hiding something from me, aren't you? It is something to do with Grandfather, isn't it?' Had he decided that it would not suit him to marry her knowing that she might not be able to give him an heir? For a moment her heart contracted with pain and she thought that she would not be able to bear it if he withdrew. Yet she must do so. Indeed, she ought to have expected it in the circumstances.

'Sir Freddie told me to tell you that he would explain tomorrow, Caroline.'

'Explain what? Has Grandfather made him angry?'

'He wasn't angry, merely determined. Oh, if you must have it—Grandfather refused permission, but Sir Freddie says that nothing is changed. He intends to apply to Mama, and of course both Tom and I like him.'

'But Grandfather is the head of the family…' Caroline was confused, upset by the news that the Marquis had refused his permission. She had expected something quite different. 'Why did he say we might not marry, Nicolas?' Caroline was very pale, for she suspected her grandfather's true reasons, whatever excuse he might have made to Freddie.

'Some tale of a quarrel between Rathbone's uncle and Grandfather,' Nicolas said. 'But you should not let it weigh with you, Caroline. He does not have the power to prevent you, though it would have been better to have his permission. I think he had promised that he would give you a substantial dowry.' Caroline made an impatient movement of her head. 'Well, I dare say it doesn't matter. Sir Freddie isn't short of the readies.'

'I do not care for the money,' Caroline said, 'but I feel hurt that Grandfather should wish to deny me this happiness.' Her eyes were stinging with unshed tears, but she lifted her head proudly, refusing to let anyone see how distressed she felt. Perhaps her grandfather had done the right thing. Oh, she did not know what she ought to do!

'Do not let it upset you,' Nicolas said, guessing at how she felt. 'Tom and I will support you and I dare say Mama will be glad if you are happy.'

Caroline heard a little cough behind her and turned to see

her grandfather's valet. 'If you would care to step up to his lordship's rooms, miss?'

'Miss Holbrook is about to dine, Jenkins. Say that she will come up later.'

'No, Nicolas, I shall go,' Caroline said. 'You and Tom must not wait. I shall come later, but I am not hungry.'

Nicolas cursed as he watched her run up the stairs. He had always liked his grandfather despite his testy ways and his faults, but he was damned if he would let the old devil ruin Caroline's life!

Caroline knocked at the door and went in, finding her grandfather sitting in his favourite chair. She was pleased to see that he was feeling well enough to leave his bed, but her heart was heavy as she saw his forbidding expression.

'I dare say you have heard the news?'

'Yes, sir. I do not understand why you have done this to me. It made me happy when Sir Freddie asked me to marry him—why could you not just accept that he was my choice?' She looked at him, feeling close to tears.

Bollingbrook did his best to ignore the signs of distress. 'There are plenty more fish in the sea, girl. He isn't good enough for you. Besides, he needs an heir and I told you that you might not be able to have a child.'

'You do not know that for sure, sir. Besides, it should be for me to decide whether or not I wish to be his wife. Did you tell him about the hereditary illness?'

'There was no point. He isn't the man for you. I shan't have it, Caroline, and there's an end to it.'

Caroline raised her head. Tears glittered in her eyes. 'I should never wish to hurt you, sir, but I do not think it is proper for you to decide. I believe my mama and Tom…' She quailed as she saw the anger in his face. 'I do not mean to be rude or disobedient, sir—nor to blame you for what happened so many years ago. But I cannot obey you in this. I love him…'

'Stuff and nonsense. You don't know what love is. Besides, in law I am your grandfather and the head of the family. You will obey me.'

'You told me yourself that love cannot be denied,' Caroline reminded him. 'You married Angelica despite everything. Why should you deny us the happiness you found with her? I would be willing to take the risks she did to give my husband his heir. Forgive me, but I cannot obey you. I do not wish to disoblige you, Grandfather, but it would break my heart.'

He gave her a stern look. 'If you disobey me, you will not get a penny from me, either when you marry or when I die.'

'I have never expected anything other than the small portion my father left in trust for me,' Caroline told him. 'If you think that I care for such things, you do not know me, sir.'

'Care for your brothers, don't you?' Bollingbrook growled. 'Well, if you go against me in this, they won't get a penny either!'

'But that is unfair,' Caroline gasped. 'How could you hold such a wicked thing over my head?'

'Didn't you tell me there were others who asked for you?' He glared at her. 'Take one of them and I'll keep my word to Tom—defy me and there's an end to his hopes.'

'You are very cruel, sir,' Caroline said, stifling a sob. 'I shall never forgive you…' She turned and ran from the room before the tears could fall.

Chapter Ten

Caroline had been lying on her bed, but sat up as her brother tapped at her door. Her tears had dried, but she knew that she must look dreadful and she asked Tom to wait. Leaving the bed, she went over to the washstand and bathed her face with cool water, then called out that he might enter.

'Nicolas told me what happened,' he said as he came in. 'When you didn't come down after dinner, I knew that I would find you crying. You must not upset yourself, Caroline. Grandfather has no real power to forbid you. I am the head of our family—the Holbrook family. I do not like to disoblige him, but in this I must think of your future. Besides, after the way he has behaved, I think he has no moral right to demand anything of us. He may decide to cut you out of his will—but you will be no worse off than before.'

'I know that,' Caroline said. 'As for myself, I do not give a fig for his money, though I would have preferred his blessing. I have always cared for him—but I cannot...' She shook her head, her voice catching. It was impossible to tell Tom what their grandfather had threatened.

'Well, I think you must make up your own mind,' Tom said. 'If you love Sir Frederick and wish to marry him then you must. Do not allow anything Grandfather said to influence you.'

'I must think about it,' Caroline said and forced a smile. She was torn in two. If she chose to follow her heart, she might destroy Tom's hopes of a future. She suspected that he liked Julia more than he let anyone see, but until his fortunes were settled he could not ask her to marry him. And there was the question of Freddie's heir. She must tell him that it was possible she could never give him a son. 'When are you going out to Jamaica, Tom?'

'Next week. I have discussed it with Nicolas and we decided that it would be best for me to go soon. As for this other business, Nicolas will shortly be back with his unit and does not fear that anything untoward will happen to him. If you were married, the threat to your safety would be at an end...one way or the other.'

'Yes, I see.' Caroline felt a surge of indignation. 'It would have been better if Grandfather had never changed his will in our favour, then we should not have this shadow hanging over us.'

'I must admit that I am grateful to him for settling the most pressing of my debts. Father had made a mess of things, Caroline. I imagine he spent much of his money on his mistresses and gambling. Not that I care for that so much. I am capable of earning my own living, I dare say. If this business goes well in Jamaica, I might even stay there for a while, see if I can make my fortune out there. Nicolas may take care of things here.'

'I do not precisely understand what it is you have to do in Jamaica, Tom?'

'Grandfather says that the estate must be sold, and that I am to have what it yields.'

'Oh…' Caroline wondered what would happen if she defied her grandfather. 'Supposing Grandfather changed his mind, Tom? Would you still wish to go?'

'I have the deed for the property and his authority to sell it,' Tom said. 'What makes you think he might change his mind?'

'Oh, no reason. I suppose he will not.'

'It is but a small part of what he intends to leave us,' Tom said as he saw her worried expression. 'Just what did he say to you this evening?'

'It does not matter,' Caroline replied and shook her head.

'You should have some supper,' her brother said and looked at her anxiously. 'Will you allow me to have something sent up for you?'

'No, please do not. I shall ask my maid for a glass of hot milk. I really need nothing more.'

'Very well,' Tom acquiesced and gave her a look of encouragement. 'I shall leave you now, but remember that Nicolas and I are on your side, Caroline. Do not let Grandfather make you unhappy.'

'No, I shan't,' she said and raised her head proudly as he went out.

After he had gone, she sat down at her dressing table and picked up a hairbrush, beginning to smooth it over her long bright hair, which hung about her shoulders in a cloud of red-gold waves. The action soothed some of her distress, but it could not prevent her mind from going round and round in circles. What was she to do? If she defied her grandfather, he had the power to deny her brothers the money that might have given them better lives. Yet how could she let him destroy her happiness? Would Sir Freddie even wish to marry her once he knew that she might carry a hereditary illness? If she had daughters, she might pass the curse on to them. It was a heavy burden her grandfather had laid on her shoulders.

At the very least, she must talk to Freddie and hear what he had to say on the matter. Even if he said it was not important, it would still not solve the problem of her brothers' inheritance. She could do nothing for the moment. She needed to talk to the one person she felt able to confide in. Having made up her mind on that point, she went to bed, and, after some initial tossing and turning, fell into a deep sleep.

Caroline did not take leave of her grandfather the next morning. When she inquired after him, Jenkins told her that he was out of sorts and did not wish to see anyone.

'You will please give him my good wishes for his health,' she said, her face pale and distressed.

'Yes, miss,' the valet said, looking at her sorrowfully. He was well aware of the dreadful ultimatum his master had delivered the previous evening, and had already tried to take the Marquis to task over it, for which he had had his head snapped off. 'He will come about, miss. Never you fear.'

'Yes, perhaps,' Caroline agreed, though she had no hope of it. 'I must not keep the horses waiting. Forgive me.'

'Keep your chin up, miss,' Jenkins said with the familiarity of a long-serving retainer. 'I shall do my best for you.'

Caroline smiled, but made no reply. She went down the stairs, taking a warm farewell of Tom, who was not accompanying them to Bath.

'If I do not see you before I leave, remember that you have my blessing, Caroline,' he told her. 'Grandfather will regret his unkindness. I think he will come to see that he has been unfair to you.'

'Thank you, dearest Tom,' she said and kissed his cheek. 'I love you. Take good care on your journey. You will write to us when you can?'

'Yes, of course. Tell Sir Frederick to take care in this mad race of yours, but no doubt he will. I have more faith in his driving than Nicolas's.'

Caroline smiled. The thought of the race lifted her spirits, for she liked nothing better than to be behind a bang-up pair of thoroughbreds, and Freddie's blacks were some of the finest she had ever seen.

She went out to join her brother in the curricle, for he had sent his phaeton on ahead with his favourite horses, and they were to drive the best part of the way in Tom's rig. A groom would stay with it when they left the Waverly Inn, and return it to the Bollingbrook estate the next day when the horses were rested.

Despite the shortcomings of his brother's pair, of which Nicolas complained bitterly at the start, they made good time and arrived at the Waverly Inn just in time for nuncheon, which had been their intention. Sir Freddie had arrived earlier, and he came out to greet them, having already secured the use of the landlord's private parlour.

He helped Caroline down, searching her strained face with a grim look of his own. 'I see that you know what took place last evening, my love. We shall discuss it at another time, if you please. It would be foolish to let such a thing spoil our pleasure in the day, would it not?'

'Yes, certainly,' Caroline replied, all heart. She gave him a sparkling smile, for her spirits had lifted at the sight of him.

'And I do not intend to do so. Tell me, Freddie—shall we put my brother to the blush?'

'Would you wish to do so—if it were possible?' he asked, a flicker of amusement in his dark eyes.

'I have always wished to beat my brother at some sport,' Caroline said, her face alight with mischief. 'I dare say it would do him no harm to lose for once. He was always faster and better at everything than Tom.'

Freddie laughed softly in his throat. 'Then we must see what we can do, must we not?'

The three of them had a pleasant lunch together. Caroline was amused to see that Nicolas drank only water, which was a sign of his respect for Freddie's driving skills. He knew that he needed all his wits about him to stand a chance of beating him. Freddie had one glass of wine, which he merely tasted as a toast to her and the future. Neither of the gentlemen ate a great deal, though they laughed and talked as if it were merely a normal day and nothing at stake.

'When are we going to start?' Caroline asked because it seemed that she was the only one impatient to be on their way.

'Patience, my love,' Freddie said, a flicker of amusement on his lips. He raised his brows at Nicolas. 'Well, shall we see what our grooms have been up to, Nicolas? It appears that at least one of us is in a hurry to be off.'

Leaving the inn parlour together, they saw that their grooms had been busy while they were dining, and had both phaetons ready to leave. Caroline looked at Freddie's blacks, which looked in the peak of condition. Her brother's greys were pawing the ground, seemingly anxious to be off, and she noticed that they were sweating slightly. Having driven with him behind them on several occasions, she knew them to be spirited creatures and she thought that the teams were well matched. It would be a close-run thing and possibly down to the skill of the drivers.

Freddie smiled at her as he handed her up. 'Are you ready, Caroline?'

'Oh, yes,' she said, her eyes bright. She had put all her problems to one side for the moment. 'I think it will be the greatest of good fun.'

Seated on the driving box beside Freddie, she glanced across at her brother. She could see that he was on his mettle, anxious to be off, and she waved to him, blowing a kiss with her fingertips.

'Good luck, Nicolas.'

He grinned at her and saluted as the grooms stood away from the horses' heads and then they were off. Caroline saw that her brother set off in a hurry, flicking his long driving whip at his horses, clearly intending to reach the turning that led to Bath in the lead.

Freddie, on the other hand, allowed his horses to begin at their own pace, holding the reins lightly, his whip propped up in the box at his side, apparently unconcerned that Nicolas had taken an early lead.

Had she been driving, she knew that she would have been pushing her horses hard to catch up, but Freddie kept his hand lightly on the reins. She frowned a little, for she thought that Nicolas would get too far ahead of them, but then she sensed that the blacks were gathering speed little by little. Freddie had done nothing that she could see, and as yet he had not touched his whip. She looked at the horses, the rippling strength of their muscles, the shine of their glossy coats, and knew that so far they were only cruising.

Freddie had not asked anything of them, but they were moving with such ease and grace that their pace was increasing effortlessly. The road ahead was quite narrow for a stretch of more than a mile or so, hardly wide enough to allow for one vehicle to pass another. And, with some sharp bends hiding any oncoming traffic, it would have been impossible to pass Nicolas even if they had caught up with him.

After they had been driving for some minutes without seeing more than a glimpse of her brother, the road ahead of them began to widen slightly. Freddie took his whip and cracked it over the heads of his team and all at once she felt the surge of speed. She glanced at him, for he seemed so calm, so certain, and it made her wonder at his patience. However, after a few minutes she saw that they were only a short distance behind her brother. Because of the difficult road, he had been unable to put enough distance between them, and now Freddie had him in his sights.

'You knew, didn't you?' she said. 'You knew that there was nothing to be gained by setting out at a cracking pace.'

'Nicolas will have found his horses hard to control on that stretch of the road at such a pace,' Freddie said, and glanced at her. 'He may have taken too much out of them at an early stage. We have some way to go yet, Caroline.'

Nicolas had clearly realised that they were behind. He was urging his horses on faster, and for the next twenty minutes or so he managed to increase his lead, the distance between them lengthening again. Freddie let him go, but then, after some fifteen minutes or so, he gave a little flick of his whip and the blacks responded gallantly. Caroline looked eagerly for some sign of her brother's vehicle, and then, just as they were approaching a crossroads, she saw it ahead of them.

'Oh, there he is,' she cried. 'We shall catch him again in a moment.'

Freddie smiled as he heard the excitement in her voice. He kept his horses steady as they approached the crossroads, which were clear on both sides, allowing both Nicolas and Freddie to maintain their speed. Ahead of them was a stretch of good clear road, with grassland to either side. Caroline felt the surge of speed as Freddie let his horses have their head, and she sensed that this was what he had been waiting for. Here at last was the space for the phaetons to race to their full potential.

She was on the edge of her seat with excitement as Freddie's blacks ate up the distance between the two phaetons; gradually, inexorably, Nicolas was being hauled back. She could see that he was using his whip frequently now, trying to urge that extra bit of speed from his horses, but he had driven them hard for the past four miles and now they had no more to give. The blacks were fresher, having been spared for the better part of the way, and now Freddie cracked his whip over their heads and they responded willingly.

Caroline hung on tightly as the phaeton seemed to almost bound forwards, holding on to her bonnet with one hand and to the carriage rail with the other. They had caught Nicolas now, and then, with a slight flick of his wrist, Freddie edged his phaeton out slightly to perform one of the neatest overtaking manoeuvres that she had ever witnessed. She held her breath as for a moment the wheels of both vehicles were side by side. A false move now and they could all be overset, but Freddie judged it to a nicety and in another moment they were past. Freddie kept up his speed for long enough to gain the lead into the next stretch of road, which was too narrow to allow for Nicolas to pass them.

Caroline looked back at her brother. For a few minutes he continued to urge his horses on, but then he seemed to realise that the race was over, for he let his pace slow and dropped behind. They were entering the outskirts of the fashionable spa town now, and the press of traffic would have made it impossible for the race to continue. As they passed the Abbey church, Caroline looked back and her brother saluted her.

She laughed and turned to Freddie. 'Nicolas has just saluted you, Freddie. He acknowledges that yours were the better horses.'

'I doubt there was much between them,' Freddie said. 'I knew the road well, perhaps better than your brother.'

'Oh, no, I do not think it was only that,' she said. 'You have the best hands I have ever seen, Freddie. It was your driving that made the difference.'

'I would not advise you to say as much to your brother,' Freddie said and grinned at her. 'I trust you are pleased, Caroline—though I noticed that you wished Nicolas luck, but did not do the same for me.'

'You did not need luck,' she said and her eyes were mischievous. 'I had every confidence in your driving, sir.'

'Thank you. I shall take that as a compliment,' he said. 'I believe I shall have to take your driving in hand before I allow you to handle my greys.'

'I love to drive,' Caroline said. 'I only wish I were able to practise more.'

'We may soon put things right when we are married,' Freddie said. 'You shall have your own rig, Caroline. Something suitable for a lady, and then you may drive yourself when you wish.'

'I wish that I might,' Caroline said, suddenly rather sad. 'I know that I said I would marry you, Freddie, and you mustn't think that I don't want to. I do love you with all my heart—only I am not sure I can marry you in the circumstances.'

Freddie glanced at her. 'You mean because of what your grandfather said, I suppose. You know that we do not need his permission? Your brothers have already signified their approval, and I dare say Mrs Holbrook will look favourably on my suit.'

'Yes, I am sure Mama will say yes,' Caroline said, but hesitated. 'But…Grandfather threatened to change his will again if I disobeyed him. For myself I care nothing for it, but Tom has had such a difficult time since my father died. And then there's Nicolas. He has only a small trust fund from his maternal grandfather, and must support himself.'

'Bollingbrook threatened to disinherit them if you married me?'

'Yes,' Caroline said, pleased that he had grasped the situation at once. 'It kept me awake all night, for I could see no way out of the predicament. I dare say you will not mind if I have no dowry, but how can I deprive my brothers of their fortunes?'

'Do you know the size of this inheritance?' Freddie had slowed his horse to a walk now. He raised his hat to an acquaintance passing in a similar vehicle.

'I believe Tom said it may be in the region of two hundred thousand pounds—divided between us and the son in Jamaica.'

Freddie whistled softly. 'That is indeed a considerable sum of money. I had not realised Bollingbrook was in possession of such a fortune—and that, I imagine, does not include the entail?'

'Oh, no, that is entirely different, and not worth the half of it, I dare say,' Caroline said. 'Nicolas wondered if my uncles might have got wind of the change to his will, and if they could possibly have commissioned the attempts to kill Tom—and me.'

'What happens to the money if you or your brothers should die before your grandfather?'

'I believe the money would go to the fourth beneficiary.'

'The Jamaican?' Freddie nodded thoughtfully. 'I think that there may be something in it after all. Two hundred thousand pounds is a great deal of money.'

'Yes, that is what Tom has always said,' Caroline told him, frowning. 'It might have been better had Grandfather never altered his will.'

'Yes, perhaps,' Freddie agreed, 'but we must not jump to conclusions too soon, Caroline.' He was drawing to a halt in front of one of the fashionable houses in the Royal Crescent. 'As for this other business—does your grandfather's blessing mean a great deal to you?'

'I would have been pleased to have it if he had given it freely,' Caroline admitted. 'I have always been fond of him—but it is Tom and Nicolas that matter most.'

'Yes, I see,' Freddie said and smiled as he handed her down. His groom, who had gone on ahead of him with the baggage coach, was waiting for them, and came to take the reins from him. Freddie knocked at the front door and stood with Caroline on the pavement as they waited for an answer. 'Do not worry too much about this for the moment, Caroline. Bollingbrook may have been bluffing—and when he thinks about it, he may wish to reconsider. I shall call another day to speak with Mrs Holbrook—but for now I shall leave you. There are some matters of business I must attend to.' As the door was opened by a maid wearing a neat black gown and white apron, he nodded to Caroline and, lifting her hand to his lips, dropped a kiss within the palm. That and the smile which accompanied it sent a little shiver of pleasure down her spine.

'Thank you for the pleasure of your company, Caroline. It was most enjoyable.'

Caroline felt a thrill of delight. She could only agree with him, returning his smile before entering the house. Her mother came into the hall as she did so, running towards her with outstretched arms.

'Caroline, my love. It is so good to see you! I had your letter about your grandfather and I wondered if you would feel that you must stay with him for a little longer?'

'He would not have it so,' Caroline said and embraced her. 'Besides, I fear that he is not pleased with me at the moment. I have a great deal to tell you, Mama.'

'Well, put off your bonnet and then come into the parlour,' Mrs Holbrook said. 'I am alone at the moment, though Mr Milbank dines with us this evening. I did not wish to go out on your first evening in Bath—but where is your brother?'

'He will be here shortly,' Caroline said. 'I came with Sir Frederick and Nicolas...followed us.'

'Sir Frederick brought you?' Mrs Holbrook was somewhat surprised. 'There was no mention of that when your baggage arrived earlier.'

'No, Mama. But I wanted to tell you...' She followed her mother into the small parlour, but just as Mrs Holbrook had finished telling the maid that she was to serve them tea and buttered muffins in twenty minutes, there was a commotion in the hall and Nicolas came striding in.

'Ah, there you are, puss,' Nicolas hailed her in high good humour. 'Sir Freddie is not here, I gather? I must seek him out to pay him the twenty guineas I owe him. That was a capital race and the way he passed me was a masterpiece. I declare he is a fine whip, one of the best I've met.'

'What is that?' Mrs Holbrook looked from her son to her daughter. 'Please tell me that you do not mean… Caroline! You did not take part in a curricle race?'

'Well, Sir Freddie was driving a phaeton, but, yes, I did, Mama.'

'You were with Sir Frederick on the high road—racing your brother?' Mrs Holbrook made a moaning sound and put a hand to her face. 'You might have been killed…both of you. Not to mention the scandal…'

'But no one knows,' Caroline said, her cheeks warm. 'And we are perfectly safe, Mama. Sir Freddie took no risks, I promise you. He has the best hands of any whip I've seen and he has promised to teach me to drive so that—' She was silenced as she saw her mother's expression. 'Honestly, Mama, no one will know that we raced.'

'Depend upon it, someone saw you,' her mother said and looked at her accusingly. 'You must know that you were the subject of some gossip in town, Caroline. We brushed through that right and tight thanks to Lady Stroud—but it is enough that you drove here with Sir Frederick alone, for I dare say you did not have a maid or a groom?' Caroline's guilty look was enough to confirm her fears. 'That on its own would cause talk—but if anyone should learn that you actually raced…' She sank down into one of the comfortable chairs with an air of despair. 'I think you have ruined yourself.'

'No such thing, Mama,' Nicolas said, guiltily aware that in his excitement he had given his sister away. 'I dare say Caroline may drive with her fiancé, may she not?'

'Her fiancé?' Mrs Holbrook stared at her, anxiety and hope warring in her breast. 'Do you tell me you are engaged to him?'

'Yes,' said Nicolas.

'Well, perhaps…' said Caroline.

'Which is it?' Mrs Holbrook asked and fanned her cheeks with the ladies' magazine she had been reading before her children arrived. 'You have quite overset me, Caroline. I am not at all sure that I should wish you to marry him. It seems to me that he is hardly a suitable husband for a young lady—where is his notion of propriety?!'

'I wanted to be part of it, Mama,' Caroline said. 'I was not frightened and it is not fair that I should be excluded from all the fun just because I am a girl.'

'I am glad that you did not say lady,' her mother said, 'for your behaviour has been anything but ladylike. I would send you to your room to reflect on your waywardness—but please explain, are you or are you not engaged to be married?'

'Freddie has asked me and I have said yes,' Caroline said, 'but Grandfather has forbidden it. He says he shall not give me a dowry if I disobey him. And…' she glanced at Nicolas '…he says he shall change his will again. You and Tom will get nothing if I marry against his wishes.'

'A fig for that!' Nicolas said and snapped his fingers. 'I ain't saying that it wouldn't be a fine thing to inherit some money—but I ain't prepared to be the cause of your unhappiness, puss. Tom would say the same.'

'I am not sure that he would,' Caroline said. 'He has had so much trouble to pull the estate together and he would have been the main benefactor, I think.'

'Well, there's no telling that the old gentleman wouldn't

pull caps with him over something else,' Nicolas said. 'We all know what Bollingbrook's temper is. He may change his will fifty times before he's done for. Besides, I should not let it worry you, puss. He will regret his harshness to you when he has thought it over. And then he will send to make things up to you, I imagine.'

'Freddie said as much,' Caroline said. 'He does not care for my dowry, no more do I—but I do care for you and Tom, Nicolas.'

'I wish that one of you would consider my feelings in all this,' Mrs Holbrook said in a faint voice. 'I declare that I have a headache coming on. You really are the most troublesome of children. I shall go up to my room and lie down.'

'Sorry, puss,' Nicolas said as the door closed behind their mother. 'I never thought she would cut up rough like that over it.'

'It does not matter,' Caroline said. 'Poor Mama. We must be such a trial to her. You will not tell her about the Jamaican business? I fear that she would be distressed by it.'

'Lord, no!' Nicolas ejaculated. 'Sir Freddie said that it was not so very terrible, but it would cause rather more scandal than the fact that you took part in a race.'

'Yes, I think it would. What Grandfather did was perhaps not so very bad, but it is best if Mama does not hear of it.'

'She shall not from any of us.'

'Do you think this other thing…the attempts on my life…? If indeed it was truly an attempt to kill me. It might simply have been a poacher misfiring, you know.' Caroline sighed. 'I do not think we should tell Mama that someone tried to kill me, Nicolas. It would upset her.'

'We did consider that it might have been a poacher, but Sir Freddie was of the opinion that it was unlikely. As for telling Mama, I would not dream of it. I dare say she would make a run for home and keep you under lock and key. Though for myself, I think you may be safe enough for a while,' Nicolas said. 'Sir Freddie winged the fellow who shot at you. We cannot know if it was merely a hired assassin or the originator of these crimes himself, but it must give whoever it is pause for thought either way.'

'Well, I shall certainly be careful not to go far alone,' Caroline said. 'Sir Freddie is coming to see Mama in a few days. If she gives her permission…'

'You must consent to an engagement,' Nicolas said. 'You cannot give up your chance of happiness for a whim of the old gentleman. He has no right to demand it of you—and to hold such a threat over your head is wicked. I think I shall tell him he may keep his money, for the promise of it has brought nothing but trouble.'

'Oh, Nicolas…' She looked at him unhappily. 'Do not burn your boats for my sake.' He must not throw his chances away, especially as it was not yet certain that Freddie would wish to marry her once he knew she might have some dreadful hereditary illness.

'I dare say I shall get along without it,' he said and grinned at her. 'I shall have to hang out for an heiress, puss.'

'Oh, dearest,' she said and laughed. 'When do you return to your regiment?'

'I shall stay with you for two days, and then I must leave,' he told her. 'I'll see if I can bring Mama round this evening. I dare say she will have forgiven us by the time she has dressed for dinner.'

* * *

Caroline watched her brother leave. She sat down and waited until the maid brought the tea tray, asking her if she would carry something up to Mrs Holbrook's room.

After the maid had gone she bit into a delicious fruity muffin, the butter dripping on to her chin as she stared at nothing in particular. What ought she to do for the best? Nicolas had been so supportive over her predicament, but she knew that her grandfather's money would go a long way to helping both of her brothers. Could she really deprive them of their inheritance? And there was the matter of her grandmother's weak heart. She did not think that she could bear to live without Freddie for the rest of her life. Even the thought of it brought tears to her eyes.

'Damn you!' the Marquis growled as Jenkins brought him a small measure of brandy. 'What is that supposed to be?'

'With your lordship in a state of choleric, brandy is the worst thing you can have,' Jenkins said imperturbably. 'And it ain't a bit of good glaring at me that way, sir. It ain't going to change a thing.'

'Do you think I don't know that?'

'Well, you ain't been thinking much of late, sir.'

'Impudent rogue! I should dismiss you instantly, do you know that?'

'That's as may be, sir,' Jenkins said without turning a hair. 'And I ain't saying as I wouldn't mind retiring to a little cottage I've had my eye on for a while. My sister is a widow and has been for this year past. I dare say she would be glad to keep house for me for what years remain to us—but it don't alter your case, sir. You've driven your sons away, and now you've seen off Miss Caroline, and I think you are going to regret that for a long time. Especially if you cut the young gentlemen out as well, sir.'

'Know everything, do you?' the Marquis said and muttered furiously to himself. 'Well, I ain't such a fool as you think. I know that girl. She won't see her brothers disinherited. She'll come back and say she's sorry.'

'Give you pleasure, will it, sir—to see her wretched? She loves the man. Stands to reason. 'Sides, I saw her woebegone face, poor little lass.'

'How dare you speak of my granddaughter so familiarly?'

'Well, seeing as you're about to set me off, it don't make much difference, does it, sir? I might as well say my piece while I'm at it. You ain't been exactly an angel, sir.'

'Are you threatening me?'

'I wouldn't dare, sir,' Jenkins said with an air of innocence. 'It strikes me that you ought to do something about all this trouble. You wouldn't want Miss Caroline's death laid at your door?'

'And what do you mean by that?' The Marquis started up out of his chair.

'Stands to reason, sir. Someone knows you changed your will and, whoever that may be, he doesn't much like it.'

'Claude or Sebastian?' the Marquis demanded.

'I should doubt it, sir. Mr Sebastian wouldn't stir himself, and Mr Claude would think it beneath his touch. It may be that Jamaican business...'

'Yes, I dare say you are right. I shall have to think about this carefully.' Bollingbrook held out his glass. 'Now fill that up and have done lecturing me, man. I'll not have harm come to Caroline, but she must come to me and apologise before I change my mind about that damned fellow!'

'Hell will freeze over first,' Jenkins said, ignoring his master's scowl as he took the glass and filled it with a more generous measure. 'Not that it makes much difference what you do. I dare say you'll finish yourself off before you have time to change anything.'

He walked to the door, leaving Bollingbrook to scowl into the glass before setting it to one side. The man was an impudent rascal, but the devil of it was he was right…

Chapter Eleven

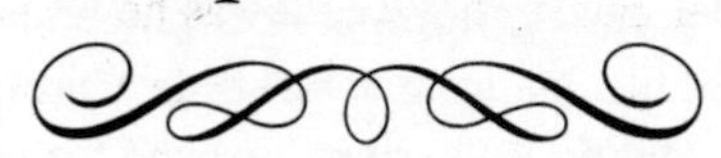

Caroline accompanied her mother to the Pump Room the following morning. She was feeling easier in her mind, because Marianne had mellowed towards her children. She had been suffering a little irritation of the nerves lest they should not approve of Mr Milbank on closer acquaintance with him. However, Nicolas had charmed all her fears away, and she was now happily describing her plans for her wedding, which was to take place the following week. For, as she had told her children, there was no point in delaying it at her time of life.

'Mr Milbank is to take me on honeymoon to Italy,' she had told her daughter before they retired to bed the previous evening. 'You have a choice, Caroline my love. You may come with us or…I had thought you might stay with your grandfather, but you might prefer to return to your aunt?'

'Perhaps I could simply go home, Mama? I should be quite happy there by myself.'

'I am not sure that that would serve,' Marianne said. 'However, we might find another alternative. I could write to my cousin and ask her if you may visit with her for a few weeks. We do not intend to stay longer than six weeks or so abroad. Mr Milbank is having some work done at his country house, and of course you will join us there as soon as we are in residence.'

'Unless I were to marry, Mama.'

'Well, yes, I suppose.' Her mother sighed. 'If you do wish to marry Sir Frederick, it might be arranged before I leave. But you were quite against it at one time, Caroline. And I am not at all sure that he is the right husband for you.'

'I know he is the one,' Caroline said. 'I love him, Mama, but as I told you yesterday, Grandfather is against it.'

'Bollingbrook may be the head of the family,' Marianne said, her feathers ruffling indignantly, 'but I am your mother, Caroline. I think I may be trusted to decide your future. Besides, Nicolas told me that Tom has given you his blessing. Bollingbrook cannot lawfully forbid the marriage.'

'I know that, Mama,' Caroline agreed. 'But would it be fair of me to take my happiness at the expense of my brothers?'

'As to that…' Marianne smiled her satisfaction. She had been at the mercy of her father-in-law for too long, and he had done little for her. Now at last she was about to become truly independent of him. 'Mr Milbank is possessed of an adequate fortune. He has already offered to set some of it aside for your brothers—and to give you five thousand pounds when you marry.'

'Mama!' Caroline was astonished. 'That is too generous. I cannot accept so much. It is kind, but—'

'Nonsense, my dear.' Marianne looked extremely pleased with herself. 'Mr Milbank suggested it without a hint from me. As I told you, he has no family of his own, and he is delighted with mine. I am sure we shall all go on very well together.'

Caroline kissed her cheek. 'Thank you, Mama. You have relieved my mind, for I do not need to feel so very guilty if I disobey Grandfather's wishes.'

'You have yet to gain my permission, Caroline. Sir Frederick may call upon me when he chooses. If I am satisfied that he can be trusted to take proper care of you, I may allow it—or perhaps an engagement. Yes, that would be much better. The wedding may wait upon my return.'

Caroline kept her thoughts on the matter to herself. Lord Bollingbrook was fond of calling his son's wife a peagoose, but Marianne could be stubborn when she chose. If she decided that Caroline must be content with an engagement until her return from Italy, there would be no changing her.

If she had known that her decision might place Caroline in danger, Marianne would have been horrified. However, her children had agreed to keep her in ignorance of the truth, and she was quite justified in thinking that if her daughter waited for a while it could do no harm. Given time to think, Bollingbrook might come to his senses and seek reconciliation.

'Yes, I think that will do very well,' Marianne said, believing that she had settled things nicely. 'If you do not wish to accompany us, you may stay with your Aunt Louisa or Cousin Amelia. And perhaps you may marry at Christmas.'

Caroline had thought about her mother's decision for much of the night, but she could see no way of changing things. With the wedding so close, something must be arranged for her, and she thought, of the two alternatives open to her, she would prefer to stay with Cousin Amelia.

Amelia Postlewaithe was the unmarried daughter of a bishop and lived with her companion and servants in an old and crumbling country house, together with her cats, dogs and a rather rude parrot that someone had taught to swear. Caroline suspected that that someone was her brother Nicolas, and the parrot had been a source of much amusement when they visited—though not shared by Cousin Amelia.

Although life would undoubtedly be rather dull with her mother's cousin, who seldom entertained, Caroline thought that she would prefer it to another stay in London with her aunt. She had no interest in continuing her Season, and wished that she might look forward to a settled future with Freddie. However, her mother's wedding must take precedence and therefore she would just have to wait.

Venturing to the Pump Room with her mother the next morning, Caroline looked around her with interest, for it was her first visit. Several ladies and gentlemen were drinking from small cups of the spa water, which was said to be beneficial for health. When Caroline took a sip, she pulled a wry face, for it did not taste as pleasant as it might.

Marianne Holbrook did not venture as far as the baths themselves. She was not in need of their healing properties and would have thought it most improper to bathe in mixed company. She knew that ladies of unimpeachable reputation did so, but she had already made it clear to Caroline that neither of them would bathe.

'For you know the water makes one's bathing dress cling to the form and is shockingly revealing,' she had confided to her daughter in the carriage earlier. 'No, Caroline. Mr Milbank does not approve and nor do I.'

Caroline was fast discovering that her mother's conversation was liberally punctuated by references to Mr Milbank. His likes and dislikes, his manners and goodwill, were all dwelled upon and examined with too much regularity for Caroline's taste. She was grateful to him for delivering her mother from the sad decline into which she had fallen, but thought that she would not care to accompany them on their honeymoon trip.

They saw nothing of Freddie at the Pump Room and Caroline was feeling low in spirits when they returned home. They were to dine with some of her mother's friends that evening, and the only entertainment offered would probably be a hand of whist.

The evening was worse than Caroline could have imagined, for it seemed that one of the ladies had heard something she thought a little odd concerning her. As yet there was no talk of the race, but Caroline had been observed arriving in Bath with Sir Frederick.

'I was told that she was with a gentleman and that they had neither a maid nor a groom with them,' Mrs Selwyn said to Marianne. 'I was sure that that could not be the case, for I know Caroline to be a properly behaved young lady. To arrive looking a little windblown and in a phaeton…I thought that some mistake must have been made?'

'Oh, she was with Sir Frederick Rathbone,' Mrs Holbrook said airily as if it were no great matter. 'You must know that he is a great friend and…' She looked coy. 'Well, I must not say more at the moment, but I assure you that it was quite proper for her to be with him. Besides, her brother was not far behind her. They met on the way to Bath, and Sir Frederick took Caroline up with him for a short distance.'

'Ah, I thought there must be some explanation,' Mrs Selwyn said, nodding at Caroline in a satisfied way. 'You are to be congratulated, Miss Holbrook. I believe Rathbone is quite a catch.'

'Well, as to that…' Marianne put a finger to her lips. 'We must wait and see, must we not? I am sure I can rely on your discretion, Susan.'

'Yes, of course. Absolutely!'

'And that means she will tell everyone that I am to marry Freddie,' Caroline said as they were driven home later. 'How could you do it, Mama? When Freddie has not even spoken to you.'

'I was left with little choice,' Marianne said. 'You will have no reputation left if the gossips hear of that infamous race, Caroline.'

Caroline crossed her fingers. She placed no reliance on her brother's keeping mum concerning the race, and it could not be long before it was noted that she had been with Freddie when he drove into Bath, her brother following shortly behind. The gossips would put two and two together, and she would be labelled as being shockingly fast, if nothing worse.

She spent another uncomfortable night, dwelling on her thoughts.

In the morning, just before they were about to set out for the Pump Room once more, the knocker sounded and Sir Frederick Rathbone was announced. He was shown into the small parlour where Caroline sat with her mother. Her heart leaped as she saw him, looking particularly handsome in his blue coat and cream pantaloons. His cravat had been tied in what was called the Waterfall style, and he looked very much the gentleman of fashion.

'I am glad to have found you at home, Mrs Holbrook,' he said and smiled at her. 'I was afraid you might have gone out.'

'We were to leave in a few minutes,' Marianne said, 'but no matter. I have no pressing appointments and we are pleased to see you, sir.'

She indicated a chair, but Freddie preferred to stand. He glanced at Caroline. 'I trust you are well? Would you wish to remain—or return in a few minutes? You know the reason for my call, I believe?'

'I shall stay, if you do not mind,' Caroline said. 'I have told Mama of the situation with Grandfather.'

Freddie inclined his head, turning to her mother. 'Then you know my purpose, Mrs Holbrook. I applied to Bollingbrook as the head of the family, but was refused on grounds which I do not think valid. Tom was good enough to say that I had his blessing, but I think Caroline will wish to have yours, ma'am.'

'I dare say,' Marianne said, but did not smile. 'However, I must pull caps with you, sir. I cannot approve of Caroline's being with you during the race you and my reckless son took part in. Not only is it shocking, and may well harm Caroline's reputation, but it could have been dangerous.'

'I assure you that at no time was Caroline's life or wellbeing in danger,' Freddie said. 'Forgive me if it distresses you, but I took care to do nothing that would risk her. She is far too precious to me.'

'Yes, well, that may be the case,' Marianne said. 'But it makes me a little uneasy. Can I trust you to take care of her? You may love her—and I believe that she loves you—but love is a fleeting thing. I believed myself loved when I married Mr Holbrook and was sadly disappointed in later life. I do not wish my daughter to suffer as I did. Her husband must be a man of character and responsibility, sir.'

'Oh, Mama, there was never any danger,' Caroline said. 'And it was I who teased Freddie into letting me be a part of the race.'

'Caroline dearest, do not,' Freddie told her gently. 'Your mama is perfectly right to make these inquiries. I understand that she may feel a little uneasy, but you know, ma'am…a young lady of Caroline's nature may fall into more trouble if her spirits are denied. Had I not taken her up with me, I dare say her brother might have been persuaded.'

'Oh, you do not need to tell me that she is reckless,' Marianne said. 'It has always been the same with that pair—and Caroline as naughty as her brother.' She looked at the gentleman standing before her, seeing the mischief in his eyes. 'And I dare say that you are another such one, sir. You will not bamboozle me! I believe that I must not deny you, for my daughter might very well do something outrageous if I tried—but you must prove yourselves to me. There is already some scandal concerning the pair of you, and an engagement would be just the thing to nip that in the bud before it goes too far—but you must be prepared to wait until my return from Italy for the wedding.'

'Thank you, ma'am, you are very generous,' Freddie said and leaned forwards to take her hand, raising it briefly to his lips. 'Do I have your permission to take Caroline driving now? When she returns I hope she will be wearing my ring. Do you go to the Assembly this evening?'

'Yes, that was my intention.'

'Then we may let it be known there, ma'am. It should help to steal the gossips' thunder, and I shall know how to deal with anyone who dares to speak ill of my intended wife.'

'Yes, that will do very well,' Marianne said and relented as she saw the pleasure leap in his eyes. 'Go along the pair of you!'

'Thank you, dearest Mama,' Caroline cried and flew to embrace her. 'I knew that you could not refuse us.'

'Well, I have always liked him,' Marianne said. 'And if he cannot control you, then I dare say no one will. But the wedding must wait—is that clearly understood?'

'Yes, Mama,' Caroline said and looked at Freddie. 'It will take me one minute to put on my bonnet and pelisse…'

As she hurried away to get ready, Freddie looked at his future mother-in-law. 'You need not fear for her future, ma'am. It has taken me a long time to find a lady that I wished to make my wife. I may not have been as circumspect in the past as I might have—but all that is at an end. Caroline's happiness will be my first concern, and I shall do everything that I deem necessary to protect her.'

'Then you have my blessing, sir.'

'I have received a letter informing me that Lady Stroud arrives in Bath tomorrow, ma'am,' Freddie said. 'She will be delighted to learn that you have consented to our engagement for I know that she liked Caroline very well.'

'I shall be delighted to renew our acquaintance,' Mrs Holbrook said. 'And I shall call as soon as she is in residence.'

'I know that Lady Stroud will be pleased to see you, ma'am.'

On that note they parted, Freddie going into the hall as Caroline came flying down the stairs to meet him.

Freddie had driven out to a local beauty spot. He stopped his phaeton and told his tiger to watch the horses while they got down to walk for a few minutes.

'So, my love,' he said when they had wandered a sufficient distance from the lad's curious gaze. 'Are you happy?' Caroline smiled up at him. Her heart was beating very fast and she was excited by his nearness.

However, there was one thing she had to do before she could accept her happiness. 'Yes, Freddie, I am happy—but there is something I must tell you. I thought Grandfather would tell you, but he did not…'

'You mean the quarrel with my uncle?'

'No, something more unfortunate…' Caroline hesitated, then, 'You may have heard of Grandfather's third wife. He loved her very much and she was my grandmother.'

'Yes, I had heard that he was very fond of her.'

'Did you know that her family refused permission for the marriage and so she ran away with him?'

'Yes. Someone told me recently.'

'Grandmother's brother told Grandfather that she was too delicate to have a child…he warned that she might die in the attempt.'

'As she did, unfortunately,' Freddie said. His eyes narrowed. 'It happens sometimes and is always tragic. Are you thinking that you might have inherited her weakness?'

'Grandfather fears it. I was afraid if you knew that I might not…be able to give you an heir…'

'If I thought it for one moment, I should be careful not to give you a child. I must tell you at once, Caroline—you are more important to me than any child could possibly be. If we were fortunate enough to have a son, I should naturally be delighted, but if I lost you…it does not bear thinking of, my dearest.'

'But surely it is important for you to have an heir—for the sake of your family?'

'It would please my family,' Freddie told her. 'But you may put such fears from your mind, Caroline. In the first place I am fairly certain that your grandmother's illness was due to a fever she caught in childhood that weakened her heart, and, secondly, I am marrying you because you are the only woman I have ever wished to marry.'

'So you would still choose me even if I could not bear a child?'

'Yes, of course. I know this must play on your mind, Caroline. Bollingbrook should never have told you the story. However, we shall arrange for you to visit an excellent doctor I know once we are married. I am certain that he will put your mind at rest. If he should confirm your fears, I shall make certain that we never have a child.'

'And you truly would not mind that?'

'I should mind it more for your sake than my own, since I believe you might be unhappy if you could not have children—but I should try to make you happy despite it. We might in those circumstances even adopt a poor child who needs a home and family.'

'Freddie…' Caroline's throat caught with emotion. 'You are so good…'

'I am selfish,' he told her and took her hand. 'I want you, Caroline, and I would move heaven and earth to get what I want.' He raised her hand to his lips, dropping a kiss in her palm. 'Are you content now, dearest?

'Yes, Freddie. How could I not be after what you have just said to me? I must be the most fortunate of women!'

'I believe I am the fortunate one, my love. I cannot wait for the day when I can claim you for myself.'

'I hope Mama may be persuaded to allow us to marry

as soon as she returns from Italy, but Christmas is not so very far away.'

'Shall you stay with your aunt while Mrs Holbrook is away?'

'Mama says she will write to her cousin, Amelia. She is a little deaf and does not entertain much, but I think I would prefer to stay with her. She lives in Yorkshire, so it may mean that we shall not often see each other.'

'I have an idea that might suit us better—if it appealed to you, dearest?'

'Please tell me,' Caroline said, smiling up at him as he reached out to touch her cheek. The look in his eyes made her sigh, for she wished that they might be married almost immediately. Her heart was racing wildly, her lips anticipating his kiss. She felt that she could swoon with the delightful sensations he was arousing in her. 'I hope it means that we do not need to be separated?'

'If you would consent to be Lady Stroud's guest at her country house, which is not much more than twenty miles from Bath, I might also visit her—and then, you know, we should be in each other's company as often as we pleased.'

'Oh, I think that is a very good suggestion. Do you think that Mama will agree?'

'I think that she might listen to my godmother, don't you?'

'Oh, yes.' Caroline laughed as she saw the mischief in his eyes. 'You wicked thing, Freddie! You always make me laugh—and to think that I did not particularly like you when we first met. I thought you arrogant and too sure of yourself—but I like you very well now...despite your faults.' Her eyes sparkled with mischief as she waited for him to take up the challenge, but he replied in a more serious vein.

'I knew that I found you very attractive at the start,' Freddie told her. 'But I was determined to hold back. I was not sure that I was ready to marry anyone, but then I realised that nothing else would do.'

'When did you know that you truly loved me?'

'I believe it was after the balloon accident. I realised that it could so easily have been you that was injured or killed—and it terrified me.'

Caroline blushed. 'I thought you were angry with me…that you had formed a disgust for my reckless behaviour, which was the cause of the trouble. For it was surely my fault that Tom was injured.'

'That is ridiculous,' Freddie said, a grim line to his mouth. 'How could you have been to blame? I was angry that it had happened and anxious, for I did not understand why.'

'It is very difficult to understand,' Caroline said. 'Tom and Nicolas seem to have settled on Grandfather's illegitimate child in Jamaica, but I cannot see why it should suddenly happen now. I know that Grandfather changed his will in our favour, but surely that cannot be the cause of these attempts on our lives? How would that person be so quickly aware of the changes?'

'Do you have any other ideas?' Freddie asked. Having turned the various theories over in his mind, he had as yet been able to come to no real conclusion. Had the attacks been made on him he might have understood their cause—but why Caroline? 'My one concern in waiting for our wedding is that this unknown assassin might try to kill you again.' He frowned as she shook her head. 'I know that you do not wish your mama to be upset over this business, but if you were my wife I could make certain that you were safe.'

'I promise you that I shall be careful,' Caroline said. 'I

think I must be quite safe staying with Lady Stroud in the country.'

'Yes, perhaps. I own I think you will be safer there than in London.' He reached out, drawing her into his arms and bending his head to kiss her. His mouth took possession of hers in a hungry yet tender kiss that made her weak with longing. 'I confess that I shall find the next few weeks very trying, my love.' He smiled at her, tracing the line of her cheek and laying his finger for one moment at the pulse spot at the base of her throat. 'I have never wanted anyone this much, Caroline. I do not know how you managed it, little minx, but you have wound yourself about my heart and it beats only for you.'

'Oh, Freddie,' Caroline said, feeling that she wanted to melt into him, to become a part of him. 'I do so wish that Mama would consent to a wedding before she leaves, but I know that she will not.'

'Then I must be content to wait,' Freddie said, 'which means that we should go now, for I am tempted to sweep you up in my carriage and run away with you to Gretna Green.'

Caroline laughed, her eyes bright with mischief. 'Oh, yes, Freddie! I should love that of all things. What an adventure that would be—to be married over the anvil and be together always.'

'I dare say you would regret it afterwards and long for all the trimmings of a big wedding?'

'No, I do not think so,' Caroline said. 'We should be able to give a dance and dinners for our friends whenever we felt like it—and, in truth, I do not care so very much for the constant round of society. It is well enough to invite one's true friends, but I was happy enough to go down to Grandfather's estate.'

'But you would not truly wish to elope?'

'Yes, I should like to…but it would hurt Mama, and we have promised that we shall wait,' Caroline said. 'So I suppose that we must.'

'Yes, I suppose we must,' Freddie said and laughed. 'Besides, I wish to let the world see how much I love and honour my bride, so we shall restrain our impatience. Hold out your left hand, my love.'

Caroline did as she was bid and he took a small pouch from his coat pocket, extracting a beautiful square emerald surrounded by diamonds and set on a gold band, which he slipped on to her third finger.

'Oh, Freddie,' she said. 'It is so beautiful. Thank you very much.'

'I am glad that you like it,' he said. 'There are many items of family jewellery residing in the bank, which I shall give you when we are married—but this ring has never belonged to anyone else. I commissioned it for you before I left London.'

Caroline tipped her head to one side, challenging him. 'Were you so certain that I would say yes?'

'I hoped that you would,' he said. 'But had you refused, I should not have given up, Caroline. When I want something, I am not to be denied—and I want you for my wife.'

Caroline lifted her face for his kiss, melting into his arms once more, feeling the wave of desire she was beginning to expect whenever he touched her. She let her hands move up the back of his neck, spreading out into his hair and holding his head as he would have moved away. Her body was demanding so much more, and she felt bereft when Freddie broke free, holding her from him.

'If we continue like this, I shall not be able to keep my

word to Mrs Holbrook,' he said. 'Come, Caroline, we must return to the carriage. Your mother will be anxious if we are gone too long.'

Caroline knew that the news of her engagement had gone round the ballroom like wildfire. She suspected that it had already been talked of, and, as soon as she walked into the room with her mother and Sir Freddie, it had been noted that she was wearing a ring on her left hand.

She had imagined that she would not know anyone, but soon discovered that several of her acquaintances had come down to Bath. The Season in London had passed its height, and some of the older ladies had decided to visit the spa for their health after so much junketing around in London.

Lady Stroud was evidently delighted. She nodded with approval as Freddie brought his fiancée to her. 'Kiss me, my dear,' she said, offering her cheek. 'Yes, it will do very well, Freddie. I am pleased that you have at last decided to oblige your family. I shall enjoy having you both to stay with me for a few weeks before the wedding.'

Caroline was congratulated on her engagement by almost everyone she met, though one or two of the ladies looked at her askance. Nicolas told her that rumours of the race were circulating, but the news of her engagement had overtaken it, and most of the younger set found it a huge jest and were applauding her courage. It would, of course, have been very different had she not become engaged to Freddie, and Caroline was a little chastened as she realised that she might have been in serious trouble.

However, no one actually cut her, and she enjoyed the evening more than any similar affair that had preceded it, for she was able to dance with Freddie as often as she liked. She did dance with one or two other gentlemen out of politeness, but her true happiness came from being with Freddie.

George Bellingham came to them as soon as he arrived, congratulating Freddie and wishing Caroline happy. He had taken a house in Bath for a few weeks, and Julia and her mother had come down to stay with him.

'It is a great pleasure to me to see you settled, Freddie,' he said. 'And I am happy that you have a good man to care for you, Miss Holbrook. Freddie is the best of good fellows and we shall all get on famously.'

'Thank you so much, sir,' Caroline said. 'You are very kind.'

George looked at his friend. 'There was something I wished to discuss with you, Freddie. It will do tomorrow, if you will call at my lodgings?'

'A little matter of business?' Freddie said, amused. 'I assure you I fully intend to settle my debt, George.'

'Oh, you mean the chestnuts?' George said and frowned. 'No, this is rather more urgent, Freddie—but it will keep for tomorrow.'

Freddie nodded, sensing that George had something of importance to impart—something that he did not wish Caroline to hear.

'Yes, of course. At about ten?'

'Excellent,' George said. 'Caroline, you will give me the pleasure of this dance, I hope?'

'Yes, of course,' she said and gave him her hand. She looked up at him as he led her into the dance. 'You and Freddie are very good friends, are you not?'

'The best,' he agreed. 'I have long wished to see him happy, Caroline—and I believe he is at last.'

Caroline enjoyed her dance with him, and when he returned her to Freddie, they talked for a while before he left. She looked at Freddie curiously when they were alone.

'What do you suppose is so important?'

'I have no idea,' Freddie said. 'Do not tease yourself over it, my love. I dare say George wants my advice on some horses that he wishes to purchase.'

Caroline thought that he was being a little uncommunicative, but was too happy to press for more information. If it was a matter of business, it was unlikely to concern her.

'What I have to say concerns Farringdon,' George said when they met the next morning at his lodgings. 'I happened to dine at the same inn as him on the way down here. He was looking most odd—not at all his usual self. And that evening he became quite drunk and abusive. He said some rather unpleasant things concerning you, Freddie.'

'Such as?' Freddie raised his brows.

'He practically accused you of cheating him out of his fortune.'

'Rubbish! No one would believe him. He is a careless gambler, reckless—and I have always been meticulous in matters of play.'

'You are perfectly right, Freddie, that was not what worried me. He seemed to be so bitter, to hate you so much. He was muttering in his cups, threatening you. Of course it was all nonsense, but I felt that you should be aware.'

'Thank you, George. What was the nature of his threats?'

'He said something like...*he will discover what it feels like to lose everything he cares for.* Clearly he was drunk, but I did not care to hear him speak so bitterly of you. I believe he means you some harm, my friend. Can it be merely a matter of his gambling debts—or have you done something more to make him hate you?'

'Nothing I can think of…' Freddie frowned.

'It may be the loss of his horses,' George said thoughtfully. 'He was very proud of both his chestnuts and the greys. He cannot enjoy seeing you driving them.'

'I do not fear Farringdon. He is a fool and might have cut his losses had he been honest. I told you that I was prepared to forgive the debt if he was straight with me, but he lied—told me that he had no debts on his estate and that he would pay in full. I had my agent investigate and he discovered that hardly anything was left. Farringdon knew that when he sat down to play. He knew that his notes were worthless. I did not wish to be lumbered with a failing estate and would gladly have returned it had there been anything to return. As it was, I took his greys in settlement of the debt and as far as I am concerned that was an end to it.'

'And he may think himself fortunate, for if you had chosen you might have had him arrested for debt or fraud, whichever you preferred—but instead of being grateful, he has dwelled on his misfortunes and now blames you for all his ills.'

'Well, he may think as he pleases,' Freddie said. 'He was already set on the path to ruin before I won a guinea from him.' He smiled wryly. 'I must settle my debt to you, George.'

'There is no hurry,' George said. 'I am happy to see you so well suited, my friend. I think she is just the woman for you.'

'How could it be otherwise?' Freddie said and offered his hand. 'The chestnuts are yours and I wish you joy of them.'

'I think I shall give them back to you as a wedding present,'

George said, shaking his hand. 'I would not wish to win such a wager, for it was taken lightly. Yes, you shall keep them, and in return you will ask me to be godfather to your first child.'

'Yes, of course. Thank you, George. I am glad to know what is in Farringdon's mind, though I set little store by it. The man is a loser by nature and I shall not let his bitterness disturb my peace of mind.'

'Well, I dare say it was merely a drunkard's loose talk,' George said and smiled. 'Tell me, when are you to be married?'

'As soon as Mrs Holbrook allows,' Freddie said. 'I am on my way to the Pump Room now, for she takes the waters most days. Perhaps you would like to accompany me?'

Caroline saw the two gentlemen come in together, and, leaving her mother to talk to companions of her own generation, she went to join them, her face alight with mischief.

'Have you come to take the waters, Freddie?' she asked innocently. 'I believe they are beneficial for all manner of ailments. Especially the rheumatics, they say…'

'Minx!' he said, giving her look of mock outrage. 'You deserve a spanking, miss, and the time is coming when you may get all that you deserve.'

Caroline went into a peal of delighted laughter. 'Have you come to take me driving? I was about to go to the lending library, for Mama has asked me to return a book for her. If you accompany me, we may go driving afterwards—should you wish for it?'

'As it happens, George and I are both on foot this morning,' Freddie said. 'But we should both be delighted to accompany you, Caroline. Afterwards we may stroll for a while and perhaps gaze in the shop windows or take a cup of chocolate and some of those delicious cakes they sell at a little shop nearby—if that would please you?'

'Oh, yes, that sounds delightful,' Caroline agreed. 'I must just tell Mama what we plan, and then we may leave. I confess I find the prospect of chocolate more appealing than a cup of this water.'

Freddie and George exchanged a few words with Mrs Holbrook and then the three set out together. Caroline found the two gentlemen good company, for they teased each other unmercifully, and made wagers on the silliest things, but only for amusement's sake.

'Shall you attend the theatre while you are here, Miss Holbrook?' George asked her. 'I believe there is a very good play on this coming week. Does Mrs Holbrook approve of the dramatic art?'

'Oh, yes, I think so,' Caroline replied, a naughty twinkle in her eye. 'You see, Mr Milbank particularly likes to visit the theatre, especially for something of a light-hearted nature—and Mama approves of most things that Mr Milbank likes.'

'Perfectly proper,' Freddie told her with mock severity. 'I hope you are taking a lesson from your mama, Caroline? I shall expect you to agree with everything I say when we are married.'

'Shall you truly?' Caroline said, tipping her head to one side. 'Oh dear, I fear you shall be sadly disappointed, sir.' She laughed softly, her eyes bright with mischief. 'Oh, do look,' she said. 'I believe that is Julia over there with her mama. I must speak to them…'

She let go of Freddie's arm, and went to step out into the road, but, remembering that he had once scolded her for being impulsive, hesitated as she saw a heavy wagon rumbling quite fast towards them. Then, as she hovered at the kerb, she suddenly felt something knock into her and she gave a little cry, almost falling from the pavement into the path of the oncoming vehicle. She was within a hair's breadth of being crushed under its wheels, for her ankle had twisted and she could not keep her balance. Fortunately, Freddie was standing close to her and he grabbed her pelisse, pulling her back out of harm's way and into his arms as the wagon thundered past over the cobbles.

'Oh,' she said as he held her. She was trembling, for the accident had shocked her. 'What happened? What is George doing?' she asked as she saw that their companion had taken off after someone who was clearly running away. 'I think… did someone push me?'

'Yes, Caroline,' Freddie said, looking grim. 'I did not notice him, for I was concerned that you meant to dash across in front of that wagon. I was watching you and only saw the rogue as he pushed you, but I think George realised what was going on, for he was after the man like a shot.'

'Oh, how horrid,' Caroline said, feeling shocked and a little sick. 'Do you think…I mean, did he actually mean to push me or was it an accident?'

'I cannot be sure,' Freddie said, though he did not believe it could have been an accident. 'Miss Fairchild has seen you, Caroline. She means to come to us. It may be best if we say nothing to anyone just yet. Invite your friend to take chocolate with us, and then we shall see what George has to say when he returns. I hope he may catch the fellow, but I make no reliance on it.'

'Caroline!' Julia said as she came across the road to them. 'What happened—did that fellow push you? I thought you were going to be hurt!'

'Oh, no, I believe it was a mere accident,' Caroline said. 'We are going to have some chocolate and cakes, Julia—do say you will come?'

'Yes, of course. I should love to,' Julia said. 'I have been to the lending library, but the book I wanted was out.' She looked at Freddie. 'I hear you are to be congratulated, sir—and you, Caroline. I wanted to tell you how very pleased I am for you both. Of course I expected it—we all did.'

'Thank you,' Caroline said and blushed as she glanced at Freddie. 'I was not aware that anyone knew until recently.'

'It was commonly talked of in London,' Julia told her and smiled a little coyly. 'I know for a fact that some of our friends had a wager that you would be married before Christmas. Everyone remarked on it, because Sir Frederick had never been known to take so much interest in a young lady before. Besides, it was obvious that he was in love with you.'

'Oh, no…' Caroline glanced at Freddie, and saw that he was looking thoughtful. 'Was it so easy to see? I confess that I did not know it myself for some time.'

'Oh, here comes my uncle,' Julia said, her attention turned. 'Did you catch that wicked fellow, sir?'

'I fear not,' George said, a trifle out of breath. 'He went into an inn and escaped out the back somehow. I'm sorry, Freddie. I should know the fellow again if I saw him, but that isn't of much use to you.'

'You did your best, George,' Freddie said. 'As it happens, Caroline was not hurt. I dare say he must have been after your purse, Caroline. It is over now—shall we all have our chocolate and cakes?'

George offered Julia his arm and the four of them went into the chocolate shop together. Caroline glanced at Freddie, for she sensed that he was playing the incident down to try to avoid gossip, which would have been bound to reach her mother's ears sooner or later.

'What are you thinking?' she asked in a low voice.

'That I must do something about this business, Caroline. That is the third time you have been attacked and it really cannot go on.'

'But what can you do?'

'Trust me, my dearest,' he said and smiled at her. 'When does Nicolas return to his regiment?'

'In the morning, I believe.'

'I must speak to him before he leaves,' Freddie said. 'But Julia is looking at us. We must behave as if nothing has happened.'

Caroline went to join her friend by the counter where delicious-looking cakes had been set out on various plates and stands. Freddie certainly had something on his mind, but there was no use in asking. He would tell her when he was ready for her to know.

When she glanced over her shoulder, she saw that Freddie was talking earnestly with George about something, and the two of them looked serious. However, when the ladies walked to join them at the table, having made a selection of cakes that they would all enjoy, they were laughing over some jest and she thought that perhaps she had imagined it.

After enjoying their chocolate, they parted company, George having agreed to escort Julia to join her mother, who had gone on to the Pump Room, and Freddie to deliver Caroline to her lodgings.

'I shall see you this evening, my love,' he told her, kissing her hand. 'Please take care of yourself until then.'

'You are very worried about what happened this morning, are you not?'

'You could have been killed or at least badly injured,' Freddie said. 'The time has come when I must do something, Caroline—but do not worry your head over it, my love. I am taking certain steps to make sure it will not happen again.'

Caroline stared after him, wondering what he meant to do. She sighed as she went indoors. It was most unpleasant that these things should be happening, and she could not help wishing that her grandfather had never thought of changing his will.

'I believe it must be for the best,' Nicolas agreed when, a little later that day, Freddie finished telling him what he planned. 'The sooner she is removed from harm's way the better, in my opinion. She should be safe enough at Lady Stroud's house, particularly if you have employed certain measures to protect her.'

'I shall be with her,' Freddie said. 'I have been giving the matter a great deal of thought recently, Nicolas. Something George told me earlier today has made me wonder if we were wrong to consider the Jamaican connection. I think that business may have rather more to do with me than your grandfather's will.'

'Yes, it had crossed my mind,' Nicolas agreed. 'But why is Caroline his target?'

'I imagine at the start it was meant to be me, for I was due to fly in that balloon, not Tom. He may have had no idea that Caroline was to be involved—but when he realised that I was planning to marry her, he turned his hand against her, thinking to cause me more grief.' Freddie looked grim. 'It is fiendishly clever, Nicolas, for I would rather die than have harm come to her.'

'Yes, I understand you,' Nicolas said grimly. 'I am very fond of Caroline and I think I might kill this rogue if I got my hands on him—whoever he may be.'

'You may stand in line,' Freddie said, a glitter of anger in his eyes. 'I have agents working on this affair, Nicolas. Do not imagine that I have been idle. They will discover who is behind all this bother and the culprit will be punished. Until then, Caroline must be protected. You must return to your regiment tomorrow and that means I must be the one to see that she is watched constantly. I shall do that best if I have her near me at all times—and there is only one way to be sure of it.'

'Yes, that is very true. Your plan is the best that can be achieved, sir. I understand what you mean to do—and I pray that all will go well.'

'If Caroline is safe, I care little for anything else,' Freddie said, and on that note of agreement they parted, Freddie to complete his plans for that evening, and Nicolas to prepare for his part in the plot.

Mr Milbank had given a small party for a select number of friends that evening. It was Nicolas's last evening with them in Bath, and was to be a celebration, for he would not get leave to attend his mother's wedding. Tom had driven over from Bollingbrook to join them, for he was about to set out on his journey to Jamaica and had been invited to the party. Naturally, Freddie was invited as Caroline's fiancé. Amongst others, Mr Bellingham, Julia and her mother made up the company that sat down to a very good dinner.

The conversation flowed easily, helped by the fine wines

and delicious food served at table. It was quite late in the evening when the party finally began to break up. Nicolas took his mother aside, asking if he might escort her home in his curricle, for there was something he wished to say to her.

'Yes, of course, dearest,' Marianne said, smiling at her son, who was her favourite, though she had always tried to love her children equally. 'Caroline may come with Tom if she pleases. Or perhaps Sir Frederick will bring her…'

'Yes, of course I shall take Caroline,' Sir Frederick said and smiled at her. He turned to Tom and shook hands with him. 'I am glad to see you again. You are looking much better. I trust nothing more has happened to disturb you?'

'No, I am sure thanks to you,' Tom said. 'I have noticed a few extra rather brawny men about the place recently. Grandfather knows and said to tell you he appreciated your interest in the business. He hasn't quite got round to sending you his apologies, but I think he may do so before long.'

'Well, I am not perfectly certain of that,' Freddie said, a flicker of a smile in his eyes. 'I may be in his bad books again soon, and in your mama's—but Nicolas will fill you in, I am sure.'

He turned to Caroline, seeing that she had her velvet evening cape about her shoulders, smiling at her as she came up to them. 'Ah, there you are, my love. Are you ready to leave?'

'Yes, thank you,' she said, and took a step forwards, standing on her toes to kiss Tom's cheek. 'I shall not see you for some weeks, perhaps months, dearest. You will promise me to take care of yourself while you are away?'

'Yes, as best I can,' Tom told her and gave her a one-armed hug, his other arm still in a sling, but no longer painful.

'Freddie sent me someone I might trust—an old soldier. He swears worse than Cousin Amelia's parrot, but I shall walk safer with him at my back.' He nodded to her. 'Go with Freddie now, Caroline. You will be married when I next see you, and I shall leave a gift for you with Mama.'

'Thank you,' Caroline said, 'but my best gift will be to see you safely home again, Tom.'

She became aware of Freddie waiting for her, and went to him, tucking her arm through his and looking up at him. 'I am quite ready now.'

'Then we must be off,' Freddie said. 'My curricle is waiting, I believe.'

'Your curricle?' Caroline asked curiously, for she knew that he more usually drove his phaeton in town. 'I thought you walked here this evening?'

'Yes, that is true, but my groom has his instructions.' Freddie offered her his arm. 'Are you tired at all, my love?'

'No, not at all,' she said. 'It was a very pleasant evening, but I do not feel like going to bed.'

'What would you like to do?' Freddie asked with a flicker of a smile.

'Oh…walk with you under the stars perhaps,' Caroline said and laughed. 'Yes, I know I am being foolish. It is just that…it becomes harder and harder to part every night.'

'Does it, Caroline?' Freddie took her hand, helping her into his curricle. His groom was driving that evening and he climbed in after her, sitting next to her and taking her hand in his. 'Why do we not take the long way home?'

'Oh, may we?' Caroline was pleased, for though she had enjoyed her evening, she did not wish to say goodnight to him yet. 'That would be lovely, Freddie.'

He kept her hand in his, stroking it idly with his thumb so that she felt her blood rush wildly through her veins and turned to him as he drew her towards him, his lips brushing hers in the softest of kisses.

'You do know that I love you and that I would never do anything to harm you?'

'Yes, of course,' she said and gazed up into his eyes. 'I love you, too, Freddie.'

He touched her cheek, his fingers shaping the contours of her face and then going behind her head as he pulled her to him for a kiss that was deeper and more hungry than any she had yet had from him. Caroline melted into him, her body aching for the release of something she hardly understood, but knew would come from being one with him.

'Oh, Freddie…' she whispered. 'When you kiss me like that, Christmas seems a very long way away.'

'Yes, it does,' he agreed. 'But we are leaving for my godmother's home this evening, and that means we shall be together constantly until we are married.'

'What do you mean?' Caroline looked at him. She was suddenly aware that they were leaving Bath. 'Freddie, this isn't the way home. What are you doing?'

'We are leaving Bath, my love,' he said and gave her a wicked smile. 'My godmother travelled home this morning and will be waiting for us.'

'No, Freddie, we must not,' Caroline said, startled and anxious. 'Mama will be so worried—and there is her wedding… No, we must not do this.'

'She will know of my intentions by now,' Freddie reassured her. 'Do not distress yourself on Mrs Holbrook's account, Caroline. Nicolas has promised to talk to her and explain why I have taken this desperate step. It is to protect you, my dearest one. I told you that I could not allow the situation to continue any longer. You were not safe in Bath, but you will be safe with me at my godmother's, I promise you. In the meanwhile I shall try to mend fences with your mama—and possibly your grandfather, if he will see us.'

'Oh…but Mama will be so upset,' Caroline said. 'Poor Mama…you really should not have done this, Freddie.'

'I am sorry if it distresses you, Caroline—and I would not have done it had I not believed it was the only way. I took precautions to protect you at Bollingbrook Place, but even though I was with you in Bath you were still attacked. I shall feel safer in the country for your sake—just until this thing is settled.'

'Yes, I see,' Caroline said. She was silent for a few moments, absorbing what he had told her, and then, 'Do you not think Mama might have agreed to our marriage sooner had you told her the truth?'

'She might,' Freddie said. 'She knew that you were to stay with Lady Stroud, though she did not know that I intended to leave Bath this evening. I did so for reasons of secrecy, of course.'

'You took a great deal on yourself,' Caroline said, for she was too disturbed to give in immediately. 'I am a little cross with you for not telling me what you planned.' She looked at him anxiously. 'Of course I do not mind—as long as Mama is not worrying about me.'

'I believe Nicolas may bring her about,' Freddie said and smiled at her. 'It will not be so very bad, my love. Your mama may tell everyone you have gone to visit friends. And then we shall invite them all to our wedding when your mama returns from her honeymoon trip.' He touched her hand briefly. 'Have I your forgiveness, my love? You do know that I have done this for your sake?'

'Yes, I know,' Caroline said and turned to face him. She leaned forward to kiss him softly on the lips. 'I still wish that we might be married sooner…'

'You are a temptress, my love,' Freddie said ruefully and eased her away from him. 'I may have spirited you away, my dearest, but I am not going to seduce you. We shall wait until my wedding ring is on your finger.'

'Shall we really, Freddie?' Caroline said and reached up to touch his face. She traced the line of his mouth with her forefinger, bringing a groan from him. 'I do not truly see why we should. We are so soon to be married…'

'And then I shall put you across my knee and give you the spanking that your mother obviously did not,' Freddie growled. 'I have no intention of giving in to you, minx, no matter how you try to tempt me.'

'Oh, dear,' Caroline said and gurgled delightfully. 'What a sad disappointment you are, Freddie dearest. I had not thought you were such a flat…'

'A flat?' Freddie looked at her incredulously. 'No, no, Caroline, I shall not have that.'

'Well, a slow-coach then,' Caroline said and pouted at him. 'I am not perfectly sure what the right word may be, but—' She gasped as he pulled her into his arms, kissing her so ruthlessly and with such determination that she could do nothing but melt into his arms. 'Oh, Freddie…' she breathed, well pleased with the result her teasing had brought. 'I do love you.'

'And I love you, my darling,' he said, grinning at her. 'I am not sure that I shall ever say no to you again, but this time I am determined on it.'

'Oh…' Caroline smiled and leaned her head against his shoulder. 'In that case, I think I may as well go to sleep for a while.'

Freddie smiled as she lay against him. He slid his arm about her, holding her more comfortably as the curricle drove on through the night. She did not fool him for one moment, and he was very much aware of an uncomfortable tightness in his breeches. It was exquisite torture to have her near like this, to know that she was ready to surrender her sweetness to him, and yet refrain from taking all that he so desperately wanted of her.

And yet he was determined that he would wait for their wedding night. Caroline was such a lovely innocent, and he would not give the gossips more fodder than he needed. Though if Mrs Holbrook played her part, there was no need for anyone to know where Caroline had gone…

Chapter Twelve

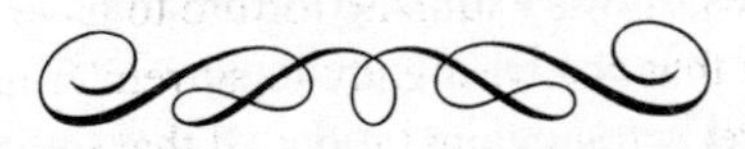

'Nicolas!' Mrs Holbrook stared at her son in shock and horror. 'Do not tell me that you were a party to this terrible deceit? I cannot believe that you would treat me so hardly…' She held a scrap of lace kerchief to her eyes. 'It is quite, quite shocking that Caroline should run off with him at the dead of night…'

'It was not Caroline's fault,' Nicolas said loyally. 'Sir Freddie and I planned it together. It was the only way to keep her safe, Mama. Caroline has been attacked three times. There was the balloon accident and then she was shot at when riding at Grandfather's estate—and this latest incident. Freddie said that he must remove her from danger and the best way to do that was to leave Bath at once and secretly.'

'Why didn't any of you tell me?' Mrs Holbrook demanded. 'If I had known…' She smothered a sob. 'I think it is most unkind of you all to keep this from me.'

'We didn't want to upset you,' Tom said, coming into the parlour at that moment. 'Stop crying, Mama. Caroline will be all right with Sir Frederick.'

'This means I must cancel my wedding,' Mrs Holbrook said dramatically. 'It cannot go on as planned…'

'That is nonsense, Mama,' Tom said. 'You will be married at the appointed time. Nicolas must return to his regiment, of course, but I shall put off my journey for a few days to see you wed.'

'Oh, Tom dearest…' Mrs Holbrook threw herself on his shoulder, weeping into his coat. 'You alone of my children even attempt to consider my feelings.'

Tom patted her shoulder, nodding at his brother over her head. 'You had best get to bed, Nicolas. You have to leave early in the morning. Leave Mama to me.' He smiled at his mother, putting her from him. 'Tell me, Mama—would you have Caroline safe at Lady Stroud's home or fatally harmed?'

Marianne gave a little shriek, her face turning pale. 'Was it truly the only way to keep her safe, Tom? Not just one of her mad pranks?'

'I am convinced that Caroline did not even know of it,' Tom said. 'Indeed, I think only Nicolas and Freddie knew what was happening. I am perfectly sure that George Bellingham did not, for he caught up with me when I was walking home. Apparently, he had just received some information that he thought Freddie should know.'

'Oh, dear,' Marianne said, looking at her son. 'Do you think it is more bad news?'

'I have no idea, but I intend to speak to Bellingham as soon as possible myself. He will be wondering what has happened, and if this concerns Caroline in any way, then I want to know about it.'

'This is all Bollingbrook's fault,' Mrs Holbrook declared,

a wrathful look in her eye. 'And the next time I see him I shall certainly tell him so!'

On that note she departed to her bedchamber, leaving the brothers together. Nicolas looked thoughtful, because he sensed that Tom was anxious about something.

'I wish I could help you out, Tom—but if I am not back on time I shall be declared absent without leave, and that will not do.'

'No, no, you must get off right and tight. My journey may wait a few days. I must keep my promise to Mama, and, if Caroline is in some fresh danger, then I must warn Freddie of it.'

'Yes, of course,' Nicolas said, frowning. 'Has it occurred to you that this business may be nothing to do with Grandfather's will?'

'Well, I have wondered lately,' Tom said and looked thoughtful. 'It may be that Sir Frederick has an enemy himself. I am damned if I can puzzle it out.'

'Sir Freddie has some idea, I believe,' Nicolas said thoughtfully. 'However, when you speak to Bellingham in the morning, you may learn something new. You will write and let me know what comes out of all this, Tom?'

'Yes, of course,' his brother assured him. 'Try not to worry about it, Nicolas. There is nothing you can do—and you may be certain that Sir Frederick knows what he is about. I dare say there is nothing for either of us to worry about at all.'

'Thank you for coming,' George said the next day when Tom called on him. 'I was worried when I found that Freddie was not at his lodgings last night. However, now I understand—and you may be sure that I shall not say a word to anyone.'

'Thank you. You may imagine that Mrs Holbrook is very distressed about all this, but she has accepted it because she believes, as my brother and Sir Frederick do, that it was the only way to keep Caroline safe.'

'That was undoubtedly his reason for carrying your sister off in such a high-handed way,' George said and looked anxious. 'The devil of it is that I think it is exactly what he ought not to have done.'

Tom felt a coldness at the nape of his neck. 'What do you mean, sir? Surely she will be safe enough at Lady Stroud's home?'

'Perhaps,' George said. 'Sir Frederick has an enemy—a man who is determined to bring him to his knees if he can. And, though I believe it would please him to see Freddie dead, I think he wants to punish him first.'

'By taking away the person who is most precious to him?' Tom nodded. 'Yes, that makes sense to me. All the attacks have been on Caroline of late. Indeed, since I took Sir Frederick's place at the balloon ascension at the last minute, he may have been the intended victim. A hired assassin would not know of a last-minute change of plans…'

'Yes, quite possibly. We have all been chasing our tails, thinking that you and Nicolas were targets as well as Caroline, but I am fairly certain that we were wrong. As I left Milbank's party last evening I met a man who had been working for Freddie. He had important information, which I persuaded him to give to me…and it transpires that I was right after all. I mentioned my fears to Freddie a day or so ago, but he shrugged it off as unimportant.'

'You know who has been threatening Caroline?' Tom asked.

'Yes, I believe so,' George said. 'It was a matter of money, but not of Bollingbrook's will. Freddie won a considerable sum from someone a short time ago. He thought he had settled the affair, for he took far less than was owed, merely warning the gentleman concerned that if he saw him gambling again he would make public that he was virtually bankrupt. The fellow is desperate, and may imagine that he is ruined, though if he had kept faith with Freddie he might have come out of it better than he has. Freddie would certainly not have done anything to harm him, but he may not have realised that the affair was over.'

'Good grief!' Tom was shocked. 'Then this is a personal vendetta against Freddie. I know that Nicolas discussed it with him, but they were not certain…' He frowned. 'This could mean that Caroline is even more at risk with him than she was before.'

'Yes, I fear that may be so,' George agreed. 'We have to warn him.'

'I shall set out at once,' Tom said and frowned. 'At least, as soon as I have told my mother that I shall not be able to attend her wedding…'

'Please do not disappoint Mrs Holbrook. It would only distress her more. I shall leave Bath in the morning. It is probable that Farringdon does not know they have left Bath, and that they are safe enough for the moment—but I think Freddie should be warned. Farringdon is the kind of petty individual who will do anything for spite—and at the moment he is like a wounded beast.'

Tom nodded his agreement and they parted, for there was little more to be done for the moment. They could only hope that Freddie was aware of his enemy and would take the proper steps to protect both Caroline and himself.

As he left George's house, Tom had come to a decision. He had been intending to wait until he returned from Jamaica to speak to Julia, but these attacks on Caroline had made Tom realise how precarious life could be. He would visit Mrs Fairchild in the morning and ask her permission to speak to her daughter. His visit to Jamaica could be put off for a few days longer, and, if Julia cared for him, as he hoped she did, they might be engaged before he left.

Caroline looked out of the upper window of Lady Stroud's country house. It was a very pretty establishment, and her hostess had made her welcome the previous evening. She had slept very well in a comfortable bed and was feeling happy and relaxed as she came downstairs that morning.

'Good morning, Miss Holbrook.' A woman that Caroline knew to be her hostess's housekeeper came to greet her as she entered the breakfast parlour, where food had been prepared and awaited her under silver covers. 'I trust you found your room comfortable?'

'Yes, thank you,' Caroline said and smiled at her. 'And thank you for the roses on the dressing table; they smelled lovely.'

'Lady Stroud wanted everything to be nice for you, miss,' the housekeeper said. 'She asks if you will attend her in her bedchamber—in about half an hour perhaps, when you have eaten your breakfast.'

'Yes, of course,' Caroline replied.

The housekeeper smiled and went away, leaving Caroline to help herself to the selection of tasty dishes on the sideboard.

She selected a little scrambled egg and bacon, and poured herself a cup of hot chocolate before sitting down to enjoy her meal. She had almost finished when the ring of boots on polished wood alerted her and she looked up with a smile as Freddie walked in.

He came to her, dropping a kiss on her cheek as she turned to greet him. 'I thought you would still be upstairs,' he said. 'I went for a ride as I usually do, but another morning we might ride together if you care for it?'

'Yes, I should like that very much,' Caroline said, sparkling up at him. 'But I should like to drive your horses even more, Freddie. Now that we are here at Lady Stroud's estate, do you think you might teach me?'

'Minx!' Freddie said and went to examine the contents of the silver chafing-dishes. 'I dare say I might be persuaded since you ask so nicely, my love. It will do no harm on the estate—and perhaps we may find you something of your own in good time.'

'Oh, Freddie,' Caroline said and got up to go to him. 'I think you mean to spoil me—do you?'

'Perhaps,' he said, giving her an enigmatic look. 'You are a temptress, Caroline, and you look beautiful this morning. Our wedding seems a very long time off at this moment.'

She gave a gurgle of laughter, reaching up to kiss him briefly on the lips. 'I think I shall enjoy being your wife very much, sir,' she said and drew back before he could prevent her. 'And now I have promised to visit your godmother. I must not keep her waiting.'

'Wicked one!' Freddie threw at her as she blew him a kiss and walked away. 'Have I met my match at last, I wonder?' He smiled at the thought, for he was feeling pleased with himself and the world that morning.

Caroline was feeling equally pleased with life as she went upstairs to Lady Stroud's private apartments. She knocked and a few moments later was invited to enter. Her hostess was sitting in bed, a pink shawl over her shoulders and a frilly cap on her head. She smiled and held out her hand, inviting Caroline to sit on the edge of her bed.

'You are up early, Caroline. I wake early myself, though I do not venture downstairs before noon these days.'

'I have always been used to rising early,' Caroline told her. 'I used to ride with my brother Nicolas when he was at home, and sometimes with Tom. If I did not ride, I went for long walks. Even in the winter I like to be outdoors as much as I can.'

'I approve of a girl with healthy habits,' Lady Stroud said. 'The moment I set eyes on you, I was sure you would make my godson a good wife. He has an old and valued name, you know, and he will inherit his uncle's estate in good time. Mine too when I am gone. It is right and proper that he should marry and marry well. We do not want any ramshackle filly in the family. No, you will make Freddie a good wife and give him several strapping sons, I have no doubt.'

'Yes…' Caroline stared at her a little uncertainly. 'I know it is important to provide sons for the family name to continue.'

'I believe in the family,' Lady Stroud said, her eyes narrowing as she saw Caroline's expression. 'Not frightened of that side of things, are you? Nothing to worry about, believe me. Freddie will look after you. He may have had his fling, but he won't let you down, child.'

'No, I did not think he would,' Caroline said, realising that she had almost betrayed herself. 'He is everything I could wish for in a husband.'

'And so I should think,' Lady Stroud said with a little frown. 'Get off and find yourself something to do then, girl. No sense in sitting here all day!'

'I shall see you later, ma'am. It is very good of you to have me here as your guest.'

'Stuff and nonsense! It was the most sensible thing in the circumstances—though why your mama would not permit your wedding immediately I do not know!'

Caroline smiled, but said nothing. She was thoughtful as she went downstairs. Freddie had assured her that she was more important to him than an heir, but she was sure Lady Stroud would be disappointed if Caroline did not produce the sons she expected.

'Ah, there you are.' Freddie came out of the parlour as he reached the bottom of the stairs. He looked at her for a moment. 'Is something wrong, Caroline? Did my godmother say anything to distress you?'

'No, of course not,' Caroline said and gave him a radiant smile. 'Lady Stroud has been everything that is kind and generous. I was merely thoughtful.'

'I have asked for the greys to be brought round,' Freddie said. 'Go up and change into something suitable, Caroline—and we shall begin your lessons at once.'

'You have done very well for a first lesson,' Freddie said as she brought the curricle to a halt in front of the house. 'You have good, natural hands, Caroline. I think we shall make a whip of you yet. I do not know that you will outshine Letty Lade at her best, but you will rival her once I have finished with you.'

'Freddie…' Caroline laughed up at him as he helped her

down. They stood for a moment in the sunshine, his hands about her waist, smiling at each other, both aware of a strong pull of sensuality. 'You are such a tease—but you do mean it? You really think that I shall be good enough to drive myself one day?'

'Yes, of course—' He broke off as a curricle came up the drive at a spanking pace. 'Now what the devil does George want here?'

Caroline turned in surprise as George Bellingham got down and came towards them. She was conscious of Freddie's hands about her waist, and moved away, a little flush in her cheeks to be seen in such an open embrace.

'George, my dear chap, what on earth are you doing here?'

'Forgive me for intruding…' George smiled at Caroline. 'How delightful to see you, Miss Holbrook. I had to see you, Freddie—just a small matter of business, you know.'

A small matter of business that had brought him here hotfoot from Bath! Freddie frowned, his eyes narrowing. Clearly George had something important to tell him. He turned to Caroline, a little smile of regret on his lips.

'We must postpone our conversation until another time, my love. I shall see you later.'

'Yes, of course, Freddie.'

She walked into the house, leaving the two gentlemen together.

'What is it, George?' Freddie asked. 'Why come all the way here, my friend? You have some news, I gather?'

'I am certain that Farringdon is behind those attempts on Caroline,' George said. 'I dare say he probably meant to harm you in that accident with the balloon, but after that he directed his malice at Caroline…to cause you more grief,

Freddie. I thought you should be warned of something I have learned…'

'Yes, that is much as I had thought,' Freddie agreed. 'It was good of you to come, my friend, but, as I told Caroline's brother, I have made certain arrangements. Even now, you are being watched—just as I have been all morning.'

'Then I need not have bothered,' George said ruefully. 'I was not perfectly sure…'

'No need to apologise,' Freddie said and grinned at him. 'Now that you are here, you must stay to nuncheon.'

'Congratulations, sir.' Tom shook his stepfather's hand. 'Mama, I wish you happy, but I know that you will be.'

'Oh, yes, very happy,' Marianne said and embraced her son. 'I am sorry that you must leave us so soon, Tom—but I know that you have much to do. You will write to me as often as you can?'

'Yes, Mama, of course,' Tom replied. 'When do you leave for Italy?'

'We have decided to postpone our trip for a week or two,' Marianne said. 'I wish to know that Caroline is safe, and I have something to say to Bollingbrook. We shall call there first and then go on to Holbrook, where I must supervise the packing of some things I wish sent down to Mr Milbank's estate—and then I intend to call on Lady Stroud to make sure that Caroline is all right.'

'Yes, well, I am sure that Caroline will be pleased to see you,' Tom said. 'I must leave now, Mama. I have much to do…'

Tom smiled as he put his other problems to the back of his mind for a moment. Before he left Bath there was one more call he must make.

* * *

'Come to gloat over me, have you?' Bollingbrook glanced askance at the new Mrs Milbank. 'Well, I cannot say that I blame you. I have not behaved well to you or your children.'

'There was a time when you might have done much to help me,' Marianne said, retaining her dignity. She had thought that she would exact revenge for past slights but, seeing him looking wretched, the desire had left her. 'However, that is past and I need nothing you can give me, sir. I have come to tell you that you have endangered the lives of my children and to ask if you will make it plain to whomever it concerns that you are no longer intending Tom, Nicolas and Caroline to be your heirs.'

'Well, I ain't able to oblige you,' Bollingbrook said, 'for I have signed most of the money over to Tom, though Caroline will have her dowry and Nicolas has something substantial. I've arranged for the funds to be available from my bank and that is that. Besides, I have news this morning that means it would make no difference if they were to die.'

'I assure you that it makes a great deal of difference to me!' Marianne looked at him indignantly.

'Oh, stop your mithering, woman,' Bollingbrook said. 'You know very well that I did not mean it that way.' He gave her a scathing look. 'Do you think I want anything to happen to that girl?'

'No, I do not,' Marianne said, 'and I suppose I must thank you for what you have done for them—though it might have been done sooner.'

'For once in your life you have said something that I agree with,' the Marquis said. 'And if you will listen, I shall tell you why you need not fear the Jamaican connection. I have received a letter just now telling me that the boy was killed in an accident some two months ago.'

'Then who is trying to harm my daughter?' Marianne was shocked. 'This changes things. Someone must speak to Sir Frederick about this, for he should be warned. It must be him who has an enemy…'

'If anyone had asked me, I would have said that that seemed the most likely in the first place.' The Marquis cleared his throat. 'We have all been damned fools! Will you forgive the past, ma'am—and will you and your husband stay to dine with me?'

'Thank you.' Marianne inclined her head. 'I think we can agree not to be enemies, sir—if only for the sake of my children. However, we wish to be at Holbrook by nightfall. I do not expect that I shall see you for a while, sir—but I wish you good health.'

Holding her head high, she walked from the room, leaving the Marquis to stare after her. He muttered beneath his breath, ringing the bell for Jenkins with some vigour. His valet, who had been hovering in the next room, came immediately.

'You rang, sir?'

'Of course I damned well rang, Jenkins,' the Marquis growled. 'Don't give me that injured look, man! I've had enough of it from that woman—though she isn't quite the milksop I thought her. At least she had the decency to tell me what was going on. That rogue has taken my gel off to stay with his godmother—and intends to marry her, I dare say.'

'Yes, sir.' Jenkins looked at a spot just above his head. 'I expect he does intend it. He loves her as she loves him.'

'Yes, I know I've only myself to blame that they've gone off without a word to me,' the Marquis said. 'Well, I can't do much about it now, but I think it's time to mend fences if we can, Jenkins.'

'Yes, sir.' Jenkins tried not to look pleased, but failed miserably. 'Your writing slope, sir?'

'No, damn you! What do I want with letters? Put up enough clothes for two days, Jenkins. We are off to Lady Stroud's estate to see how the land lies!'

'Ah…' Jenkins said, a gleam in his eyes. His master had hardly left his room in the past year. 'Are we certain about that, sir?'

'Damn your eyes, man! I'll get there if you have to carry me.'

'Yes, certainly, sir,' Jenkins said. 'And when do you wish to leave?'

'As soon as you can be ready, of course. You may give my instructions to the rest of the household and then come back and help me. And I shall want my knee breeches. Lady Stroud is a stickler for dress, as I recall…' He smiled as his valet went off to do his bidding. It might be the last thing he did, but he was going to see what could be done about this wretched business.

'Ah, there you both are,' Lady Stroud said, coming into the parlour where Freddie and Caroline were sitting together that afternoon. 'What are you doing indoors on a day like this? You should be out enjoying the fresh air, my dears.'

'Yes, you are perfectly right, Godmother,' Freddie agreed and looked at Caroline. 'I was just about to ask if you would like to take a turn about the gardens, my love?'

'I should enjoy it very much,' Caroline said, and gave him her hand. He pulled her to her feet and into his arms, looking down at her for a moment before he kissed her forehead. 'It is so warm that I do not think I need to put on my pelisse and I shall not bother with a bonnet.'

'Then let us go,' Freddie said, offering her his arm.

Caroline took it and they went out into the hall and through the door that an obliging footman opened for them. The garden was a riot of colour and perfume, for Lady Stroud was very fond of her borders, which were beautifully kept. A gardener was busy taking the dead heads from the rose bushes, and, seeing Caroline, he broke off a perfect pink rose bud and handed it to her with a little bow.

Caroline thanked him, and they strolled off. Birds were singing their hearts out because it was such a lovely day, and, as they walked towards the woods that lay beyond the wall at the end of the long garden, they were both aware of a feeling of perfect peace. It was a little cooler in the woods, but that was only to be welcomed on such a warm day.

'It is lovely here, isn't it?' Caroline said, looking up at him. They had been walking for a few minutes in perfect harmony. 'I was only thinking last night that I should like to walk in these woods…' She frowned as she remembered something. 'I forgot…I meant to tell you that I saw someone lurking out here last night when I glanced from the window—twice, actually.'

'Indeed?' Freddie arched his brows at her. 'I shall have to reprimand them, Caroline. My men are supposed to be guarding us, not frightening you.'

'Oh, no, I wasn't frightened,' she said. 'I remembered that you said you had set someone to watch over me in London—and I thought perhaps it was them.'

'Does nothing frighten you?' Freddie asked with a smile. 'Most young ladies would be near fainting if they thought that their lives might be in danger. But hopefully it will all be over soon, and you must not be distressed whatever happens, my love.' Something in his eyes seemed to carry a warning, and a little chill started at the nape of her neck.

'What do you mean?' she asked, gazing up at him in surprise. 'I thought…' The rest of her sentence was lost as she saw something in the trees just ahead of them, and then a man stepped out, and instinctively she knew what was happening. 'Freddie…be careful…'

'Yes, I know,' Freddie told her in a low voice. 'He has been following us since we entered the woods.' He let go of her, his hand moving slowly towards the deep pocket of his coat. Only when his fingers had closed over the pistol he sought did he turn his head to look at the man, noting the pistol in his hand, and the desperate look on his face. Freddie smiled slightly. 'Good morning, Farringdon. I have been expecting you. Your rogues have not served you well, I think? I thought you might feel it time to step out of the shadows and do the business yourself.' He took a step forwards, standing just in front of Caroline, shielding her from the line of fire. 'I hope you mean to be sensible? This business may all be settled without need for bloodshed. If you feel yourself ill used, I am sure we can come to some arrangement.'

'Damn you, Rathbone!' Farringdon snarled. 'It is always so easy for you, isn't it? You made it easy for me, but you humiliated me…stripped me of my pride and my pleasure in life by taking my horses. If I have nothing left, I may as well be hanged—but I'll see you and her dead first…'

He raised his arm, pointing his pistol at Freddie's chest. Caroline saw what he meant to do and launched herself at Freddie's back, pushing him so hard that he stumbled. As Farringdon fired, the shot went over his head and Caroline gave a cry as she felt his ball strike her arm. And then another shot rang out…

* * *

Moments after Freddie and Caroline had entered the woods, the noise of thundering hooves and clattering wheels announced the arrival of an old-fashioned coach at the front of the house. Grooms came running to attend it, for it bore the arms of a marquis. One of the grooms jumped down, and rapped at the doorknocker with some urgency. He was admitted into the hall, and asked for Sir Frederick.

'Sir Frederick has just gone out, but my mistress is at home,' the footman told him. 'May I ask who is calling, sir?'

'You may say that the Marquis of Bollingbrook has arrived and asks if Lady Stroud will see him.'

'Certainly,' the footman said. 'Be so good as to ask the Marquis to step inside, sir. I shall inform her ladyship that he has arrived.'

'What is it, Blake?' Lady Stroud had heard the voices and came out into the hall just as the Marquis had stepped out of his carriage. She went to the open doorway to look at her visitor and frowned. 'Damn my eyes, if it ain't Bollingbrook,' she said. 'All it wants now is for Southmoor to turn up and I shall think myself twenty years old again!'

'Harriet,' Lord Bollingbrook said and doffed his hat to her, with a creaky attempt at gallantry. 'I hope you won't refuse to put me up. I've travelled a deuced long way in too short a time and I'm done up. If you turn me away, I must go to an inn and it will probably be the end of me.'

'Burned your boats, have you?' She gave a cackle of laughter. 'Serves you right, you old rascal. Very well, I'll give you a bed, but if you upset Caroline I'll have my servants throw you out without the blink of an eyelid! I've become very fond of that gel, and that's the truth of it.'

'And you would,' Bollingbrook said, a glint of laughter in his eyes. She had swept him back to the old days when he had wanted to make her his mistress and she had shown him the way home. 'Like her, do you? She's a grand girl, ain't she?'

'Come about, have you, you old fool?' Lady Stroud eyed him severely. 'Well, you had best be prepared to grovel, for she will be back soon—' She broke off, for she had seen them advancing across the lawn, and she sensed that something was wrong. Freddie was supporting Caroline, and, even as she watched, he suddenly bent down and swept her up in his arms.

Bollingbrook turned and saw them. 'Something has happened,' he muttered and would have gone to them had his valet not forestalled him, hurrying to reach them and confer with Sir Frederick. He returned almost immediately.

'Miss Holbrook has been winged, sir. It is just a flesh wound and Sir Frederick has sent for the doctor—but I've told him that I'll see to her for the moment. It wouldn't be the first time I've patched up a similar wound.'

'Damn it!' Bollingbrook said wrathfully. 'What has that idiot been up to with my gel? If she takes harm from this, I'll have his hide!'

'Stop your mithering, you old fool,' Lady Stroud said. 'Whatever happened, it will not have been Freddie's fault.'

The Marquis glared at her, but Freddie had reached them now. He paused for a moment to glance at the Marquis, and then down at the girl he carried in his arms.

'Your grandfather is here, dearest.'

'Put me down for a moment, Freddie.'

He set her gently on her feet, keeping an iron grip about her waist, supporting her as she smiled at her grandfather. 'Do not worry, sir, it is merely a little scratch,' she told him, though her face was deathly pale. 'I shall be better in a moment, but please do not quarrel with Freddie, for I cannot bear it. Besides, it was entirely my fault that I was shot.'

'Well, I shan't quarrel with him,' the Marquis said, 'for you've set your heart on him and I don't want to be at odds with you, Caroline. I've come here to tell you that I'm sorry and ask you to forgive me.'

'Of course I forgive you,' she said, and then looked at Freddie. 'Do you think you could carry me upstairs? I am feeling a little odd…' She was swooning as Freddie lifted her into his arms. He nodded curtly to the others and went on into the house, swiftly followed by Jenkins.

Lady Stroud turned her fearsome gaze on the Marquis. 'You had better come in, Bollingbrook. You can tell me why you saw fit to forbid that gel to marry my godson in the first place!'

Caroline was barely conscious as Freddie gently deposited her on the bed. However, she revived under the gentle ministrations of the Marquis' valet, her eyelids fluttering open as he finished binding her arm.

'Thank you, Mr Jenkins,' she said, giving him a brave smile. 'You were very gentle and did not hurt me at all.'

'You are a brave young lady,' Jenkins said. 'You'll be as right as ninepence in a day or so, don't you worry. And don't worry about the Marquis, Miss Caroline. His bark is worse than his bite and he thinks the world of you.'

'Thank you.' Caroline looked beyond him to where Freddie still hovered, his expression grim. 'Please do not be cross with me, Freddie. I knew he meant to shoot whatever you said and I couldn't bear it if he had killed you.'

Freddie came to the bed as the valet moved away, discreetly leaving the room. He stood looking at Caroline for a moment, and then he smiled.

'How do you think I should have felt if he had killed you instead? You were very foolish, Caroline…reckless…but I know that you did it because you love me, and that makes me feel humble. I did not expect to be loved that much, my dearest. I have never truly known love before this.'

'Have you not, Freddie?' Caroline asked. The look in his eyes made her want to hold him and never let go. 'I do not see why you should not be loved that much. I think you are everything that is good, honest and decent—and I am very lucky that you love me.' She drew a shaky breath. 'If only we were sure that we could have a child…it would be my dearest wish…'

'Did I not tell you to forget this nonsense, my love? Believe me, you are perfectly healthy, and should have no trouble in bearing a child. There is no hereditary weakness, my love.'

'What makes you so sure?'

'Because my uncle Southmoor told me. He knew Angelica as a child—they were neighbours—and he remembers what happened. She caught scarlet fever as a child and almost died. In the end she recovered, but it left her with a weak heart. He did try to tell your grandfather once, but they had quarrelled years before and Bollingbrook would not listen.'

'Then it could not have been passed down to me through Papa?'

'No, definitely not,' Freddie said. 'My uncle tried to tell Bollingbrook. Angelica's brother lied to him because he wanted to prevent the marriage. It was a cruel lie, my darling, nothing more. Bollingbrook was too proud to listen.'

'So you knew all the time…'

'I wish I had mentioned it the last time we spoke of this,' Freddie said. 'But I thought I had set your mind at rest.' He smiled and leaned forward to kiss her. 'Remember, you are more important to me than anything else. Rest for a while now, my love. The doctor will be here soon, though I believe Jenkins has done all that need be. Your arm will be sore for a while, but no lasting harm has been done.'

'Your men killed Farringdon after he shot me,' Caroline said, remembering the second shot that had felled their enemy. 'So there will be no more attempts on either my life or yours.'

'It is over now,' he said with a grim look of satisfaction. 'But I must talk to your grandfather. It is time that we settled our differences.'

'You won't quarrel with him?'

Freddie smiled. 'I promise not to quarrel with him, Caroline—but I cannot promise that he will not quarrel with me…'

Caroline lay back against her pillows with a smile. Her arm was very sore and she thought that she might like to sleep for a while.

Caroline was feeling much recovered when she went downstairs at just after noon the following day. Lady Stroud was concerned and asked if she felt well enough to be up, but Caroline smiled and told her that there was no need to worry.

'My arm is a little sore,' she said, 'but the medicine the doctor gave me ensured that I slept and I do not care to lie abed too long.'

'I dare say my gel is as strong as an ox,' Bollingbrook said, looking at her with pride. It was obvious that Freddie had passed on the good news and he was now able to face the idea of her marriage with equanimity.

'Grandfather—' she began when the sound of a door-knocker and voices in the hall was heard. The next moment the parlour door opened and Mrs Milbank came in, shortly to be followed by her husband.

'Mama…' Caroline was astonished as she saw her, for she had imagined her on board a ship bound for Italy. 'Why are you here? I don't understand…'

Mrs Milbank was looking decidedly young and fashionable in her green silk gown. 'Caroline, my love,' she cried and opened her arms as Caroline went to embrace her. 'I could not rest for thinking of you, and so Mr Milbank said we should come and see if you were all right for ourselves before we leave for our honeymoon.' She suddenly realised that Caroline's arm was in a sling and gasped. 'But you are hurt! What has happened to you?'

'Stop fussing, woman,' Bollingbrook said, glaring at her. 'She is quite able to take care of herself without you mewing over her like a broody tabby. If you must know, my girl is a heroine and saved Sir Frederick's life!'

'I think I know my own daughter, sir. And I shall thank you to keep your opinions to yourself!' Mrs Milbank gave him a furious look, which startled him and then made him chuckle with laughter. 'I do not see what is so funny, sir, when my poor daughter is injured…'

'Damn me, Mrs Milbank, but it seems you suddenly acquired the spirit of a lion. I shall have to revise my opinion of you.'

'Caroline?' Marianne ignored Bollingbrook's sally, her anxious eyes on her daughter.

'It is nothing much, Mama,' Caroline said. 'Please, come up to my room where we can be private and I shall explain everything to you.'

Mrs Milbank stared at her in silence for a moment, and then sighed. 'It seems that I was wrong to delay your wedding, Caroline. You are not a little girl any longer, and I dare say you know your own mind. Yes, I shall come with you and you may tell me everything...'

'I was beginning to despair of ever having you to myself,' Freddie said to Caroline as they walked in the garden that evening. 'But perhaps it is as well that Bollingbrook and your mama are both here. They have finally settled it between them that we are to be married without more delay.'

'Now they are falling out over who is to pay for the reception,' Caroline said and gurgled with laughter. 'But Mama is no longer afraid of him and I think that they are secretly enjoying the battle. Indeed, they may even end up liking each other!'

'I am sure they already do,' Freddie said. 'I have invited my uncle to come for the wedding. I dare say there may be fireworks when he and Bollingbrook meet, but I believe we shall weather it.'

'Oh, I do not fear any of them,' Caroline said, gazing up into his eyes. 'I have nothing to fear now, dearest Freddie.'

Freddie reached out for her, gathering her into his arms, careful to avoid touching her right arm, which he knew to be a little sore. 'I love you so much, my darling girl. You do know that I would have married you even if you had inherited a weakness that prevented us having children, don't you?' he said, a growl of passion in his voice. 'You mean everything to me, Caroline. I want your children, but more than anything

I want you…' He kissed her hungrily, the desire flaring between them. 'Oh, God, I want you so much…'

Caroline melted into him, her body seeming to dissolve in the heat of their desire. She let herself drift on the pleasure of his caress, which was more intimate and passionate than anything that had passed between them before that night, his fingers lightly brushing her breasts.

'I love you…' she whispered, knowing that if he asked she would give herself to him now this night. Indeed, her body was clamouring for his touch.

With a groan of resignation, Freddie moved away. He had been swept to the brink, but drew back at the last. 'You are a sweet, wicked minx,' he muttered hoarsely. 'But torment me as you will, I shall wait for our wedding night.'

The sun was showering its blessing on them as they came out of church that morning. The bells rang out and a small crowd had gathered to wish the bride well, throwing handfuls of rose petals at her and Freddie as they walked to the carriage waiting to take them back to Lady Stroud's house, where it had been decided the wedding would be held to save more delay.

Freddie leaned forward to kiss Caroline on the mouth as the horses started forwards. 'Did it please you to have most of your family there for the wedding?'

'Oh, yes, very much,' Caroline said, smiling up at him. He looked so very handsome and she was so much in love. 'I was glad to hear that Tom doesn't have to go to Jamaica just yet after all—and the news that he is to marry Julia is wonderful! It has all worked out very well, has it not?'

'Yes, very well,' Freddie said. 'Now, tell me, my love—

do you wish to give a ball for our friends or travel abroad immediately?'

'I think perhaps I should like to spend a little time alone with you at your estate, Freddie,' Caroline said. 'And then we may give a ball before we go travelling—if it pleases you?'

He reached out to touch her cheek, trailing one finger down to her throat and sending little shivers of delight down her spine. 'You must know, my beloved, that for the rest of my life I want only to please you. I told you that I should probably never say no to you again, Caroline, and I meant it.'

'Oh, no, you will spoil me,' she said. 'Besides, you have said many things to me, Freddie. I seem to recall that you have several times promised to spank me.'

His eyes danced with amusement, for she was teasing him more often these days, and he liked it. 'Ah, yes, so I did,' he said, 'but do you know, my love, I think that must wait for a while. Our guests are expecting us at the reception my godmother has given for us, and, much as I shall look forward to the prospect, I do not think that we should keep them waiting—do you?'

Caroline smiled. They had reached the house now and all their guests were waiting to greet them. They had invited only their closest friends, most of whom had been in Bath and not forced to travel too far.

Caroline passed from one to the other, receiving congratulations and gifts. It was not until just before she was about to go up and change into her travelling gown that Julia asked to speak to her.

'You look so happy,' Julia said and there were shadows in her eyes that made Caroline reach out to take her hand. 'I am so happy for you, dearest Caroline.'

Caroline leaned forward to kiss her cheek. 'I am so glad that we are to be sisters, Julia.'

Julia blushed. 'I had almost given up hope. I could not believe it when Mama told me he had asked for me.'

'I knew he loved you, but he had such a hard struggle with the estate after Papa died. I suppose he needed to be sure he could support a wife before he dared think of approaching you.'

'I would have married him even had your grandfather not given him such a generous gift,' Julia said. 'I love him.'

'I know.' Caroline embraced her. 'I am so pleased for you both.' She kissed her cheek again and then saw her mother coming towards her. 'I must go and change, Julia. It will be your wedding soon…'

Caroline woke and yawned, a smile forming on her lips as she realised how good she felt. Freddie's passionate love-making had kept them both awake for much of the previous night. She stretched, remembering the sweetness of being loved by a man who had taken every care to please her. She had never realised how delightful the pleasures of loving could be.

The bed was cold beside her, and, glancing at the small enamelled clock on the chest beside the bed, she realised that she had slept long after her normal hour. Freddie must have left her to sleep on, which was very considerate of him in the circumstances.

Looking about her, Caroline saw that her maid had been in earlier and left a tray on the table near the window, but when she got up to investigate, she discovered that the chocolate pot had gone cold. She was about to ring for someone to come when she glanced out of the window, and what she saw there sent all thoughts of breakfast from her mind. Freddie was talking to some men on the lawn and they were preparing a balloon for flight.

She gave a shout of glee, flinging off her nightgown and hurrying behind the dressing screen to wash and dress in one of her simplest gowns, for which she needed no help from her maid. Within a few minutes she was running down the stairs and out of the front door, which the footman opened for his popular young mistress with a smile. Her hair was flying about her face, for she had not bothered to tie it up. She looked much younger than her years, the glow of excitement in her eyes as she ran across the smooth lawns towards the small group of men. And then Freddie turned and saw her.

'Ah, there you are, my love,' he said, smiling at her, a gleam of amusement in his dark eyes as he recognised that she had dressed hurriedly. 'I was about to come in search of you. We are almost ready for flight. I take it that you wish to go up?'

'Oh yes, please,' she said, her eyes bright with pleasure. 'You know that I do. It is so good of you to arrange this for me.'

'You were disappointed the last time,' Freddie said, 'which was possibly my fault for arranging such a public display. But you know this is a hobby of mine, and you will be able to go up quite often should you wish it. We are always trying new things—are we not, Mr Jackson?'

'Yes, sir,' the balloon master said and smiled at his sponsor's lady. Sir Frederick had some ideas for flight, which had not yet been thought of, and one day they would no doubt put the theory to the test. 'We have a fine day for it, Lady Rathbone. The wind is in the right quarter and we should be able to stay up for some time—if you wish it?'

'Oh, yes, please,' Caroline said, giving him her hand as he helped her to climb into the basket. Freddie hopped in beside her, and the other men on the ground began to cast off the ropes that were anchoring the balloon to the earth. As it started to lift, Caroline felt a little strange. She watched the people on the ground become smaller as the balloon started to drift across the sky, rising higher and higher until they looked down on the treetops. 'Oh, Freddie,' she breathed as he came to put his arm about her waist, 'isn't it wonderful? I never dreamed anything could be this exciting.'

'No,' Freddie agreed, but he was looking at her, at her lovely, expressive face and her glorious hair tumbling about her shoulders. He was remembering the previous night when he had seemed as though he could never have his fill of her, thinking of the pleasure she gave him with every word, every smile. Had he been bored with his life only a few short months ago? He certainly wasn't now, for every day seemed fresh and new. 'Do you know, my darling, neither have I…'

* * * * *